RIDE OR DIE

Also by Solomon Jones

The Bridge

RIDE OR DIE

SOLOMON JONES

St. Martin's Minotaur

New York

RIDE OR DIE. Copyright © 2004 by Sola Productions. All rights reserved. Printed in the United States of America. For information, address St. Martin's Press, 175 Fifth Avenue, New York, N.Y. 10010.

www.minotaurbooks.com

Design by Phil Mazzone

Library of Congress Cataloging-in-Publication Data

Jones, Solomon, 1967—
    Ride or die / Solomon Jones.
        p. cm.
    ISBN 0-312-30616-4 (hc)
    ISBN 0-312-33989-5 (pbk)
    EAN 978-0-312-33989-0
    1. North Philadelphia (Philadelphia, Pa.)—Fiction. 2. African American teenagers—Fiction. 3. Conflict of generations—Fiction. 4. Children of clergy—Fiction. 5. Police murders—Fiction. 6. Drug traffic—Fiction. I. Title.

PS3560.O5386R53 2004
813'.6—dc22

                                                                        2004046681

10 9 8 7 6 5 4 3 2

FOR MY MOTHER, CAROLYN JONES,
WHO HAS ALWAYS BEEN OUR ANCHOR IN THE STORM

Acknowledgments

First, I must thank my Lord and Savior, Jesus Christ, who snatched me from the deadly streets portrayed within these pages. I am forever grateful for His grace. But all that I do as a writer would be irrelevant without my readers. One in particular comes to mind: Gloria Patricia Bennett, who passed suddenly, was an enthusiastic reader whose effusive praise, pointed questions, and humorous commentary made the solitary hours spent writing well worth the sacrifice. I met Gloria through Barbara Woods, a member of one of the hundreds of book clubs that have invited me into their homes to discuss my work. My sincerest thanks to Gloria and to all of you for making my stories part of your lives. To my editor, Monique Patterson, thanks for being the best at what you do. To Victoria Sanders, thanks for giving me my start. To my agent, Manie Barron, thanks for embracing the vision. To my lovely wife, LaVeta, thanks for seeing me for what I could be.

I love you. To my daughters, Adrianne and Eve, thanks for being hope for the future. To my brother, Brian Jones, thanks for being the picture of perseverance. To my father, Solomon E. Jones Sr.; my grandmother, Lula Richards; my aunt, Juanita Bryant; my uncle, Gerald Richards; and my cousin, Melanie Bryant; thanks for loving me as I love you. To my in-laws, Jose and Eva Andino, thank you for being steadfast examples of the Christian walk. Thanks to Sue and Harold Jacobs, Ben Jacobs, and all Sue's children and grandchildren, for your friendship. Thanks to W. Wilson Goode Jr. and the members of the Philadelphia City Council. Working with you has been a true learning experience. Thanks to Darwin Beauvais, quite simply the best lawyer I've ever seen. You made what could have been a stressful time a lot easier to handle. To the leadership and members of the Calvary Baptist Church of Philadelphia, thank you for your support and spiritual guidance. And again, thanks to you, my readers. You are the mirror that reflects the truth in each story that I tell.

RIDE or DIE

1

The sway of Keisha Anderson's hips
stirred the still summer air as she climbed the subway steps and
began the walk up Broad Street.

She'd spent the last few Wednesday evenings the same way—
rushing from her summer job to church in an effort to maintain
the illusion that was her life.

But tonight she didn't want to rush. As she passed the poster-
laden remains of the Uptown Theater, she slowed down and allowed herself to drink in the sights and sounds of North Philly.

She listened as an ambulance screamed past, and watched as
a young mother dragged a toddler by the arm. She heard a basket-
ball smacking against the sidewalk while a passing car blasted
Jay-Z.

The song's infectious rhythm took Keisha to a place she'd
come to know intimately since reuniting with her childhood love,

Jamal. It was a place that allowed her to straddle the line between her own world, with its hard-and-fast rules, and a world where the do's and don'ts were as fluid as the sound of his name.

Jamal. She mouthed it silently, turned it over in her mind, and tasted it on her tongue. It was smooth and buttery sweet, like the secret kisses he'd pressed against her lips.

But at the same time, Jamal's name was bitter. It was a reminder that she'd had to look to him for the love she'd always longed to receive from her parents. Love she'd watched them give to their parishioners instead of her.

Keisha shook her head. She didn't want to think of the years of service that had caused her family a misery she wanted no part of. She only wanted to think of the streets that provided sweet escape from it, the streets whose forbidden pleasures she longed to taste.

As she approached the drug dealers who were posted on the corner of Broad and Dauphin, her soft lips curled in a mischievous smile. She fixed her smoldering gaze on them and invited their lustful stares.

They happily complied. Their eyes roamed everything from her honey-brown eyes to her gently rounded hips as a rare summer breeze caused her white cotton sundress to cling to her ample curves.

Seconds later, the catcalls began in earnest. But rather than enjoying the attention, Keisha grew angry at their raw, disrespectful words, and whipped around to face the tallest one.

"What did you say?" she snarled with a hand on her hip.

Surprised, he coughed, and his white T-shirt, already too large, seemed to swallow him whole.

"I just wanted to holla at you for a minute," he said, trying not to buckle under the weight of Keisha's stony stare.

"I'm standing right here," she said, tossing her hair and looking him up and down with an arched eyebrow. "Holla."

He looked around at his boys, who urged him on with solemn nods and knowing grins. Tugging at his low-slung pants, he ambled over to Keisha.

He tried to take her arm to move her away from the crowd, but Keisha wouldn't budge. She wanted all of them to hear the exchange.

Pulling the curved bill of his baseball cap down over his eyes, the boy looked down into Keisha's ginger-colored face, with its soft lines and flawless beauty, and tried to act composed.

"What's your name, baby?" he said with a crooked smile.

She rolled her eyes. "A minute ago, my name was bitch."

"Naw, I ain't—"

"When I walked by," she said, cutting him off, "you said, 'Look at *this* bitch.' You didn't care what my name was then, so why do you care now?"

"Hold up, baby, I wasn't—"

She raised a single finger. "Next time you want to talk to me," she said, "you call me by my name. It's Keisha."

There was shocked silence as she stepped forward and put a hand in his face.

"And if you can't remember that," she said, her voice low and threatening, "maybe I'll send somebody by to remind you."

Before he could respond, she turned on her heel and crossed Dauphin Street, her sundress billowing behind her as she passed a gray stone church whose walls climbed silently into the evening sky.

As she rounded the corner of Fifteenth Street and headed for the playground, she could hear the sound of the drug dealers laughing at their humiliated friend.

She almost joined in. But her smile quickly disappeared as the atmosphere around her began to change.

Fifteenth Street was filled with closed auto repair shops and cold yellow streetlights. Abandoned houses lined one side of the block. Barren, packed earth and cracked sidewalks lined the other.

Seeing it all made the night feel colder than it had been just minutes before. And that coldness, more than anything, frightened Keisha.

Walking through the gates of the playground, she saw soiled diapers and used condoms. Trash cans filled to overflowing. Broken overhead lights. And dank air whispering through the darkened doorway near the playground's locked office.

Keisha felt her chest tighten as she made her way toward the steps between the building and the swings. There were no more sounds to tempt her. No more voices to anger her. Only an ominous silence that seemed to grow deeper with every passing second.

She climbed the first step and caught sight of the alleylike street on the other side of the playground. Just beyond it, there was a rocky dirt path that wound between tree-sized weeds to York Street.

The path was the last thing she saw.

Someone grabbed her from behind, slapping a hand over her mouth and pressing himself against her as he dragged her backward.

Keisha bit down hard, and her teeth tore through his skin, causing warm blood to flow into her mouth.

The man grunted, released her, and swung his fist. Keisha saw a flash of light, and her eyes filled with tears as the pain of the blow shot through her body.

He grabbed her again, and she reached back to claw at his

face. He ducked and continued pulling her backward. She tried to twist her body to face her attacker. Then another man emerged from the shadows and swept her feet out from under her.

"No!" she shrieked, catching a glimpse of the second man's scarred face.

They covered her mouth again, dragging her into the shadowy doorway and pulling her cotton dress over her head. The one with the scar pried her legs apart. The other placed a knife against her throat. Her stomach turned as the stench of urine mingled with the odors of garbage and sweat.

"Give it up or I'ma kill you," said the one with the knife, kneeling next to her and undoing his pants.

"Stop!" she shouted while trying to kick her legs free.

There was a muffled sound behind them. The one with the knife turned to see where it came from. But it was already too late for him to respond.

The first punch was delivered with such force that the scar-faced man at Keisha's feet tumbled into the other one, who dropped his knife and tried to stand. Before he could do so, a boot landed against his temple. Seconds later, both men went down in a barrage of flailing fists.

Keisha wanted to run, but she couldn't get out of the doorway. Neither could her attackers. They were hit again and again, as fists and feet flew at them faster than they could fend off the blows.

Keisha crawled backward as grunts and the thudding sound of hard punches filled the closed-in space. Flecks of blood dotted her white dress. One of her attackers reached back for the knife he had dropped.

Her rescuer stepped on his hand and the man screamed. After that, the struggle ended. And the violence that had filled the doorway was replaced by a deep, resonant voice.

"Both o' y'all get outta here," her hero said slowly. "And I bet' not ever see y'all around here again."

As her attackers ran away, Keisha looked up at the silhouette of the man who'd saved her. He was bathed in the pale moonlight that shone on him from behind.

His broad shoulders extended almost the length of the doorway, while his torso tapered down to a small waist. His muscled arms extended to his thighs, where his clenched fists rested. His chest heaved up and down as steam poured off his dangling dreadlocks.

After she'd filled her eyes with the familiar shape of him, Keisha pursed her lips and tried to be brave. But the façade was short-lived. Tears burst from her eyes as she stood up and rushed into his arms.

"Jamal," she said through tortured sobs. "Thank God you were here."

"You all right?" he muttered as he cradled her like a baby.

She nodded and held him tighter. "Who were they?"

"I don't know," he said, looking around to make sure they were gone. "I never saw 'em before."

Keisha's sobs subsided as he held her in his arms.

"I want you to go home," he said calmly.

Keisha loosened her grip and backed away from him. "Not by myself," she said nervously. "You have to come with me."

He took her face in both hands and stared into her eyes. "I can't."

"Yes, you can," she said, searching his eyes in the dim light. "I've already decided to tell my parents all about us."

The gentleness left his voice. "You can't do that, Keisha. Not yet."

Her eyes filled with confusion. "But why?"

He didn't want to lie to her. But he couldn't tell her the truth.

"I need you to trust me," he said, wiping an errant tear from her cheek. "Go home. Tell them what happened, but don't mention me. I'll come see you tonight, and I'll explain everything. I promise. Okay, Keisha?"

She wanted to refuse him, to make him bend to her will. But she was too shaken to do anything but agree.

"Yes, Jamal," she whispered.

"Good. I'll call you on your cell in an hour."

He kissed her lips tenderly. Then he nudged her out of the shadows and pointed her toward the church.

She almost turned around and ran to him. But she knew, now more than ever, that there was something forbidden about the man she loved.

Still, she couldn't help wondering, as she ran from the playground, if Jamal was what she'd been hearing about all her life.

She wondered if he was a savior.

"The doors of the church are now open," said the Reverend John Anderson, his black robes dangling from his outstretched arms as he stood in front of the altar.

With a face the color of black coffee and smooth skin stretched taught over high cheekbones, he was an imposing figure. His parishioners were drawn to that, even more than to his fiery preaching, because they lived in a world where strength often overshadowed faith.

"If anyone here doesn't know Christ as their personal savior," Reverend Anderson continued, "come down the aisle right now, and . . ."

His words trailed off as the doors in the back of the sanctuary swung open. The street light streaming in from the stained glass windows seemed to dim, and the parishioners' faces dropped as they turned and watched the trembling figure lurching down the aisle in a ripped and bloody dress.

"Oh my God," said one of the church mothers, nodding her head in prayer and pulling her sweater tight around her shoulders.

Whispering voices filled the sanctuary. But most of them weren't praying. Somehow they knew that prayer might not be enough to change what they saw in the center aisle of their beloved sanctuary.

The girl they watched approaching the front of the church—the one whose smiling face they'd seen from the time she was a baby—was not the same. Something had changed. Her innocence was gone.

"Daddy," Keisha said, her voice going from that of a young woman to that of a little girl. "They tried to hurt me."

She ran into his arms and wept in front of the altar. And though no one left their seat, the entire congregation embraced her along with her father.

Tears filled Reverend Anderson's eyes. Then he motioned to a deacon.

"Give the benediction," he said, gently moving his daughter toward the door behind the pulpit. "Bible study's over."

Keisha's mother, Sarah Anderson, got up from the front pew, following them through the door and into the pastor's office. But she didn't cry.

Reverend Anderson slammed the office door, glanced at his wife, then wheeled to face his daughter.

"Are you all right?" he said, throwing off his robe and shoes as he angrily reached into his closet for a pair of boots.

Keisha sat down. "I'm a little scared, but I think I'll be okay."

"What happened?" Sarah asked, sitting down next to her.

"I cut through the playground on Fifteenth Street. Somebody grabbed me, and . . ."

Keisha's thoughts were lost somewhere between the terror of the attack and remembrances of Jamal. It wasn't that she couldn't speak. She just didn't know what to say.

Her father grabbed her shoulders and looked into her eyes.

"And what?" he said.

"They tried to rape me."

"Who's *they?*"

"There were two of them. I don't know who they were. But one of them had a scar on his face."

"You didn't see anything else?" her father said, reaching into the back of his closet.

"It was dark," she said, allowing her pent-up tears to flow. "They grabbed me from behind."

Reverend Anderson emerged from the back of the closet holding a bat. His eyes were red and swollen, and his tear-streaked face was filled with rage.

"Sarah, I want you to take Keisha home," he said quickly.

"John, don't be foolish," Sarah snapped. "She doesn't even know who it was."

"She might not know who it was," he said as he moved toward the door. "But I know who to start with."

"You need to start with the Lord," Sarah called after him.

"When I find the man I'm looking for," the reverend said, pulling a pair of leather gloves onto his massive hands, "he'll need the Lord a whole lot more than I do."

Thick cigar smoke wafted through the back room at Frank Nichols's bar, floating toward vents in the ceiling and disappearing as if it were never there.

Though the bar had always been the only profitable business on Fifteenth and Dauphin, it was nothing spectacular up front, where the regular patrons drank. But the back room, with its ventilation system and entertainment center, was where Frank ran his real business—drug dealing.

The back room, where murders had been planned and takeovers mapped out, was where Frank felt most comfortable. And so, whenever he was here, the mood was festive. Tonight was no different.

Frank and his lieutenants ate fried shrimp and coleslaw as scantily clad barmaids shuttled back and forth with glass upon glass of Jack Daniel's.

Frank sat facing the door, his high yellow skin and honey-colored eyes shining in the dim light. He was a small man, no more than five-eight. But beneath his pretty-boy looks and conservative suits, there was strong, wiry muscle, and the heart of a lion. At fifty-five, after nearly forty years in the game, his mind was sharper than ever.

His lieutenants were lined up around a flat-screen television, watching a rebroadcast of a heavyweight bout in which a too-prim Englishman beat a brash former champion from Brooklyn.

Frank had brought his men together this way at least once a month for the past four decades. He liked to study them away from the corners where they plied their trade. He wanted to see their habits, observe their desires, and note their weaknesses.

If voluptuous barmaids in thongs could distract them from the business at hand, their weakness was flesh, and they could betray him for a whore.

If they were eager to refill their glasses after more than two or three shots, their weakness was strong drink, and alcohol could loosen their tongues.

If they hoarded the food for themselves, they were gluttons, and their greed would eventually spill over into business.

Over the years, his formula for evaluating his men had proved valuable. So had keeping his ear to the street.

Frank pointed the remote control at the television screen and turned off the fight. When he did, everyone turned to him. Because at these gatherings, where security was minimal and business was almost never discussed, such an action meant something was wrong. The room went silent as they waited to hear what it was.

Frank sipped from his glass and lowered his eyes.

"Colorado Street was short a thousand dollars this month," he said, staring at the man who ran the crack trade on the tiny block off Dauphin Street. "You replaced it outta your pocket, Raheem. But that don't solve the problem. I wanna know why it was missin' in the first place."

Raheem was six-five, thirty years old, and built like a linebacker. But Frank's stare was enough to cause him to tremble. He sipped at his drink to calm his nerves before he spoke.

"Young boy told me he wanted a job," Raheem said nervously. "I knew the family was strugglin', so I gave him a package. He decided he wanted to trick with the money. Took this young girl up New York on a shoppin' spree. When I heard about it, I went up there and found him."

Raheem took another swig of his drink.

"He won't be workin' for us no more," he said firmly. "I told his mama, 'When they find him, I'll pay for the funeral.'"

Frank looked around the room, studying the faces of his lieutenants, until his gaze was once again fixed on Raheem.

"So why somebody tell me you took the money?"

"'Cause they lyin'," Raheem said evenly.

Frank stared at him for a moment longer. The tension in the air was palpable.

"I know they lyin'," Frank answered. "But it's still your fault. You never give a package to somebody that's hungry. You give it to somebody who already know how to hustle. And if they mess it up, you don't do 'em soon as you hear about it. You wait."

As Frank spoke, there was a rumbling outside the door. The single guard who was posted there yelled at someone to stop. There was the sickening sound of wood against flesh, and a body tumbling to the floor. It sounded like it could've been the police, so no one fired. They simply placed their hands on their weapons and waited.

Seconds later, the door burst open and a man wielding a bat stepped through. The men in the room leveled their weapons, but Frank raised his hand before the bullets could fly.

Reverend Anderson stopped when he saw the guns pointed in his direction. He lowered the bat, stood in the middle of the floor, looked around him, and observed the faces of the men who ran the neighborhood crack corners.

None of them bore the scar he was looking for. But that didn't mean they were blameless.

"I came for the man who tried to rape my baby," he said, his right hand tightly gripping the handle of the bat as his eyes bulged with rage.

Frank Nichols leaned back in his chair and smiled.

"See, that's what I was just talkin' about," he said coolly. "You don't go out right after somethin' happens and try to settle it. You give yourself time to think about what you gon' do. Otherwise you end up bringin' a bat to a gunfight."

"There won't be no gunfight, 'cause y'all ain't trying to go to prison," Anderson said, mocking them. "They make you check your guns at the door of the prison. Guys like you can't survive without them."

"Is that right, Pastor?" Frank said smoothly.

"Yeah, that's right," Reverend Anderson said. "And so is this: if anything else happens to Keisha on these streets, Frank, I'm blaming you. And when I come, I'm coming correct."

Nichols grinned knowingly. "Seems like every time somethin' happens to your family, you blame me," he said.

Reverend Anderson dropped the bat and lunged at Nichols, but two of his lieutenants grabbed the pastor and dragged him back before he could swing.

Nichols took a sip of his drink and sat back. "John, I don't know what happened with your daughter, but I'll try to find out. And if I hear anything, I'll handle it."

Reverend Anderson wrenched free from the men who were holding him. "I don't need you to handle mine, Frank. I can handle my own."

Frank stood up and walked toward the pastor. When they were just inches from one another, he stopped and looked up at the taller man.

"We used to be like brothers, John," he said solemnly. "What happened?"

"You *know* what happened," said the pastor, looking around the room before settling his hate-filled gaze on Frank. "*This* happened. But I'ma shut this down, too. I promise you that."

"Well, I hope we can settle our differences before one of us dies," Frank said with a deadly calm. " 'Cause you never know. That might be sooner than later."

"You're right, Frank," Anderson said, echoing the underlying threat. "It just might be."

As Frank ambled back to his seat and the pastor turned to

leave, Frank's men put their weapons away in the belief that the altercation was over.

Only three people knew that it wasn't: Frank Nichols, John Anderson, and the young man with dreadlocks standing silently in the corner, watching as his father played God.

2

Sarah and her daughter exchanged few words during the short walk from the church to their home. But that wasn't unusual.

Sarah was most often withdrawn from her daughter. And Keisha resented it. That was why Keisha sat in silence while Sarah dressed the wounds she'd sustained in the attack, and afterward she stalked into her room, hoping that Sarah would stay away.

Sarah felt her daughter's bitterness, and indeed she shared it. She resented Keisha because she still had youth and opportunity, two commodities that Sarah had long ago squandered.

But in spite of the tension between them, Sarah knew that her daughter needed her now, because those men had attacked much more than Keisha's body. They'd attacked her very soul.

Tapping lightly on Keisha's door, Sarah twisted the doorknob and walked in.

Keisha, who was standing in front of the mirror, glanced at her mother and resumed staring at the bruises on her neck.

"Sit down, Keisha," Sarah said casually. "I want to talk to you."

Keisha hesitantly took a seat, though she didn't want to be bothered. Sarah sat next to her, wearing a look of uncertainty that Keisha wasn't used to seeing on her mother's face.

"A lot of things are different than they were when I was sixteen," Sarah began. "You see things we only whispered about in the girls' bathroom. You hear things we never said out loud. I know that, so don't think I'm sitting here trying to preach about things I don't understand."

"Mom, I've had a really long day. I just want—"

"I know what you want," Sarah said. "You want me to leave you alone and let you see things for yourself. You want me to stop quoting the Bible, stop trying to make you into the kind of woman you need to be. You want to be like everybody else, right?"

Keisha lowered her eyes and didn't answer.

"See, that's the thing that hasn't changed, Keisha. When you're sixteen and your hips are round and your breasts are full, and men start looking at you like they want what's between your legs, you start to wonder. You start to think, 'Maybe it wouldn't be such a bad thing to try it.'

"You see your girlfriends riding around with drug dealers and wearing the finest clothes and going shopping every day. You learn that all you have to do is open your legs and the world is yours. And you start to think, 'Maybe the streets aren't as bad as they tell me they are. Maybe they're trying to hide something from me.'"

"What does that have to do with what happened tonight?" Keisha said, sensing the accusation.

"I just want to know," Sarah began, already regretting the question she was about to ask.

"What is it, Mom?"

"I want to know if things really happened the way you said they did. I want to know if there's anything else you need to tell me."

Keisha thought of Jamal. She wanted badly to tell her mother that she was wrong—that not every man wanted her simply for what he could take.

But Keisha couldn't break her promise to him. And even if she could, she was too hurt by her mother's suspicions to speak of anything else.

"Two men threw me down and tried to rape me," Keisha said, a tear rolling down her cheek. "They choked me and punched me and put a knife to my throat. They told me they would kill me if I didn't do what they wanted. And you're sitting here saying that it might be my fault?"

"I'm saying that I know what it's like to wonder," Sarah said defensively.

"Wonder what?"

"What life would be like if your father wasn't a pastor."

"So you're saying I went out looking for this?"

"No, I'm saying *I* did!"

Keisha reared back, the shock of her mother's words hitting her like a sharp blow.

"I'm saying I did things when I was your age because I was tired of being a preacher's daughter," Sarah said, her words tumbling out before she could stop them. "I see a lot of myself in you, Keisha. The only difference between us is this: you still have a chance to change your future. I don't."

They sat in silence, each of them tasting the bitter truth of Sarah's words.

"I wish you'd known your grandfather," Sarah said with a sad smile. "He was a good man. But he didn't leave me much breathing room, so I had to take it."

"But that's not what I'm doing," Keisha said defensively.

"That's what I told my parents, too," Sarah said. "But I was just like you. Smart and pretty and mature. I had my own job and my own money and I didn't have time for boys my age. I wanted men. So I sneaked around and got just what I wanted. And then I got a little something extra."

Keisha felt a chill run down her spine as her mother turned her face away in shame.

"This man I knew took me to dinner at some fancy restaurant downtown," Sarah said. "And when he drove me home, he went right past the corner where he usually dropped me off, and he took me out to the park."

Tears filled Sarah's eyes, and her voice broke.

"Then he raped me."

Sarah broke down. Keisha wanted to hug her, but she couldn't. The gulf between them was too great.

It hadn't been bridged by the scripture they'd shared, or the sermons they'd heard. It wouldn't be bridged by their common experience.

When Sarah stopped crying, Keisha looked her mother in the eye. "I didn't ask for what happened, Mom. You have to believe that."

Sarah searched her eyes. "I know you didn't. But I need you to promise me something."

"What?"

"Promise me you won't let yourself get sucked in by these streets. Because once you do, getting out will be harder than you could ever imagine."

"I promise, Mom," Keisha said.

But as soon as she'd said it, Keisha knew it was a lie.

As Sarah exited the room, she knew it was, too.

A half hour passed, and Keisha was still reeling from Sarah's accusations. The revelation that her mother had been raped was of no small consequence. But it wasn't enough to win back Keisha's respect.

Keisha had spent years watching her mother wither under the strain of being a pastor's wife. And listening to her tonight made Keisha even more determined to follow a different path.

It was with that thought in mind that she snatched the vibrating phone from beneath her pillow when the call she'd been expecting from Jamal came through.

"Hello?" she whispered into the receiver.

"Meet me outside," Jamal said. "I'm at the end o' the alley, on Twentieth Street."

The call disconnected, and Keisha felt the blood rush to her face. The secrecy of their meetings was as exciting as the taste of his lips. But tonight's rendezvous would be different from the ones they'd been having since he'd shown up in her life again. Tonight he would have to tell her why.

Lifting the thin sheet that covered her, Keisha took off her cotton nightgown, revealing the tight jeans she wore underneath. She slipped on a T-shirt and crept down the hallway, past Sarah's locked bedroom door. She could hear Sarah talking on the phone—probably to one of the sisters from church.

Taking a deep breath, Keisha descended the steps, walked to the front door, unlocked it, and went outside. She moved quickly down the block and rounded the corner.

Jamal stood in the shadows and watched as her eyes lit up at the sight of him. The look on her face made him think of the first

.time they'd met, five years before, during one of his rare visits to North Philly.

He still remembered every detail.

He'd walked down Fifteenth Street and peered through the playground gate, where he spotted her playing double Dutch.

Her long, curly hair fell against her back each time she jumped, and her honey-brown eyes sparkled in the sun. Even then, when she was eleven and he was thirteen, he believed that she was beautiful.

He'd stared at her from a distance until he walked through the gate. And when he passed by her with a look in his eyes that conveyed a message beyond his years, she'd lost her balance and tripped between the ropes, falling to the ground in a heap.

Rushing to her side, he'd helped her up. And that simple act of kindness led to a first kiss, beautiful and sweet, between two children on the cusp of adolescence.

He never told her where he'd come from. And to Keisha, it made no difference. She defied her parents, who forbade her to date, and continued to meet with him secretly in the heat of Friday afternoons. That summer, she and Jamal shared the innocence of first love.

They stared into each other's eyes, whispering things that only they could hear, and talking of plans that only they could know. They held hands and shared laughter. And sometimes they just sat in comfortable silence, knowing that there was no need to fill it with words.

When the summer ended, Jamal's mother forced him to stay away from North Philly and, consequently, from Keisha. But, of all the girls Jamal had known in the five years since, Keisha was the only one to show up in his dreams.

But he wasn't prepared for what happened when she showed

up in the flesh, looking like a woman, though her parents treated her like a child.

It amazed him that she was willing to sneak away to be with him, when she knew that her parents would never approve of her spending time with a boy who was clearly from the streets.

"Come on," Keisha said, breaking into his thoughts. "I don't have long."

They rushed into his black Lexus, and once they were behind its tinted windows, their lips joined in a lingering kiss.

Jamal pulled away, and looked into her eyes. "Are you all right?" he said, genuinely concerned.

Keisha nodded. "I will be."

"I'm still tryin' to find out who them dudes was," Jamal said. "When I do, I'll take care of it."

"My father said the same thing," Keisha said worriedly. "I hope he doesn't do anything crazy."

At the mention of her father, Jamal's facial expression turned hard, and at the same time terribly sad.

Keisha hated it when he looked that way. At times like these, his true feelings were obscured by the mask of anger that he'd learned to wear over the years.

She didn't want to deal with the truth beneath his scowl, so she quickly changed the subject.

"You know, Jamal," she said with a smile, "these last few weeks have been wonderful. It's almost like it was when we were kids."

"Yeah, but we ain't kids no more. It's a whole lotta stuff we gotta deal with now."

Keisha glanced at him, confused. "What kind of stuff are you talking about?"

"Your father, for one thing," he said, without returning her gaze.

"Jamal, it doesn't matter what my father thinks about us."

"That ain't what you said three weeks ago."

"Well, this isn't three weeks ago!" she said heatedly.

Jamal was surprised by her fire. She was, too.

Taking a deep breath, she tried to explain. "Jamal, I've spent my whole life in a little box—worrying about what my father thinks, or what my mother thinks, or what the church folks think. All I want to do now is be free. Free to choose who I am, free to choose what I believe, free to love who I want to."

She reached out her hand, gently touching his face. "And I love you."

"You don't even know me," he said, turning to face her.

"I knew you the first time I kissed you, Jamal," she said, as a smile spread across her face. "I never forgot the way it felt. Maybe that's why, when I bumped into you when I started working at Strawbridge's, it was like nothing had changed. It was easy to sneak away with you, the same way we used to sneak away and watch the sun set when we were kids."

Jamal shook his head. "You don't understand, Keisha."

"You're right," she said, searching his eyes. "I don't. I thought I was the one who had to run and hide."

She reached for the handle and opened the door.

"My mother's not right about much," she said. "But she's right about men. I guess I'm not giving it up fast enough for you."

"It ain't about that, Keisha."

"You're not ready for me, Jamal," she said bitterly. "Hopefully, I'll still be around when you are."

She was about to get out when Jamal grabbed her arm. "Wait, Keisha."

"You're hurting me, Jamal," she said, looking down at his hand. "Let me go."

Jamal stared into her eyes menacingly.

"Close the door," he said. "I need to talk to you."

Keisha felt a surge of fear overtake her anger, and she did as she was told.

Jamal released her arm. And as his heart and mind engaged in a tug of war, he told her the truth he'd thus far managed to avoid.

"Two months ago, your father started talkin' 'bout gettin' crack outta North Philly," he said, staring straight ahead, as if in a trance. "Frank asked me to make him stop."

Keisha's face creased in a look of confusion. "Frank Nichols?" she said in disbelief. "What, do you *work* for him?"

"Yeah," Jamal whispered. "You could say that."

Jamal paused as if to detach himself from the cruel reality of his admission.

"We sent your father money. He sent it back. We sent him women. He ignored 'em. We sent threats. He ain't budge. For a while we thought he ain't care about nothin'. But we was wrong. He cares about you."

Jamal avoided looking at Keisha's eyes as he spoke. He didn't want to see the hurt they contained.

"I started followin' you," he said matter-of-factly. "I learned what you did, where you went, and what you liked, so if we ever needed to put our hands on you, we could."

"Is that what you were doing at my job a few weeks ago?" she asked suspiciously. "Following me?"

"Yeah."

"And were you following me tonight, too?"

"Yeah, but—"

"So that's all I was to you?" Keisha said angrily. "Something to report back to Frank Nichols about?"

"Keisha, you don't understand."

"You keep saying that!" Keisha shouted. "But I do understand. I understand that you work for the biggest drug dealer in North Philly—the same man my father's wanted to bring down for years. I understand you acted like you cared about me when all you were doing was keeping tabs on me for your boss."

"Frank Nichols ain't just my boss!" Jamal shouted.

"Well, who is he, then?"

"He's my father."

The words hung in the air between them. They answered Keisha's questions about Jamal's penchant toward secrecy. And it raised yet another question that Keisha was forced to ask.

"Why are you telling me this?"

Jamal turned to her. "I'm tellin' you 'cause it ain't just a job to me, Keisha. I loved you since I was a little boy, and I'll be damned if I'ma sit here and let somethin' happen to you 'cause o' my father."

"And what about my father?" Keisha asked.

Jamal paused. "That's the other thing I wanted to tell you, Keisha. Your father might be in trouble."

After leaving Frank Nichols's bar, Reverend Anderson wandered Diamond Street, thankful that the streets were bathed in a quiet that was rare for a North Philly summer.

The stillness allowed the murderous rage within him to subside. But it also brought back memories of a time he'd taken pains to forget.

Anderson had seen this type of silence before, in the days when he was destined to live a life like Frank Nichols.

It was nearly forty years before, when his father's bootlegging and speakeasies and numbers running had finally given way to heroin dealing.

John Anderson Sr. wasn't like other dealers of the sixties.

There was no credit, no competition, and no mercy. He was before his time, really, in that he was the most ruthless man North Philly had ever seen. That would have been bad enough. But he was training his son to be his successor. So when competitors rose up to overtake them, or when customers took too long to pay, John Junior, who was just seventeen years old when he joined the family business in 1962, was sent to do his father's bidding.

He broke arms with his hands. He cracked heads against sidewalks. He broke ribs with baseball bats.

He had done other jobs on the very block he was now passing through. Jobs that kept him looking over his shoulder even now.

John glanced behind him and saw a blue car rolling slowly along the street, its windows sliding down about halfway. When the barrel of the nine-millimeter poked out at him, John hit the ground and rolled. And as the bullets hit the sidewalk, sending sparks into the air, he jumped up running, keeping his body low as the bullets whizzed over his head.

There was the hum of the car's engine as it rode alongside him, then the quick, repeated tap of the gunshots, then the unmistakable and sickening thud of a bullet hitting flesh. Someone screamed, a body fell, and he felt something warm and sticky running down his face.

He kept running, half expecting to feel the burning sensation of a bullet boring into him. When he didn't, he ran right, onto Sixteenth Street, then ducked left, through the alleylike street that ran from Sixteenth to Seventeenth. About halfway through, he heard the car skid to a stop behind him. A door opened and shut, and footsteps slapped against the sidewalk as someone gave chase.

John knew he couldn't outrun his pursuer, so he stopped and dived into a vacant lot that had overgrown with pungent, tree-sized weeds.

He tried to hold his breath, and listened as the man walked

the length of the alley. He wanted to look out and see the man's face, to remember it so that he could repay him for the attempt on his life.

But a look might cost him too much. So he waited. And when he heard the footsteps go past him again, he glanced out from behind the weeds and saw the back of the shooter's head. It was covered in thin dreadlocks, tied together and hanging to shoulder length.

As the sound of sirens drew closer, the shooter got back into the car and drove away, turning the corner with screaming tires and heading west on Diamond toward the projects.

John reached up and touched his head, and when he looked at his hand, he saw blood. He reached up again to find the wound. That was when he realized that the blood wasn't his.

"Mama!" The bloodcurdling scream split the air, and John Anderson ran back toward Diamond Street.

When he turned the corner, he saw an old woman sprawled on the sidewalk, close to a large brownstone.

As he approached her side, he saw blood crisscrossing her chest like thick, red spiderwebs. He saw her arms stretched out at her sides. But it wasn't until he saw her face that a sick feeling overtook him.

He walked up to her and knelt down next to the middle-aged woman who sat on the ground, crying uncontrollably over her mother.

"Oh, Mother Johnson," he said to himself, as he looked at her soft brown eyes, staring skyward, and her lips curled in a satisfied smile. "You're in a better place now."

"What happened here?" said a cop who jumped out of his car and ran over to the victim.

"Somebody was shooting and this lady got hit," John said. "I guess she was coming home from bible study and she got caught in the crossfire."

"And who are you?" the cop asked, taking out a notepad.

"I'm the one they were shooting at," he said, standing up to move as Fire Rescue workers arrived and ran over to the body.

"I'm her pastor."

3

It Was seven o'clock in the morning, and Homicide lieutenant Kevin Lynch was in his office at police headquarters, drinking bitter coffee and flipping through a file from the night before.

As he leaned back in his chair and moved the file from one side of his battered wooden desk to the other, his shaved head gleamed in the fluorescent light, his strong shoulders slumped, and his tired eyes glazed over.

He was looking at the words on the pages, but he wasn't really reading them. He already knew that they recounted the shooting death of a seventy-one-year-old woman named Emma Jean Johnson.

Her death marked the twentieth homicide of the summer, and the two hundredth of the year. The numbers were the lowest in a decade.

But the statistics didn't make it any easier for Lynch.

Whether it was one homicide or a thousand, he privately mourned every victim whose name came across his desk. He was especially dismayed by murders in North Philadelphia, because he'd grown up there.

It didn't matter if it was east of Broad, where the projects of his youth had been razed and replaced by tidy twin houses on manicured plots of grass, or north of Diamond, where the gleaming halls of Temple University gave way to crumbling row houses and time-worn streets.

To Lynch, North Philadelphia was one neighborhood divided along fabricated lines that did nothing to change the lives of the people who had no choice but to live there.

He was attached to those people, because he was those people. His inability to disconnect from that reality was his greatest strength as an investigator. And it was his greatest weakness as a man.

Though he'd learned to hide his feelings from fellow cops, his wife and daughter had watched the weight of dozens of murder investigations eat away at him over the years. And in some ways, the job had done more harm to him as a father and husband than anything in his life.

Even his wife's miscarriage some years before, which had brought tears and regret, and healing, and scarring, hadn't affected them as much as his career. His job required time. And time created distance, a distance that at times seemed insurmountable.

He'd often asked himself if a career of solving other people's problems had exacerbated his own. Yet the question wasn't enough to make him walk away from law enforcement. In fact, he'd fought to stay, even as cases like that of Kenya Brown, the nine year old who'd been murdered in his childhood home, The Bridge, threatened to destroy his community, his marriage, and his career.

Now, nearly ten years after witnessing the devastation that resulted from Kenya's death, Lynch was still watching people die for little or nothing, and he was still asking himself why.

Opening the file on his desk, he looked again at the photographs from the Johnson murder scene. There were bullet casings on the ground, along with blood, a handkerchief, and a Bible. And then there was Mrs. Johnson, her eyes fixed on some unseen point in the sky. She looked almost like the woman Lynch had known as his grandmother.

He wondered if the scene the officers described in their report was genuine. Did Emma Jean Johnson's daughter kneel by her dying mother's side because she grieved her violent and senseless death? Or did she, like Lynch, mourn her squandered chance to have one last conversation with the woman who'd raised her?

A detective knocked on his door and stirred him from his memories. He was glad, as always, to get back to work. It was the work that prevented the past from consuming him.

"Lieutenant," the detective said. "We've got problems with that shooting from last night."

Lynch sighed, leaned forward in his chair, and opened the file. "Didn't Reverend Anderson already give a statement implicating Frank Nichols?"

"Yeah."

"So bring Nichols in."

"We sent detectives to get him at six o'clock this morning, but Anderson already had five hundred people outside Nichols's bar."

"So move them."

"We tried, but they're saying they want Nichols." The detective leaned across Lynch's desk. "And we don't think Nichols is about to go quietly."

Reverend John Anderson stood atop a car outside Frank Nichols's bar, his tired, red-rimmed eyes surveying the crowd of hundreds who'd come from congregations all over the city.

After giving his statement to detectives, he'd spent the remainder of the night making phone calls to organize the gathering.

It was a protest that was thus far peaceful. But he didn't know how long it would stay that way. And he didn't know if he wanted it to.

The crowd had marched the six blocks from his church on Twentieth and York to the bar at Fifteenth and Dauphin, and now they were leaning forward, watching and waiting as Anderson raised the bullhorn to his lips.

"Last night," he said, pausing to lock eyes with several men in the crowd, "they tried to rape my daughter."

There was a shocked silence. Then the crowd pressed closer to the makeshift stage.

"My only child came to me with blood on her dress and tears in her eyes and said, 'Daddy, they tried to hurt me.'

"I turned to my wife, and she said, 'John, turn to the Lord.' "

Reverend Anderson paused and looked down at his daughter, who was standing directly in front of him, trying not to allow her divided allegiance to show on her face.

"But when I looked in my baby's eyes and saw hurt," John continued, "I wasn't a pastor anymore, I wasn't a preacher anymore, I wasn't a teacher anymore. I was just a father. A father whose child was in pain."

There was a smattering of amens as heads began to nod in agreement.

"I grabbed the nearest thing I could get my hands on," the pastor said, pointing to the bar on the corner. "And I came here, and told Frank Nichols that if one hair on my baby's head was ever harmed on these streets, there would be hell to pay!"

The crowd began to clap wildly as Anderson's jaw jutted out defiantly.

He suddenly grew solemn. "And through it all, Mother Johnson was praying," he said, his voice beginning to rise. "Praying that these drugs, and these rapists, and these thieves, and these murderers, would be wiped from our community!"

The clapping resumed in earnest, and as Lieutenant Kevin Lynch's black Mercury Marquis pulled onto the sidewalk across the street from the spot where Anderson was speaking, the pastor found his stride.

"Mother Emma Jean Johnson laid down her life so that God could answer her prayer!" he shouted to thunderous applause. "She was cut down like a dog in the street so that we could come here today and say, 'No more!'"

As the crowd worked itself into a frenzy, Lieutenant Lynch looked up at a three-story abandoned house that stood just a few feet behind Anderson. He saw a man walk to the edge of the rooftop and lie down. There was something in his hands. But it wasn't until he pointed it that Lynch realized what it was.

He grabbed his handheld radio. "Dan two-five, we've got a gun on the roof."

Voices exploded over the radio as Lynch pushed through the crowd.

Plainclothes officers from Civil Affairs moved rapidly toward the building where the gunman crouched on the roof. Uniformed officers removed barricades. Command officers called for additional units.

And Anderson called for Nichols to come outside.

"Frank Nichols!" he screamed into the megaphone. "It's judgment day!"

At that, two of Nichols's men emerged from the bar: Raheem, who ran Colorado Street, and an older man who ran Fifteenth Street. They closed a steel door behind them to prevent the increasingly hostile crowd from storming the place.

"Murderers!" someone yelled, and the crowd took up the taunt.

As the chant grew louder, Keisha looked over at Nichols's underlings, then scanned the crowd and saw Jamal standing about twenty feet to her left. They locked eyes, and Keisha's heart fluttered as she stood between the two men she loved.

Her feet were rooted to the spot as Lynch came within a yard of her father. The police commissioner and several commanders who'd just arrived on the scene were also pushing toward him.

"Get him down!" the commissioner screamed into his radio. "Get Reverend Anderson down!"

Lynch, who was now standing directly behind Keisha, looked up at the roof and took out his weapon just as Keisha tore her gaze away from Jamal.

"Daddy, get down!" Keisha yelled as Lynch's gun went off near her ear.

A second later, Dauphin Street disintegrated into bedlam.

The crowd that had pressed itself together to hear Anderson was now trying to tear itself apart. Old women were trampled. Children were separated from their parents. Men were trapped against cars. And the police were powerless to maintain order.

Keisha saw her father one minute, and the next minute she was knocked to her knees and swallowed up in the panicking mass of people. There was screaming, then several gunshots, and suddenly someone hit the ground just a few feet away from her. She looked over and saw one of the protestors—an older man with bloodstained gray hair. He was struggling to breathe, and blood leaked like tears from the corners of his eyes.

Keisha screamed and tried to rise to her feet. But someone ran past and kicked her in the head. As she began to lose consciousness, she felt an arm reach down and grab her.

Then everything went black.

Keisha awakened on a couch in a dimly lit, dank basement, squinting to adjust to the light as a man sat perched in front of her on a barstool.

She tried to speak, but her tongue was thick in her mouth. She attempted to rise, but her head swam. She sank back into the couch, which sat against a crumbling cement wall on a dirt floor.

Fighting to correct her blurry vision, she blinked, and the man's face came into focus. When it did, she saw black skin framed by long, thin dreadlocks. And perched above his chiseled nose and thick lips were dark, intense eyes, staring tenderly into hers.

She was dizzy, floating as if in a dream, and reached out to steady herself. As she did so, her fingertips grazed the fine, shiny stubble that covered his face. She traced his cheekbones, which rose at sharp angles. Then she followed the path of his jaw and ran her fingers down to his chin, and up to his lips.

"What happened, Jamal?" she asked, trying hard to regain her equilibrium.

"You bumped your head," he said, leaning forward to stroke her hair. "They was 'bout to run over you, so I brought you in here."

She couldn't understand everything he was saying, but she

knew that his touch caused something to go through her. Something that was exhilarating and frightening, just like the muffled sounds of screaming and pounding that she heard coming from somewhere above her head.

Her thoughts were still muddled. But when she forced herself to look away from Jamal's hypnotic gaze, one thought jumped to the fore.

"Where's my father?" she asked anxiously.

"The cops scooped him up. He all right."

"I need to see him," she said, leaping off the couch and trying to push past him.

He placed his arm in front of her. "Not yet," he said quickly.

"Let me go!" she said, pushing more violently. "I have to see my father!"

"If I let you go," he said, his tender gaze hardening, "you might not ever see him again."

She suddenly stopped struggling as her face clouded with a mix of anger and realization.

"You knew!" she shouted while punching and slapping at him. "That's why you told me my father might be in trouble last night. You knew they were gonna try to kill him!"

He grabbed her hands and tried to calm her down. "Listen to me, Keisha."

"No!" she said, kicking wildly in an effort to get away from him. "You knew!"

"Keisha, stop!" He took her by her arms and forced her down onto the couch, then knelt on top of her and held her there.

The two of them sat there for a moment, gulping air as they tried to recover from the brief struggle.

"I didn't know," he said, staring into her eyes. "I just know they told me to get your pop to stop gettin' in our business."

"You're lying," she said.

"Keisha, listen to me," Jamal said earnestly. "I don't know who tryin' to kill your father. All I know is, it ain't me. Did my father get somebody else to do it? I don't know. But I do know this. My pop kills people. He don't care no more about me than he do about you or anybody else. And if he find out what I'm 'bout to do, he'll kill me, too."

Keisha looked into his eyes, searching them for the lie she believed was there. She couldn't find it.

"And what are you about to do?" she asked.

He reached out and held her fingers between his own. "I'm leavin', Keisha," he said gravely. "I'm walkin' away from my father's business."

Keisha could hear in his voice that he was serious.

"Why would you do that?" she asked, hoping he would give her the answer that she wanted.

Jamal's eyes took on a faraway look as he tried to find the right words.

"My mother hated me 'cause I was too much like my father," he whispered. "My father couldn't love me 'cause he ain't know how. So if I gotta choose between love and hate—between them and you—I'm takin' you, and I ain't lookin' back."

He took her chin in his hand and turned her face toward his own.

"I'm makin' my choice, Keisha," he said earnestly. "I need to know if you gon' make yours, too."

There was a lull in the shooting, and John Anderson felt like he was in the midst of a dream.

As the police officers' hands guided him away from the car

where he'd given his speech and he listened to the garbled sounds of shouting voices all around him, he could feel that he was in the eye of a storm. And it was troubling, because he knew in his spirit that the thunder and lightning were about to begin anew.

Earlier, he had come there in the belief that trouble was what he wanted. But he wasn't so sure anymore. He was, after all, a man of peace, he thought as the officers pushed him through the crowd. But as the moments stretched out, allowing him to see things clearly through the mounting confusion, he realized that he hadn't known peace in forty years.

As he absorbed the various sights around him—a woman running with a baby, an injured man lying on the asphalt, one car crushed against another, police officers shouting into radios—he saw the same type of confusion that often raged in his mind.

Thoughts from his past cropped up on a regular basis, challenging the very essence of who he was. These were the thoughts that mocked him for the sermons he preached, and the service he rendered, and the faith he claimed to hold dear.

These thoughts grew into action. And every day, they caused him to fail when his faith was tested. There were tests of the flesh, and tests of his convictions, tests that repeatedly showed that he, like any man, was driven by his desires.

But while other preachers proclaimed that their desires were in line with God's, John Anderson knew that the desires that drove him were anything but godly. They were sometimes downright wicked. And if he'd learned anything on this day, it was that wicked desires bred wicked results.

The police moved him past the car, too slowly it seemed, in an effort to get him away before the shooting resumed.

When it did, John turned, and for the first time recognized the police commissioner on his right.

But as John opened his mouth to shout a warning, the sound of his voice was swallowed up by the thud of a bullet, smacking against flesh like the sound of wood against bone.

John watched the police commissioner fall to the ground in a heap, and in the next moment John was pushed down next to him.

As he lay there, behind the open door of a police car, he prayed that there would be no more death today.

Keisha sat on the couch and stared across it into the face of the man she'd fallen in love with as a child. It was a face that had matured over the years.

But the boy she'd known was still there, in that face. He lived in those smoldering eyes. She could see him still, staring at her across the playground and speaking without words.

He was saying that the dreams they'd shared as children were going to live or die based upon what happened in the next few moments. There would be no more playground sunsets or secret kisses. There would be no more childhood laughter or shared innocence.

Right here, right now, in the dank air of a basement, Keisha would have to make a choice that only a woman could. And she didn't know if she was ready for that.

"What you thinkin' about?" Jamal asked.

"I'm thinking about the freedom I told you I wanted," she said thoughtfully. "And I'm wondering why it doesn't seem that important now."

"Maybe you just scared," he said, taking her hand in his.

Keisha looked up into his face. "Why would I be afraid?"

"'Cause now you gotta do more than just talk about bein' free. You gotta decide if you really want to."

"Suppose I'm not ready to decide now?"

"Then I guess you already made your decision," Jamal said sadly.

Keisha wasn't sure what she wanted. But she knew what she didn't want. She didn't want to watch her parents' marriage break under the weight of the ministry. She didn't want to spend the rest of her life wondering what could have been. And most of all, she didn't want to lose Jamal.

"Why can't we just stay here and be together?" she said with upturned eyes.

"'Cause people who don't follow my father's orders don't live long."

"Where will you go?"

"I don't know," he said, stroking her hair.

Keisha looked straight ahead and spoke, almost to herself. "How can you live your life, knowing your own father would want to kill you?"

"How can you live in a place where they talk about love, but you never see it?" Jamal retorted.

"How do you know what I see?" she asked saucily.

"'Cause if you saw love, you wouldn't be tryin' to get it from me," Jamal said, matching her tone.

"If you loved me, you wouldn't talk about my family that way," Keisha said.

"This ain't about our families, Keisha. It's about us."

Jamal got up slowly from the couch and walked across the basement floor.

"But since you want to make it about families, let me tell you 'bout mine," he said quietly.

He paused to allow his mind to unlock the memories.

"My mom was a college girl—a good girl who met my pop one night in a club. He told her he was a businessman. She believed him.

"They dated for a minute, and when he got her pregnant, she found out what his business really was. She hated him for how he made his livin', and she made sure I ain't see him, 'cause she ain't want me to turn out like him. Problem was, she hated me, just like she hated him."

"That summer I spent comin' down here to see you? I had to sneak down here, 'cause I knew she ain't want me nowhere near my pop.

"When she heard what I was doin', she sent me down South. When that ain't work, she bought me back home. When I got popped the second time for hustlin', she told me what her eyes had told me all my life. She said I wasn't shit. She said, if I wanted to be like my father, I could go 'head and do that. Then she put me out her house, and told me to forget I was her son."

Jamal turned and faced Keisha, and she thought she could see the reflection of his tears.

"You ask me how I know you don't see no love?" he said quietly. "I know, 'cause I can see it in your eyes. They look just like mine."

Keisha got up from the couch and threw her arms around his neck. He wrapped his arms around her waist, and the two of them hugged one another in an effort to squeeze away their pain.

Keisha kissed Jamal's cheek, released her embrace, and turned away from him.

"I want to be with you, Jamal," she said, biting her lip. "But there's so much I want to do with my life. I've been working with this lady at my job who says I have a good eye, and I could probably work in fashion."

She turned to him. "I want to do that, Jamal. I want to see the world. I want to make a mark."

"And you can't do that with me?" he said with resentment.

"Haven't you ever wanted anything, Jamal?"

"Yeah," he said, his voice cracking. "I wanted you."

The words struck her like lightning, making her forget everything that had come before.

And when she looked into his eyes and saw the depth of his love for her, she knew that her decision had been made. Yes, she wanted the freedom to choose her own path. Yes, she wanted the chance to succeed. But more than any of that, she wanted love. And she knew that she would get that from Jamal.

She kissed him gently on the lips. "I want you, too," she said tenderly.

Placing her palms against his face, she put her lips against his ear.

"Tell me what I need to do to come with you."

In the quiet, damp air of the basement, Jamal sat her down on the couch, and began to lay out the plan of escape he'd been formulating since the night before.

"I'ma have to act like I snatched you like my pop told me to."

He pulled back his shirt to reveal the gun he was carrying in his waistband. "I'ma have to use this."

She looked at him with a question in her eyes, and he took her hand in an effort to answer it.

"Touch it," he said, guiding her fingers to the barrel of the gun.

She did, and at once felt something awaken deep inside of her. It was an excitement that was almost sexual.

Her lips parted slightly, and her mouth watered with anticipation. She was finally going to taste the world she'd always seen around her—a world that was reflected in the dim light that played upon the gun's gray steel.

"I'ma carry this gun," he said with a sly smile playing on his lips. "But I want you to know my gun belong to you."

Keisha felt herself blush at the underlying message.

"I want you to understand somethin' else, too," he said, stroking her cheek.

"What's that?"

"No matter what happen in the next few hours, no matter what it look like I'm doin', I want you to understand that I love you. And I would never let nothin' happen to you."

She placed her hand against his, and guided it along her face. "I know."

Jamal kissed her tenderly. Then he pulled out a cell phone and called one of his father's people to say he had the girl.

As he spoke, Keisha could hear the shooting outside begin anew. The sound of the bullets made her feel alive.

Lynch crouched behind the car where Reverend Anderson had stood and listened to the high-pitched whine of bullets as they ricocheted off nearby parked cars. From where he was kneeling, it was hard to tell whom the gunman was targeting, or if he was aiming at all.

He knew that the shooter was on a rooftop, and that it was his job to remove him.

He watched as panicked protesters ran one block east and charged onto Philadelphia's main thoroughfare, Broad Street, stumbling into rush-hour traffic.

He saw cars swerve and crash to avoid fleeing people as screams pierced the air and bodies were flung skyward. And when the crumpled wrecks had filled the intersection and the injured lay moaning in agony, he watched traffic back up in all directions, leaving the crowd trapped between twisted metal and flying lead.

As the gunfire continued, residents of the block shut their doors and huddled inside. Police were pinned down near their vehicles. Children cried for their mothers. Husbands called to their wives. And Lynch jumped out from behind the car where he'd been hiding. He ran full speed toward an alley on the north side of the street.

Once there, he pulled his weapon and looked down the alley to see if there was clear passage to the other side. But he couldn't see anything beyond the weeds and trash in front of him.

"Dan two-five!" he yelled into his handheld radio. "Get me some more units on Dauphin Street!"

The sound of sirens filled the air in response to his call. But even if backup could get there, they'd have to abandon their vehicles and make their way to Dauphin Street on foot.

Lynch didn't have time to wait for that.

Holstering his gun, he covered his face with his arm to shield himself from the tear-shaped leaves that whipped back at him as he pushed through the trash-strewn alley.

As he passed through, he peered to his right, through the man-sized weeds, and saw children staring out at him from a kitchen window. Their faces were etched with the same emotion that pervaded the nearby streets—fear.

Just across from them, on the other side of the alley, he found what he was looking for. Removing his gun from its holster, he stepped over knee-high trash and pushed through a dry-rotted wooden gate to an abandoned house.

The back door was gone, so he stepped through the opening and thrust his hand out in front of him, feeling his way through the darkness and hoping that he wouldn't fall through the creaking floor.

He could smell the charred wood from the fire that had long ago gutted the building. He could feel the dampness from the water that had failed to save it. And as he made his way through the dining room and to the steps that led to the second floor of the three-story house, he felt something else that he couldn't quite place.

There was a hiss, a sudden rumbling, and something ran toward him, its claws scratching against the floor before it lunged at him. He ducked sideways and it flew past, landing a few feet behind him and running toward the back door.

"Damn rats," he muttered.

Moving quickly up the staircase, he jogged to the second floor, then rounded the landing and skipped every other stair until he made it to the third.

Tiptoeing through the hallway, he stepped over missing floorboards on his way to the back window, where he knelt down and listened to the gunshots outside.

He quickly realized that he was just a few houses from the rooftop where the shooter was positioned.

Lynch opened the window and slithered out to the roof. He lay flat, facing the direction of the shooter, whom he could see kneeling behind one of the century-old chimneys that topped the houses on the row.

He was a dark-skinned man with dreadlocks, a muscular build, and a face that was fixed in an enraged expression. With each shot from the AK-47 that he held, his rage seemed to transform into a self-satisfied sneer.

Lynch could see from his demeanor that he wasn't shooting merely because someone had paid him to do it. No. This was personal.

Lynch aimed his weapon and looked for a clear shot, but the chimney that stood between them prevented it.

Then the shooter stopped to change the banana clip that held his bullets.

Jumping to his feet, Lynch leaped over a large hole in the burned-out roof, charged full speed across the forty feet that separated them, and unleashed a barrage from his semiautomatic pistol.

The shooter didn't stop to look for the source of the bullets. He merely ducked behind the chimney and hunkered down. In three seconds, Lynch was upon him.

The shooter didn't have the time to snap the new banana clip into his rifle. But he didn't need it.

Popping up from behind the chimney while clenching the barrel of the rifle, the shooter swung the butt and hit Lynch's arm, knocking Lynch's gun from his hand. Lynch fell down, and the shooter stood over him and swung the rifle again. This time he missed.

Lynch rolled away and stood to his full six feet. He charged at the shooter, who ducked sideways, causing Lynch to tumble toward the chimney. He turned to avoid hitting the bricks head-first, and there was a cracking sound as Lynch's shoulder slammed into the chimney.

The pain blurred his vision as he turned to face his adversary. Then the younger, more agile man grabbed the rifle again and swung it, hitting Lynch in his head.

Lynch saw a flash of light and felt a warm liquid flow down the side of his face. He heard gunshots and approaching voices. And the last sound he heard before losing consciousness was the sound of footsteps running away.

A minute later, Lynch heard words through a velvet haze, but was unable to respond.

"Lieutenant," a police officer said, kneeling over him.

"Lieutenant Lynch!" the officer shouted, shaking his shoulder.

The pain pierced Lynch's body like an arrow and snatched him back from the fog that had enveloped him after he was struck with the rifle butt.

"Where's the shooter?" Lynch said, trying to sit up and wincing with the pain before two Fire Rescue workers arrived and told him to stay down.

"He's gone," the officer said. "But he couldn't have gotten far."

"Is anyone hurt besides me?" Lynch asked, trying and failing to laugh, because the pain was just too great.

The cop looked at the Fire Rescue workers, who looked down at Lynch and busied themselves treating his wounds, because they didn't think it was their place to answer such a question.

"I said, is anyone hurt?" Lynch asked, more forcefully.

"A protestor was shot," the officer said. "It looks like he's gonna be okay."

"Thank God," Lynch said. "It could've been a lot worse."

"There was one more," the officer said, dejectedly looking down as he uttered the news.

"Commissioner Freeman was hit. He's dead."

4

One minute after the guns fell silent, a thin veil of white smoke filled the air around Fifteenth and Dauphin, giving the street an otherworldly glow.

Injured and frightened protesters, some bloodied and scarred, roamed the pothole-ridden asphalt, trying in vain to make sense of what they'd just witnessed. For a few moments, they all stumbled about in silence. Then a few of them began to call out to those who'd been lost in the mêlée. It was then that the street came back to life.

Police commanders barked orders as uniformed officers arrested the men who'd emerged from the bar during the protest. Officers in black combat fatigues set up a staging area across the street from the bar.

Those who'd been caught in the middle tried to regroup as well. Sobbing children ran to their mothers' outstretched arms.

Crouching protesters rose up from their hiding spaces. Cars began to navigate the maze of accidents that had brought Broad Street's rush-hour traffic to a standstill.

And then, as the smoke began to clear and the slowly spinning lights atop police and Fire Rescue vehicles swept over the frightened faces and century-old brick houses of Dauphin Street, camera- and microphone-wielding reporters rushed into the crowd.

A cameraman from Channel 6 approached a group of scarf-bedecked young women whose curvaceous figures and world-weary eyes belied their tender ages. They giggled and jockeyed for position when they saw him, jumping at the chance to be on television.

As the cameraman hoisted his camera onto his shoulder, one of the girls pushed her way to the front of the group and was speaking even before he held out the microphone.

"I seen the rifle on the roof and I just ran," the fifteen-year-old said, gesturing with one hand while holding a baby with the other. "Seemed like it was just all these bullets comin' from everywhere."

"It seemed like more than one guy to me," said another girl, her slippers whispering against the asphalt as she worked her way between her friend and the camera.

Several members of the media spotted the young women talking to the cameraman and converged on them. Within seconds, tape recorders and cameras were thrust at them from every angle, and they were fielding questions from ten people.

"What did the shooter look like?" shouted a grizzled white reporter from the *Philadelphia Daily News*.

"He damn sure ain't look like you," said the young woman with the baby, enjoying her moment of celebrity and milking it for all it was worth.

There was a smattering of laughter, and the reporter looked away, red-faced, as the girl in slippers spoke up.

"He was black," she said, her lips creased in a half-smile as cameramen trained their lights on her. "*Real* black."

"Looked like he had dreads," the girl with the baby chimed in.

"Did you see where he went?" asked a young blonde reporter from the *Philadelphia Inquirer*.

Before any of them could answer, an older woman came running over to the gathering, pushing reporters out of the way until she'd made her way to her daughter.

"Gimme this baby," she said, snatching the child from the arms of the fifteen-year-old. "And get your little dumb ass in the house."

"Ma, what you—"

"You don't be out here talkin' 'bout what you seen," she snapped. "They shot the damn police commissioner. You think they give a damn about shootin' you?"

A cameraman from Channel 10 tried to turn his camera on the woman, but she reached out with one hand and pushed it away.

"When they play this on the news, Nichols and them ain't gon' go lookin' for these white people you talkin' to," the woman said, staring into the crowd of reporters and locking eyes with each of them. "They gon' look for you. Now get in the house and stop runnin' yo damn mouth."

She pulled her daughter by the arm and the girl reluctantly followed, then glanced back at her friends, who'd already begun to walk away from the reporters. This, after all, was North Philly, a place where one's own words could be a death sentence.

That knowledge wasn't lost on the police. And though there was the potential for them to be overwhelmed with the minutiae of the incident—from traffic accident reports to hospital cases to accounting for the bullets fired by police—they had not lost sight of the biggest loss of the day.

The police commissioner was dead. And while the death of a black commissioner meant nothing to people in other areas of the city, it was devastating to those in the North Philadelphia community he'd come from.

Darrell Freeman's first experience with leadership was during the 1960s. After King's assassination and the ensuing riots that destroyed much of North Philadelphia, Freeman quickly learned that black men's lives meant little. As the leader of a gang from the Raymond Rosen housing projects on nearby Diamond Street, Freeman put that lesson to devastating use.

The chestnut-brown teen with the piercing eyes, scowling mouth, and hulking arms was ruthless in his takeover of the neighborhood, torturing rivals and crushing opposition. And though the police had never pinned anything on him, the streets knew of his bloody record, as did the other gangs.

It wasn't until his brother was killed in the crossfire during a gang war in the early 1970s that grief led Freeman to lay down his arms. When the House of Umoja began a movement in West Philadelphia to convince gang members to do the same, he turned that grief to purpose, and became one of their chief ambassadors.

A few years later, when the gang wars ended and poverty and crime tightened its grip on the neighborhood he'd once ruled, Freeman knew that there was only one battle left for him to fight. So he went to the only gang that was left. He joined the police department.

While his thirty-year rise through the department's ranks had surprised his fellow officers, those who'd known him from the streets wondered what had taken him so long.

Now the very streets he'd come back to save had taken him.

Someone would have to pay for that. And they would have to pay for it soon, because if they didn't, North Philly would erupt in the same kind of anarchy that Freeman had vowed to fight. The cops couldn't allow that to happen.

As police detectives waded into the crowd, searching desperately for willing witnesses, everyone began to disperse. And with good reason. The people of Dauphin Street had lived through fifteen years of drug-related violence. They didn't plan to say anything to the police that would bring about any more.

And so, as the injured received treatment from paramedics and the cameras recorded the aftermath of the confrontation, detectives took down the names of witnesses who would no doubt have memory lapses that would significantly lessen the DA's chance to build a case against anyone.

But this was no ordinary case. And Deputy Commissioner Dick Dilsheimer, who'd taken command in the wake of Commissioner Freeman's death, didn't plan to treat it as such.

The police veteran had been summoned from police headquarters in the aftermath of the shooting to take command from his fallen comrade, and he didn't plan to waste any time waiting for the streets to give up their own.

As the ex–Marine captain walked the 1500 block of Dauphin Street, his military carriage making him seem taller than his six-two, his steel-blue eyes were filled with a rage he hadn't known since Vietnam.

He approached the staging area where the elite Strike Force unit waited anxiously, and his closely cropped brown hair, which barely touched the collar of his black fatigues, stood on end.

His jaw clenched with determination, Dilsheimer scanned the quickly shrinking crowd. Then he nodded to a nearby lieutenant who was clad in black fatigues.

The lieutenant acknowledged his order. The chase was about to begin.

The young man with the shoulder-length dreadlocks watched the police from a nearby window. But he wasn't frightened, because the playing field was skewed in his favor.

His name was Ishmael, and he was as much a part of Dauphin Street as asphalt and concrete. He'd spent his early years climbing the walls of the neighborhood's demolished row houses by using their ragged bricks as footholds.

He and his friends had run over their tar-covered rooftops countless times. In the process, they had learned the neighborhood's layout from a vantage point that an outsider could never know, and trained themselves to disappear at will.

Today the knowledge had come in handy, as Ishmael used it to become invisible in streets choked off by police.

After cutting down the police commissioner and escaping from Lynch, he'd carried his weapon across the rooftops, pulled back the wooden cover on the second-floor rear window of a storefront church, and made his way inside while whispering a derisive "Thank you, Lord" to a God he didn't believe existed.

After replacing the wooden cover, he'd walked to the front of the building and settled down near a curtained window while regarding his crumbling surroundings.

The chipped paint, damp plaster, and dry-rotted floors made the space virtually uninhabitable. But from the outside, the building looked to be fully occupied, because the church folks—much like the neighborhood's store owners—had repaired the bottom floors of the building, while leaving the remainder a shell.

He would be safe there, at least for a little while. But as Ishmael broke down his semiautomatic rifle and hid its pieces in holes in the wooden floor, he looked out the window and saw twenty police officers split into two groups across the street from Nichols's bar.

They wore the black camouflage-type outfits of an elite unit, and they carried assault rifles.

Reaching into his pants pocket for the cell phone he'd carried with him, he dialed the number he'd been given by the woman who'd sent him. He needed to tell her that something had gone wrong.

But when an automated voice came on to tell him that the wireless customer he was calling was not available, he put the phone away and told himself he'd try again later.

Settling down by the window, he watched as the police surrounded the door of Nichols's bar.

And then he watched them storm the place.

The sound of the battering ram slamming against the reinforced steel front door was like the crash of thunder.

"What's that?" said a startled Keisha.

"Sound like the cops," Jamal said nervously. "They probably lookin' for my pop."

He held Keisha at arm's length. "If we gon' do this, we gotta go now."

"What if it doesn't work?" she asked.

It was the same question that had lingered in Jamal's mind since the moment he'd laid eyes on her at the protest. He didn't want to give her the answer, because he didn't want to know it himself.

"It will," he said, taking her by the hand.

The battering ram crashed against the door again.

"Come on," he said, reaching into his waistband for his gun and pulling her toward the basement's back wall.

He guided her into a dingy bathroom in the corner of the basement, then pushed out its wooden back wall.

"We gotta go through there," he said as a damp draft blew out from the crawl space he'd just revealed.

Keisha stared into the pitch-black tunnel. Jamal grabbed her around her waist and helped her inside. Then he crawled in behind her, turned around, and replaced the wooden wall.

She crawled on her hands and knees as he followed, urging her to move faster up the slightly inclined and curving passageway. As they made their way along the hundred-foot tunnel, crawling ever faster through the escape route that Frank Nichols had long ago paid contractors to dig from the bar to the safe house, the banging sound grew louder.

Behind her, Keisha heard the steel door give way to the battering ram, the sound of footsteps charging into the bar, and the echo of many voices yelling a single word: "Police!"

A few seconds later, they reached the end of the tunnel. Jamal reached past her and pushed out a metal grate. And then he nudged her through the opening.

Keisha fell down from what looked to be a vent for an air-conditioning duct. The fall was short, and cushioned by plush white carpeting. She looked around quickly at a living room filled with plants, leather armchairs, and a television that seemed to cover an entire wall. By the time she spotted a door, he'd come down behind her, pushing his gun down into his waistband and helping her up from the floor.

"You all right?" he asked, looking into her eyes.

Keisha didn't answer. She was too busy trying to sort through the love and fear, lust and anxiety that wrestled for control of her mind.

"I'm fine," she said finally.

Jamal reached back and replaced the metal vent in the wall. Then he took out a cell phone and pushed a single button to make a call.

It didn't go through. He tried again. Nothing.

"Who are you calling?" Keisha asked.

"The lady who gives the orders," Jamal said. "Once she hear I got you, she'll call my pop, and that'll buy us some time. By the time they figure out what's goin' on, we'll be out."

There was a short, skidding sound on the street outside. Jamal and Keisha hurried to the front window, looked out, and saw an old Buick idling in the middle of the whip-thin street.

Jamal closed the shade. "That's the driver."

"So what do we do now?" Keisha asked nervously.

Jamal paused long enough to kiss her on her lips. "We trust each other," he said quickly.

Too nervous to speak, Keisha nodded.

Jamal walked her through the living room and out the front door. Keisha turned right and saw people straggling up Dauphin Street, walking away from the botched protest. She turned left and saw a deserted Susquehanna Avenue.

A second later, the Buick's back door was flung open for them, and Jamal pushed her inside. When he got in behind her and closed the door, it was like a cold breeze blew in with them.

She shivered, knowing that what she felt was a sense of dread. As the driver pulled away and the car disappeared into North Philadelphia's maze of tiny streets, she watched Jamal dial the number on his cell phone again.

———

The call connected just as the statuesque brown-skinned woman took her seat on the Acela Express that was departing New York's Penn Station. She tried to answer, but she lost the signal as the train entered the tunnel.

A business-class regular on the train that shuttled between New York and Philadelphia, she was something more than a cog in the machine that was the Nichols empire. She was the linchpin, and a beautiful one at that.

Everywhere she went, with her flawless skin, smoldering eyes, and curves that twentysomethings envied, she drew stares from every man within eyeshot. Today was no different.

Her champagne-colored silk blouse, revealing just the hint of cleavage, was the perfect complement to her bone-colored miniskirt and matching jacket. She wore no stockings with her open-toed, high-heeled sandals. And her crossed legs were covered with smooth skin stretched tight over muscle that she'd earned with countless trips to the gym.

Nola Langston carried her forty-four years well. And though her work as a buyer for a high-end department store took her around the world and paid for the endless pampering that helped to maintain her stunning looks, she had never been the type to settle for a lot. She wanted it all. And she got most of it from Frank Nichols.

She'd been seeing him for over a year, and despite his mistrust of nearly everyone, she had touched him in a way that few women ever had, partly because he wanted more from her than she was willing to give, but also because she was smarter than any man he'd ever known.

With an MBA from the University of Pennsylvania's Wharton School and a fashion industry pedigree that few Philadelphians could match, she was a model-turned-businesswoman who'd helped Nichols to start several legitimate ventures under a fictitious name. His Internet cafés and coffee shops near Temple's campus were her ideas, as were his vending machines in and around the department stores of Center City.

She'd nearly doubled his income in less than a year, and made almost half of it legal. In the process, she'd given herself to him in ways that she'd never imagined she would, ways that transcended the physical. She'd become a go-between for all manner of communications, delivering his messages in cryptic words, via cell phone.

She'd also become his lover. And on mornings like this, when she was aboard the train and thinking anxiously of seeing him again, she often closed her eyes and imagined his lips on hers.

She thought of his moist tongue, probing every crevice of her body, and she blushed as the thought made its way from her head to her thighs. Crossing her legs tightly, she hoped that the thought wouldn't overflow in a liquid gush.

Nola wanted more than just his body, after all. And she couldn't allow the fringe benefits of being Frank Nichols's lover to keep her from attaining her ultimate goal.

Still, it was nice to have someone who understood her desires and could fulfill them. Until she could get him where she wanted him, she would enjoy the ride. And she would make sure that he did, too.

When the train emerged from the tunnel, she took her cell phone from her purse and dialed his number to let him know she was returning early from her business trip. When his voice mail came on, she disconnected and retried the call. Voice mail again. No matter. He'd enjoy the surprise.

As she began to put the cell phone away, she received a call. She looked at the number and recognized it as a number belonging to Frank's son, Jamal.

She connected the call and said nothing, just as Frank had instructed her to do.

"It's Jamal," he said quietly. "I got the package."

"Okay," she said, looking around carefully, as if the other passengers could hear her conversation.

Reaching into her purse, she retrieved a small, folded strip of paper. Opening it, she read the message that it conveyed.

"Keep the package for an hour," she said. "If you don't hear anything, get rid of it."

She hung up when she'd relayed the message. Then she turned the phone off, and waited for the final result.

5

It Was eight o'clock, a half-hour removed from the end of the botched protest, and John Anderson—witness to two murders in less than twenty-four hours—had already given the police another statement.

Sitting in a scarred wooden chair at the Homicide Division, his face fixed in an expression of shock, he looked around the quiet, antiseptic room with its metal file cabinets, scuffed floor tiles, and dull beige walls, and watched the detectives, whose facial expressions mirrored his own.

They'd each seen their own mortality flash before their eyes when the police commissioner was caught in the crossfire of a war that Reverend Anderson had begun. And in their minds, Anderson was as much to blame for the commissioner's death as the man who'd pulled the trigger.

It had happened so quickly: the protest spinning out of con-

trol, the clap of gunshots echoing through the streets, the commissioner and one of his men dragging Anderson from the top of
the car.

Even as he sat in the room filled with detectives, Anderson
could hear the gunshot and sense the commissioner's grip on his
arm loosening. He could see the body dropping to the ground,
and the red, gaping hole where the right side of the commissioner's face had been.

As Anderson recounted the shooting in his mind, a door
opened, dragging him from his thoughts. When he turned
around, he saw a bald, black plainclothes officer walking toward
him with a bandage on his head.

"I'm Lieutenant Lynch," the officer said, extending his hand.

Anderson took it and gripped it tightly. "I'm sorry about the
commissioner. He was a good man."

"I'm sorry, too," Lynch said, releasing the handshake and turning toward a back room. "You can come on back here with me."

Anderson hesitated. "I already talked to the detectives about
the shooting," he said politely. "I'm just waiting for my wife to
pick me up."

Lynch was surprised. "I thought your wife was with you at
the protest."

"Protests make her nervous," Anderson said, smiling stiffly.

"I see." Lynch walked to the door and opened it. "This'll only
take a minute."

Anderson sighed, then got up and followed him inside.
Lynch closed the door, and the two men sat down on opposite
sides of a steel table that had seen better days.

"Can we get you some coffee or something?" Lynch asked.

"No," Anderson said, placing his hands on the table.

"Okay, then I'll get right to the point," Lynch said, opening a
file and looking through it as he spoke. "You've been at the center

of two shootings in less than twenty-four hours. If I didn't know better, I'd think you were the drug dealer."

"Well, I'm not."

Lynch looked up from the file. "Not anymore, you mean."

Anderson could tell that Lynch knew more about him than he was letting on. So he perched his hands in a steeple and tapped his forefingers against his lips, contemplating what he should say.

"You know, Reverend Anderson, I had a case a few years ago in the East Bridge Housing Projects that kind of reminded me of this one," Lynch said, breaking the silence. "A little girl disappeared, and I went in to try to find her.

"It took me back to my roots, I guess, because I grew up there, watching the people in that building destroying each other, a little at a time."

Anderson looked up at him. "What's that got to do with me?"

"You said this whole thing was about someone trying to rape your daughter," Lynch said evenly. "I've got a daughter of my own, so I can understand that. But it's not just about your daughter, is it? It's not even about that woman they shot last night. It's about you and Nichols destroying each other a little at a time. Except now you're destroying other people, too."

"Look, I just wanted to help—"

"Help who?" Lynch snapped. "You took matters into your own hands. Now the police commissioner's dead, and right this minute, cops are on every street in this city trying to find his killer, and they don't care who gets in their way."

Anderson started to speak, but Lynch wouldn't allow it.

"That means people are gonna die, Reverend Anderson. So if you really wanna help as much as you say you do, you'll tell me what I need to know, and you'll tell me now."

Anderson wanted to attack Lynch for having the audacity to look beyond his rhetoric. His war against North Philly's drug trade was, after all, a just war, waged to take back the souls of mothers who'd become whores, fathers who'd become murderers, and sons who'd become victims. It was a war to save his people. At least, that's what Anderson told himself.

But now, as he sat at the table, with Lynch waiting for him to offer something real, he knew that it was time for him to admit the truth. Not only to the cop, but to himself.

Anderson folded his hands on the table and took a deep breath.

"Frank's parents died when he was seventeen," he said haltingly. "Got killed in a bus accident on a trip to visit relatives down South. Since Frank and I were pretty good friends and my father needed another set of hands in the family business, we took him in."

"And what was the family business?" Lynch asked.

"Drug dealing, numbers, prostitution. My father ran his business like the mob. Had it all set up in crews with lieutenants and captains and a boss."

The pastor looked up at Lynch uncomfortably and waited for judgment to sweep across his face. When it didn't, he went on.

"My father was John Anderson Sr. They called him Johnny Hands, 'cause he could strangle a man with one of them."

"I remember the name," Lynch said. "First real gangster in North Philly."

"Yeah," Anderson said, nodding his head. "And he taught us well, me and Frank. Taught us according to our strengths."

"And what were your strengths?"

"Me? I was strong and big, so I was an enforcer. You crossed my pop, he sent me out with one of his soldiers, and we handled it. After a while, I got so good at it, he started sending me out on my own."

"So you hurt people for your father?"

"I knocked a few heads here and there," Anderson said. "Nothing major. But what I did is beside the point, if you wanna know about me and Nichols."

"Okay," Lynch said. "Go on."

"The same way my father trained me to my strengths, he trained Frank to his. And Frank's strength was his mind. After three years in the business, my father made him a lieutenant, and then a captain, gave him a few corners to run and taught him how to get men to do things. Terrible things."

"And your father didn't do the same thing for you?" Lynch asked.

"He tried, but when I saw what it would take for me to be like my father, I couldn't do it. I didn't have the stomach for it. But Frank did."

Lynch nodded and sat back in his seat.

"When I was about twenty, there was a problem with my father's corn liquor suppliers in North Carolina," Anderson said. "Frank suggested that I take care of it, and my father agreed.

"It was the first time I'd ever left my father for more than a day, but it was okay. Frank was like my father's second son, the one who would watch his back if anything ever went wrong. Not that anything could. My father was so strong, not even the white boys down South Philly would mess with him.

"So when Frank put together this big surprise party for him at the bar on Eighth and Diamond, nobody batted an eye. They just came. Everybody who worked for my father was there. All his dealers, all his whores, all his soldiers. Everybody except me."

Anderson laughed bitterly. And then he shook his head slowly from side to side.

"Frank had these strippers come in," he said, as if in a trance. "And right behind them, these guys came in and shot up the place. My father and three of his closest lieutenants died. Frank took a bullet in the shoulder. But none of the men in Frank's crew were shot. And the guys who shot my father got away clean.

"I got word down South that something had happened, and Frank was handling it. They told me that it was too dangerous for me to come back. I ignored them and drove back here as fast as I could. And when I walked into my father's bar, there was Frank, sitting there in my father's seat, with his arm bandaged, red-eyed, like he'd been crying, with three of my father's men around him.

"I ran to him and we hugged and cried together, swearing we were gonna get the men who'd killed my father. *Our* father. But I knew in my heart that I couldn't do it anymore. So I just backed further and further away from the business. And Frank got more and more ruthless. Before I knew it, he had everything that had belonged to my father. And he offered me crumbs. Crumbs I didn't want."

Lynch looked over at him. "How long did it take you to figure out what happened to your father?"

Tears welled up in Anderson's eyes. "I guess I always knew," he said. "I just didn't want to believe the man I'd loved like a brother, the man my father had treated like a son, would turn around and set him up that way."

Lynch nodded and waited for Anderson to wipe the tears from his face.

"Even after I got saved and went into the ministry, I didn't want to believe it. But I knew. I knew in my heart that Frank had killed him. And I hated him for it. Still do."

"And you never tried to avenge your father's death?"

Anderson stared at Lynch for a long while before he answered. "I guess I'm like the people you grew up with in the projects," he said finally. "I just want to destroy him a little bit at a time."

As Anderson's words hung in the air between them, the door opened and a police officer rushed in and whispered something to Lynch, whose deep brown face turned ashen gray.

When the officer left, Lynch turned to the preacher. "Reverend Anderson," he said. "Your wife is downstairs."

"Good," Anderson said, getting up from his chair. "You can call me if you need me."

"Wait, Reverend Anderson."

"I've had a rough day, Lieutenant. So if it's all the same to you, I just wanna go home with my wife, hug my daughter, and forget about this for a little while."

"That's just it," Lynch said solemnly. "Your wife hasn't seen your daughter. She's been missing since the shooting."

Ishmael squinted as the sun shone through the front windows of the storefront church.

With the temperature outside approaching ninety and the windows of the church shut tight, the entire second floor was stifling. But he couldn't afford to leave, because the police still believed that he was somewhere close to the crime scene. And they were right.

Sitting shirtless in the window, with his strapping frame drenched in sweat and his dreadlocks draped about his shoulders, he would have made for an imposing figure if anyone had seen him. But he didn't care to be seen. At least not yet.

For now, he had to do what he'd done for the last forty minutes—watch the police milling about on the street below, and wait for her to call him with the next move. In the moments in between, he tried to remember what had brought him to this point.

When he looked in his past, he saw heartbreak and fear, anger and hurt, betrayal and pain. But all of those things had been there for as long as he could remember. None of them had ever caused him to want to kill.

He hadn't known bloodlust until he'd known pleasure unimaginable. And he hadn't known such pleasure until he'd met her.

She had walked into his life three months ago, and told him that there was hope for something more. And when he looked at her, he couldn't help believing her, because he couldn't see anything beyond her smoky eyes, seductive curves, and creamy skin.

He was captivated by her husky voice, echoing through his mind in the quiet of his dreams. It was a voice that seduced him with half-truths and beguiling flattery.

She told him that his crime-riddled past didn't matter, that the only thing that counted was his future. She told him that his black skin reminded her of sunsets on the African savannah. She told him that his mind was keen, that he would someday lead men to greatness.

She told him everything that he had always longed to hear. And then she used the very things that had always made him feel inferior, and she turned them to rage.

It was like she knew everything about him. From his tortured childhood, spent moving from one house to another, to his adult dreams of becoming something more than what anyone had expected him to be.

She was the only person who'd ever truly understood him. Based solely upon that, he would have done anything she asked. But when she wrapped herself around him and showed him how love should be made, slowly and deliberately, with each touch serving a purpose, each movement taking him higher, each kiss stoking the flame, he was enslaved.

That's why he didn't question it when she told him what she

wanted him to do. If it meant that they would be together, he was willing to do anything.

Sitting there on the stifling second floor of the storefront church, with police milling about below, seeking to arrest him for a murder that would surely bring the death penalty, he didn't ask himself if he had done too much. He asked himself if he had done enough.

Extracting his cell phone from his pocket, he tried calling her once more. The line rang busy.

He put the phone away and settled back to wait. Soon he would make his move. And then she would finally be his.

Keisha stared at the bearded driver's thick neck over the Buick's backseat and refused to acknowledge Jamal's frequent glances in her direction, lest her true feelings show in her eyes.

She was determined to play the role he'd asked her to. But as she looked out the tinted window at the ramshackle houses and vast empty lots they were passing on the east side of Glenwood Avenue, she wondered how long it would be before Jamal played his.

Her trust in him eroded with each passing moment. After all, Jamal had the gun and could very well use it against her if things went wrong. But it wasn't the gun that kept her there, waiting for the game to play out. The thing that kept her there was her heart.

The circumstances surrounding their love didn't matter to her. What mattered was that she'd given her heart to him all those years ago. And now she was giving it to him again.

Since seeing him at Strawbridge's three weeks before, she'd spent a portion of each day trying to recapture the innocence of their secret summer, and a portion of each night attempting to rekindle their love.

For the first few nights, she snuck out of the house and rode with him to Fairmount Park, to laugh and reminisce about the time they'd spent together, and to vow, in the quiet of her heart, not to lose him again.

By the second week she was stealing moments during the day to talk to him on the cell phone he'd given her as a gift. And when they weren't together, she spent her time anticipating the moments when they would be.

Through it all, she ignored the telltale signs of his profession. She saw the fancy car and the seemingly endless amount of time he had to spend with her. She saw the wad of cash that bulged from his pocket, and the jewelry that dangled from his neck.

In truth, she'd known from the time they'd reunited that he was a drug dealer. And though she pretended not to notice or to care, there was something about it that excited her. It pulled at her, even now, as she watched the back of the driver's head and tried not to think of what could happen if things went wrong.

Jamal turned and glanced at her yet again, and wondered what was going through her mind. His thoughts were of her kiss. He could still feel it lingering on his lips and causing warm blood to run to his loins.

He looked away from her, knowing he couldn't allow himself even one moment of fantasy. He had to be patient, as did Keisha.

If he made his move before the hour was up, his father would know that something had gone wrong. And he couldn't chance that.

He knew that she was growing impatient. But he hoped that she could hold on for a few minutes more. A second later, when Keisha broke the silence, it was apparent that she couldn't.

"I have to go to the bathroom," she said, hoping Jamal would take the cue and do something.

The driver looked at her in the rearview mirror. Then he cut his eyes toward Jamal.

"Shut up," Jamal said coldly. "It ain't time for you to go to bathroom yet."

"I have to go *now*," she said with an attitude.

He looked at her as the driver turned right on Allegheny Avenue and drove them into the heart of North Philadelphia's Badlands.

"You can't always have what you want," he snapped.

And with that he turned away from her, and waited for the hour to expire.

6

By nine o'clock, Lynch had five teams of detectives searching for Keisha Anderson. He didn't plan to lose another girl the way he'd lost nine-year-old Kenya Brown. And he certainly didn't plan to lose his leading suspect, Frank Nichols.

Though his homicide detectives had failed to turn up anything in Nichols's North Philadelphia houses and bars, they were determined not to give up. They would find Nichols within the hour, or they would convince one of his many associates to give him up.

What they didn't realize was that Nichols wasn't running. He'd spent the night at his girlfriend's three-story townhouse in an affluent Center City neighborhood called Rittenhouse Square. And just as he always did when he was there, he cut off contact with the outside world.

He'd driven there himself, without any of his men, in a Volvo station wagon that blended in nicely in the neighborhood.

And the only thing he brought with him was a cell phone, which he didn't answer.

He didn't know that a protest at his bar had gone horribly wrong. And in truth, he didn't care.

Frank Nichols was in the place he'd wanted to be since his girlfriend had taken him to her home for the first time, over a year before. He'd seen what he wanted then. And nothing was going to prevent him from having it.

As the morning sun crept through the slightly open blinds in the master bedroom, casting strips of yellow light across his back, Frank Nichols was on his knees, oblivious to everything but the soft, yielding flesh stretched out before him.

He bent to kiss buttery legs, parting his lips until his tongue was against one and then the other. And as he moved his mouth to the place where her thighs met and felt her lips quivering against his, he thrust out his tongue to taste her, and she gasped.

He reached up to caress her and heard a rumbling deep inside her throat as her nipples grew hard beneath his touch.

He rose up and traced a moist path to her navel, and then to her neck, and finally to her lips. He kissed her, and she greedily sucked her essence from his tongue.

He pulled away to look into her eyes, and he saw what he already knew he would. Everything that she'd been holding onto, waiting to give to someone special, was there for him. All he had to do was take it.

She wrapped her arms and legs around him and pulled him down until he stiffened against her softness. Moaning in spite of himself, he reached around to her ample bottom and held it in his hands as he began to thrust, softly at first, and then more forcefully, taking the virginity she so willingly gave.

She knew she shouldn't be there with him, knew that she shouldn't want it. And as sweat beaded up between them and their wet bodies slid against one another, she was caught in the throes of their passion.

She bucked her hips as they danced to the rhythm that their bodies demanded. Moans, then squeals, then shouts filled the air as their voices echoed through the house.

Nichols's head swam with the movement of her hips. He felt as if he were about to burst. But the glass at the back door broke first.

He bolted upright when he heard it, and put his hand against his lover's mouth. There was the squeaking sound of the back door easing open, and the thud of running footsteps making their way through the living room.

Nichols knew there wasn't much time.

Taking his lover by the hand, he rolled off the bed and onto the floor, grabbing his clothes and his gun in the process.

She opened her mouth to scream, but he covered it again while pulling her across the floor to the master bathroom and locking the door behind them.

"Don't say nothin'," he whispered as he listened to them creeping up the stairway.

His lover trembled with fear as she heard the footsteps approaching.

Nichols pulled on his pants and gave his shirt to her.

"Button it," he whispered urgently. "Hurry up."

He held the gun aloft as the footsteps stopped outside the bedroom door.

Grabbing her by her hair, he pulled her toward the laundry chute that descended from the bathroom to the basement of the century-old brownstone.

He opened the door. "Get in."

She hesitated as tears streaked down her cheeks.

"I said get yo' ass in there," Nichols hissed menacingly.

He picked her up and pushed her into the chute, then jumped in behind her.

Her scream faded quickly to silence as the chute's trap door swung back and forth behind them. A moment later the bedroom door crashed open.

"Police!" a burly white man shouted as he rushed into the room with his gun out in front of him.

Two more officers barreled in behind him, pointing their weapons at either side of the room, while a third ran in and checked under the bed.

They searched quickly, bursting open the closet doors and hunting behind furniture, before running into the bathroom as the chute's swinging door came to a standstill.

Kevin Lynch was the last to enter the room. As he did, he heard the sound of a car engine come to life on a side street to the east of the house. He rushed to the window just as the car pulled off with a skid.

"Dan two-five, he's in a white Volvo!" Lynch screamed into his radio as he ran to the steps and descended them. "It's heading north on Twentieth Street!"

The police car in front of the house backed up in an effort to get to Twentieth Street, but a sudden rush of traffic blocked it in.

By the time Lynch and his men got out to their cars, Frank Nichols was gone.

The Andersons sat in Lynch's office at the Homicide Division, watching a small television perched above the lieutenant's desk and searching for some clue about their daughter's whereabouts. The uncertainty was unnerving. But watching the pictures from the morning's shootout as they were played over and over again, that was almost unbearable.

Channel 3 was on its fifth consecutive replay when Sarah Anderson got up from her hard wooden chair and turned to the local cable channel in the hopes of escaping the round-the-clock coverage. But even Comcast had a reporter on the scene.

Sarah went back to her seat and sat down. John, sitting in a chair next to hers, looked at her and tried to speak. But instead of allowing her husband to comfort her, as he'd tried to do countless times since they'd found out that Keisha was missing, Sarah turned away, because in her mind there was only one person who could be blamed for Keisha's disappearance. And it wasn't Frank Nichols.

Glancing up at the television, she watched as the reporter took up station across the street from Nichols's bar on Dauphin Street, holding a notepad and staring into the camera with his clean-shaven brown face creased in a grave expression.

She tried to tune out what he was saying. But no matter how hard she tried, she still caught snippets of his report.

"Alleged longtime drug dealer Frank Nichols . . . protest . . . gunman on a nearby rooftop."

Sarah's mind drifted to her daughter. She wondered if Keisha could survive in the midst of so much death.

"Police Commissioner Darrell Freeman . . . shot in the face . . . died instantly . . . dozens of protesters injured."

Sarah pictured Keisha's smiling face, and then thought of her tears the night before. Tears that she'd cried because of men who'd tried to hurt her. Sarah knew those kinds of tears. She'd always hoped that her daughter would escape them. But that hope, like most other hopes she'd had, was gone now.

"Gunman . . . still at large . . . armed and dangerous."

At this, Sarah was snatched back to the moment. She listened intently as the reporter described the man who'd gotten away.

"Black male, in his early twenties, about six feet tall with dreadlocks. Police are asking that you call nine-one-one immediately if you have any information concerning this case. This is Greg Connors, reporting live from—"

Sarah had heard enough. She turned off the television. Then she turned around to face her husband.

He hadn't been listening. He was past that. And he wasn't going to try to comfort her anymore. Instead, he was sitting there with his eyes closed, his body rocking slightly, and his lips moving almost imperceptibly. He was doing the only thing that could give him comfort. He was praying.

Sarah watched him for a moment, the way his clenched eyes and closed lips quivered. She almost felt sorry for him. Almost.

Sarah felt more pity for herself. She had, after all, spent years trying to be the woman that the Lord wanted her to be, and the wife that her husband wanted her to be. She'd covered her still-smooth cocoa-colored skin and round, voluptuous curves. She'd worn frumpy glasses over her large, glistening eyes. She'd submitted to her own husband as the Word commanded her to do. And in all this, she'd given away her happiness and her freedom.

They'd settled into a relationship that was steady, but not passionate; stable, but unexciting. It was a marriage filled with fake smiles and empty reassurances. There was nothing in it that was theirs alone. He was, after all, a pastor, and so he belonged to everyone and everything but her.

His identity was in his flock, and his cause, and his cross. They received his passion. Just like her father had given his passion to his ministry, rather than his home. She'd hated it then, just as she hated it now.

"What are you doing?" she asked impatiently.

He opened his weary eyes and looked at her. "What does it look like I'm doing?"

"Don't pray now," she said, her tone mocking. "You shoulda

prayed before you went out there in that street last night, like you were gonna do something to Frank Nichols."

"Sarah, listen—"

"No, *you* listen. I've been by your side, John. I've watched you do right, and I've watched you do wrong. But I always told myself that whatever you did, you were doing it because you loved the people you were supposed to be serving."

"What do you mean, 'supposed to be'?"

"You strut around talking about how God delivered you from your past," she said, making his testimony sound like some cruel joke. "You talk about how you could've been what your father was, how you could've ended up a drug dealer, how you—"

"Sarah, this isn't the time to get into this," he said, his voice laced with an unspoken warning.

"Well, when is the time for this, John? Huh? When is it time for us to step back and look at what our lives are really like— what *my* life is really like?"

"Our lives are fine, Sarah," he said, his voice weakening, as if he didn't believe his own words. "We've been blessed."

"And we've been cursed, too, John. Cursed because you sit up in that church, day after day, week after week, solving everybody else's problems, when you can't even solve your own. Cursed because you can't see anything beyond your precious ministry. Cursed because you're so caught up in what the Lord did for you thirtysomething years ago that you can't even see what you need Him to do for us now.

"I'm lonely, John," she said, trembling with quiet rage. "I cry myself to sleep at night, waiting for you to come home and be a husband. And Keisha, she's starving for your attention, too. But you can't even see it, because you spend so much time down at that church."

"You wanna blame me for Keisha?" he shouted, standing up. "Go ahead, blame me! Blame God! Blame everybody but yourself!"

"I didn't take her out there to that protest," she snapped. "You did!"

"I was trying to teach her how to care about somebody other than herself," he said. "But you wouldn't know anything about that, would you?"

"I don't go out to those protests because there are better ways to make a difference," she said defensively.

"You don't go out to those protests because you don't care!"

"I care about one thing, John," she said evenly. "Our daughter's missing. And if they don't find her, I will never forgive you."

"That's not biblical," he said quickly.

"Since when do you care about what's biblical?" she shot back. "If you cared about what's biblical, you wouldn't have put our daughter in harm's way just to make yourself look like more than you really are.

"That's in the Bible, John. Don't think more highly of yourself than you ought to."

She paused before she threw his own words back in his face. "You wouldn't know anything about *that*, now, would you?"

The pastor's mouth dropped open as his wife walked across the small office and snatched open the door to leave.

She gasped and jumped back as Lieutenant Lynch almost walked into her.

"I'm sorry, Mrs. Anderson," he said, as she stepped aside. "I didn't mean to startle you."

He walked into the office sensing that there was something in the air. He didn't want to add to the tension, but he had no choice.

"About a half hour ago, we spotted Frank Nichols at his girl-friend's house on Rittenhouse Square," he said. "He got away from us, but we think we should be able to find him fairly soon."

"And what about Keisha?" Reverend Anderson asked hope-fully.

"We haven't found her yet. But we've been studying some of the footage that the news crews took this morning."

He stopped and looked at them both. "We've got an ID on the man who was last seen with her."

"Well, who is it?" Sarah asked anxiously.

"Looks like it may be the same man we're looking for in connection with the commissioner's murder. Frank Nichols's son, Jamal."

Ishmael smiled when he heard Jamal's name blaring over the police radios on the street below in connection with the commissioner's murder.

He didn't care that the police had it wrong. He was only sorry that he'd gotten it wrong. By missing his intended target, he'd prolonged the first step in the plan she'd told him to carry out, and created complications that would delay his ultimate reward.

But if delaying that step meant hurting Frank Nichols, even hurting him through Jamal, then he'd killed two birds with one stone.

Not that it mattered. Neither Frank nor Jamal Nichols was his first concern. The most important thing on his mind was her. She was the reason he was here. She was the one who gave him purpose. Indeed, she had become his reason for being.

He hadn't talked to her since seven o'clock that morning. And he didn't know if he could go on without at least hearing her voice once more.

He'd tried calling her three times from his cell phone, and each time he'd gotten her voice mail. Not that he was worried. Knowing her as he did, he knew that she was probably a step ahead of everyone else. More importantly, he knew that she would be there for him in the end.

Thinking of that brought a smile to his lips, even as he hid like a rat on the dank, crumbling second floor of the house-turned-storefront-church.

He wiped a bead of sweat from his eyes and leaned forward to peer out the window at the Strike Force and SWAT units searching empty buildings and questioning tight-lipped neighbors. He knew that there was a chance that time, and the police, could catch up with him.

Ishmael couldn't allow that to happen. Reaching into a hole in the wall, he retrieved the semiautomatic handgun he'd hidden there several days before. He reached further into the hole and grabbed three fully loaded clips.

Then he put on his shirt, stood up, and set out toward the staircase. Calmly making his way downstairs, he walked through the makeshift sanctuary and out the back door of the church onto narrow Sydenham Street.

As police milled about just half a block away, in front of the bar at Fifteenth and Susquehanna, he crossed the alleywide street, his dreadlocks flopping against his back, and walked onto one of the lots of overgrown and rock-strewn earth where houses had once stood.

Walking between the man-sized weeds that seemed to grow on every lot during North Philadelphia's long, hot summers, he made his way to a shack made of rusted, corrugated tin.

He paused to look behind him. When he was sure that no one had followed, he pulled back the rusting metal to reveal a motorcycle.

Calmly, methodically, he removed his clothes and changed into the denim jacket and jeans she'd left for him in a neatly wrapped brown package next to the bike. He put on the helmet that rested on its back seat, tucking his dreadlocks beneath it. Pulling a cell phone from the pocket of the jacket, he pressed a button. When the call connected and her computerized voice mail picked up, he left a message.

"Don't worry about what happened this morning," he said, his voice deadly calm. "Everything is still on schedule. I'll meet you at the safe house tonight."

He disconnected the call and snapped the helmet's dark visor into place.

Seconds later, he was gone.

Keisha listened to the radio news emanating from the Buick's static-filled radio. She was hoping to hear word of her father. But in the sixty minutes they'd been driving, she hadn't heard his name even once.

But that was the least of her worries.

Both Jamal and the driver were now ominously silent as they circled a Hispanic neighborhood where drowsy-eyed zombies with swollen hands stumbled toward corners manned by boys yelling brand names like Tombstone and DOA, Pac Man and Grim Reaper. She saw cars lining up as if they were at a drive-through, their drivers rolling down windows to trade cash for heroin-filled plastic bags.

She noticed that Jamal was no longer trying to steal glimpses of her, as he'd done so many times throughout the morning. And the driver, a husky young man whose beard was split by a scar that ran the length of his jaw, wore a scowl on his wide, flat face.

Both of them looked like they were preoccupied. And so was Keisha. She was growing more anxious by the moment, trying to fight her growing suspicion that Jamal was about to betray her.

Her stomach knotted as she observed Jamal looking down at his watch. He glanced at her before looking in the mirror at the driver, who was watching him and waiting for orders.

"I guess we ain't gon' get that call," Jamal said, his face growing hard as he steeled himself for what he had to do.

The driver nodded, reached into his jacket for his gun, and laid it on the seat beside him as Keisha felt her heart beating wildly against her chest.

Jamal pointed to a nearby street. "Turn in there. Stop at the alley at the end of the block."

The driver hung a left at a deserted street where abandoned factories with broken windows loomed on one side, and a vast stretch of packed earth spread across the other.

Keisha pressed her face against the window and saw women parading the desolate strip, wearing little more than hard looks. There were cars parked along the crumbling sidewalks, rocking to and fro as men took what they had paid for.

"Let me out of this car!" Keisha shouted, turning to him as her eyes filled with tears.

The driver parked and turned around for the first time. His eyes were cold and hard. "Shut up," he said through clenched teeth.

Jamal felt a twinge of anger as he watched fear overtake Keisha. She looked at him with a question in her eyes, and he refused to answer it.

The driver watched them both as Keisha began to sob. He could see that Jamal cared for her. Indeed, he had seen it from the time they'd picked up the girl. He knew he couldn't allow Jamal to make any foolish decisions. So he turned up the radio to drown out the sound of Keisha's weeping, and prepared to do what they'd come there to do.

At that moment, a radio announcer's voice made them all go silent.

"Police have identified Jamal Nichols, son of alleged drug dealer Frank Nichols, as the man wanted in connection with the fatal shooting of Police Commissioner Darrell Freeman and the disappearance of sixteen-year-old Keisha Anderson. A six-foot-tall black male with dreadlocks, he is considered—"

The driver turned off the radio, looked at Jamal, and started to get out of the car.

"What they talkin' about?" Jamal said, his voice panicky. "I ain't shoot nobody!"

Keisha began to cry uncontrollably. The driver reached back to smack her, but Jamal caught his hand.

"Don't do that, man," Jamal said with an edge to his voice.

The driver locked eyes with him for a moment, then snatched his hand away. "Look, man, this bitch drawin'."

"Let her go, then," Jamal said quickly. "They already tryin' to gimme a body. I don't need another one."

"You don't need a lot o' things, Jamal," the driver snapped. "And I don't, either. Now if we fuck this up 'cause you feel some type o' way about some bitch, you takin' *my* life in your hands. And I can't have that."

Keisha couldn't wait any longer. She turned suddenly and kicked open the door. She was halfway out when the driver grabbed his gun and jumped out of the front seat. He gripped Keisha's arms and pulled her out of the car as she screamed out to Jamal for help.

Jamal froze, because he knew that the next few moments would forever define him. For the first time, he was unsure of what he wanted.

"Jamal, come on, man!" the driver yelled over his shoulder as he carried Keisha into the alley. "You know what we gotta do!"

Jamal wrestled with his conscience for all of five seconds. His decision made, he got out of the car.

Keisha bit the driver's hand and punched him as he carried her through the alley. And when he loosened his grip on her legs to turn his gun on her, she launched her foot into his groin.

His gun dropped to the ground as he fell to his knees in agony. Keisha hit the ground as well, and scrambled on her stomach toward the gun. Squinting through the pain, the driver reached for her. But she kicked his hand away and grabbed the gun.

By the time Jamal entered the alley, she had flipped onto her back and was aiming the gun at the driver's face.

"Look, baby, just gimme the gun," he said nervously.

"Get away from me!" Keisha said, her voice quivering.

When the driver saw that she was afraid, he smiled and began to move toward her.

Keisha gripped the gun tightly as her hands began to tremble, because she knew that she would have to pull the trigger.

With most of East Division reassigned in the wake of the commissioner's murder, Officer Chuck MacAleer and his partner were working half of the Twenty-fifth District by themselves. That would have been quite a strain if they were actually patrolling. But police work was the last thing on their minds.

From the time they'd hit the street at eight o' clock, they'd engrossed themselves in their own brand of policing, the kind that allowed the drug scourge to flourish.

Almost everyone who plied a trade in MacAleer's sector knew. When his paddy wagon came by, someone had to pay. On some days, it was the dealers. On others, it was the addicts. Today, it was the prostitutes. And as always, the officers had taken the pick of the litter.

The girl they'd chosen was about twenty, and had yet to surrender her curves to the ravages of the crack pipe. She was so new to the game that she didn't know about street tax. So they plucked her from the corner, handcuffed her, and locked her in the wagon. Then they went back and showed her the price she would have to pay for feeding her addiction on their streets.

They subjected her to all kinds of indignities, forcing her to endure perversions that even her worst trick wouldn't dare request. They humiliated her with their viciousness. She cried, and they smacked her. She screamed, and they covered her mouth. She begged, and they exploded with laughter.

Now they were finished, at least for the moment. And as the girl remained handcuffed in the back of the wagon, they parked just half a block from the strip, watching the other whores work in the shadow of the abandoned factory.

The officers smoked cigarettes and prepared themselves for another round with the girl as they listened absently to the dispatcher read the general radio message describing Jamal Nichols.

MacAleer reached over and turned down the radio.

"I'm tired of hearing about this Nichols kid," he said.

"If you ask me, he did us a favor," his partner said with a smirk. "Who needs a nigger running the department, anyway? That's like the fuckin' inmates runnin' the asylum."

"You got *that* right," MacAleer said with a nod.

His partner extinguished his cigarette and plucked it out the window. "What do you want to do about our girlfriend back there?"

MacAleer's face creased in a sickening leer. "I'm gonna have another talk with her," he said. "Just in case she didn't get it the first time."

His partner shook his head and chuckled as he got out of the wagon. "I'm gonna take a piss. I'll be right back."

He walked up the block toward an alley. The prostitutes he passed along the way ignored him, knowing that the girl had already paid for their privilege to work that day. In turn, the officer ignored the cars that were parked along the street. All of them were occupied except for one. And as he drew nearer to the Buick with the open doors and blasting radio, he sensed that something was wrong.

Slowing down, he sidled up to the alley and peered around the edge of the brick wall. When he did, his suspicions were confirmed.

The girl with the gun in her hand was holding one man at bay, while a second man with dreadlocks stood in back of the first, holding what looked like a gun of his own.

The officer's eyes stretched wide as he ducked back and flattened himself against the wall. His suddenly damp blond hair matted against his scalp as he drew his gun.

He looked toward the wagon and saw that his partner was in the back with the girl. He reached for his radio, and realized, with a muffled curse, that he'd left it on his seat.

As he did so, he remembered the description he'd heard just a few minutes before. And his anxiety became full-blown fear.

"I ain't gon' hurt you, baby," the driver whispered as he inched ever closer to Keisha. "Just like you ain't gon' hurt me. Right?"

She was still trying to convince herself to shoot when, suddenly, he lunged at her.

She shut her eyes and gripped the gun. A shot split the air like thunder, and the driver fell just inches from her lap.

When Keisha opened her eyes, she saw the dead man lying on his side, his lifeless eyes stretched wide. Jamal was standing at the end of the alley, his right arm still pointing the gun as the smoke that rose from the barrel shrouded his face.

His dreadlocks draped his shoulders as his chest heaved up and down, and his brown eyes stared into hers.

These were the eyes that she remembered. The eyes of the boy who'd picked her up after she'd fallen and carried her to safety. They were the eyes of the boy who'd shared her first kiss, the eyes of the man who'd fought off her attackers and saved her life, not once, but twice. These were the eyes she'd seen every night for the past few weeks, and fallen in love with yet again. They were eyes that she wanted to gaze into for the rest of her life.

He watched her with those eyes, unable to move, unable to do anything but hope that she hadn't changed her mind about going with him.

He had disobeyed his father's orders, and killed one of his best men in the process. He was wanted for the police commissioner's murder, and he'd cut almost every tie to his past. His life was as good as over, unless he could live it with her.

As Jamal began to lower the gun and walk toward a frightened Keisha, he didn't care about his life. His only concern was her.

That's why he didn't hear the footsteps approach him from behind.

"Jamal!" the voice came from the end of the alley. "Drop it!"

He dove to the ground, twisting his body in an effort to get off a shot. The figure at the end of the alley took aim and a bullet whizzed past Jamal's ear, striking the ground beside him.

He tucked his chin into his chest, closed his eyes, and rolled left as another bullet flew. There was a thud, the release of air, and the sound of a body hitting the ground.

This time it was Jamal who opened his eyes to bloodshed. The police officer who'd tried to arrest him lay on his face, and a widening pool of blood spread out from his head. Keisha sat on the ground, her breath coming in quick gasps as she held the gun in her still-trembling hands.

It was all Jamal could do to grab Keisha and run toward the other end of the alley.

It was all she could do to let him.

7

Frank Nichols parked the Volvo at Six-
teenth and Girard, between a hospital and the sprawling campus
of a century-old private school. The car would be inconspicuous
there, at least for the time being.

Throwing the car in park, he grabbed his lover by the hand
and bolted toward one of the tiny, crumbling streets that lined the
surrounding community.

He dragged her up three steps to a seemingly abandoned
house and banged on the door while holding his gun at his side.
His eyes darted up and down the block, watching for the police.

"How many?" said a voice from behind the tin-covered
window.

"Open the damn door!" he snapped. "It's Frank."

He listened, along with the girl, as a series of locks was dis-
engaged. When the door cracked open, Frank pushed his way inside with the girl in tow, and slammed the door behind him.

"You all right, Frank?" said a young dealer as he looked at his boss with a confused expression.

"Gimme some clothes," Frank said, ignoring the question as he stomped into the living room.

Without a word, the dealer pointed to the closet, where he and the other dealers kept extra clothing in case they had to change and leave quickly to elude the police.

Frank pulled the girl to the closet with him and began rummaging through it. As he did so, another dealer walked in from the back room with a nine-millimeter tucked into his waistband.

"Frank, I don't want to be here," the young woman said in a timid voice as the stocky young man groped her with his eyes.

Frank ignored her. "What happened at the bar this morning?" he said, pulling on a pair of jeans and a hooded sweatshirt.

"John Anderson bought some people down there," said the young man who'd answered the door.

As he spoke, his eyes weren't on Frank. His gaze was on the half-dressed, petrified young woman at Frank's side.

"Somebody started shootin'."

"Who?" Frank said.

"I don't know. But whoever it was, they killed the commissioner."

"And nobody called me?" Frank said while stepping into a pair of sneakers.

"Everybody was tryin' to get you, but you ain't answer your phone."

The woman's eyes grew wide with fear as she listened.

"Frank, I want to leave," she said in a trembling voice. "I don't want to be involved with this."

"Shut up," Nichols said dismissively.

She looked at him, and for the first time saw him as he was, and not as the debonair older man she'd wanted him to be.

Frank was oblivious to the hurt look she wore on her face.

"Where's Jamal?" he asked the one with the gun.

"They said somethin' on the news about Jamal snatchin' Keisha Anderson and shootin' the commissioner," he answered. "But ain't nobody seen him since this mornin'."

Frank grinned. "You ain't supposed to see him," he said. "When he get everything straight on his end, he'll call me. In the meantime, I got some other shit to take care of."

The dealers both nodded while the frightened girl tried to get his attention.

"Frank, please," the girl said, almost begging. "I want to leave."

"Shut up," Frank said menacingly. "I ain't gon' tell you again."

Unaccustomed to being talked to that way, she looked angrily from Frank to his minions.

"Oh, so it's shut up now?" she said, saucily. "Is that what you're gonna tell my mother when she comes back from New York and finds out her man was fucking her daughter in her own house?"

Frank took her face in his hand and roughly pulled her close to him.

"Your mother?" he asked incredulously. "You think I give a fuck about your mother?"

The two young dealers took a step backward as Frank's face contorted into that of a madman.

The girl opened her mouth to speak. But before she could make another sound, Frank slapped her hard across the face, and she fell to the floor in a heap.

"I *own* your mother," he said, standing over her with a wild-eyed stare. "And I own you, too."

He looked at his dealers, who smiled like the yes-men they were while the woman tried to drag herself from the floor.

Frank reached down and slapped her again. "You don't get up 'til I tell you to, you understand me, bitch?"

The petrified girl nodded vigorously.

"Good," he said, reaching into the closet. "Put on these clothes while we shut this house down. Then you got a phone call to make."

Nola got off the train at Philadelphia's Thirtieth Street Station, walked across the dimly lit platform, and climbed aboard the escalator for the trip upstairs.

She'd turned off her phone for the final half-hour of the trip, preferring silence to the mangled signal that often made cell phone calls on the train undecipherable.

As she rode up to the terminal, she looked at her screen and saw that she had four messages. She was walking across the terminal, about to check the messages, when her phone rang. She smiled expectantly as she answered.

"Hello?"

"I'm . . . so . . . sorry," someone whispered, then broke down in heart-wrenching sobs.

Nola's smile faded as she listened to the distraught voice on the other end. She stopped walking and stood in the middle of the Thirtieth Street Station, holding the phone to her ear, a dark suspicion rising in her mind.

"What is it, Marquita?" she asked in a demanding voice.

"I didn't mean to do it," her daughter said, sobbing all the while.

Nola could feel the bile rising in her throat, even before her daughter spoke the truth she already knew. And along with the sick feeling, something else rose up. It was anger, pure and simple, the kind of anger that a woman feels when she's betrayed.

"I tried to walk away, Mom, but I couldn't," Marquita said, breaking into her mother's thoughts. "I just couldn't. But I want you to know that I didn't mean to hurt you."

"Just say it," Nola spat. "Say it and get it over with."

There was a long silence on the phone, punctuated by the sound of Marquita's tortured whimpering.

"Tell me!" Nola yelled, as passersby looked at her quizzically.

"I spent the night with Frank," Marquita said softly.

Nola said nothing. She stood there, her breath barely a whisper, and allowed her daughter to twist in the wind.

She'd always known in the back of her mind that this was a possibility. She'd seen the way his eyes had roamed over her daughter's body on the few occasions when she'd allowed the two of them to meet.

Still, it was a shock to know that he would actually do this to her. No matter how much he wanted to.

It didn't matter that she didn't love him. Nor did it matter that she had other men. The thought of her daughter taking something that belonged to her was galling. It brought her face-to-face with the realities of age. There was always someone younger, and prettier, and more vulnerable. But as Frank and her daughter were about to find out, there were few people who were smarter or more vicious than Nola.

"Can I ask you something, Marquita?" she said coolly.

"Yes," her daughter said, her voice barely a croak.

"Why would you tell me about it? I mean, why not just keep it to yourself? Let it be your little secret?"

Marquita was silent for a long time.

"The police came to the house this morning," she said, sounding every bit the little girl again.

"Did they disturb any of my things?" Nola asked.

"No. They just wanted Frank."

Nola thought about what her daughter had just told her.

"Why would they come to my house for Frank?"

"I guess you didn't hear about it since you were on the train," Marquita said. "Somebody killed the police commissioner this morning, and some girl is missing, too. Keisha something. They think Frank had something to do with it."

"Where's Frank now?"

Again, there was a long pause. "I don't know. He got out of the house before they could get him."

"And where are you?"

"I'm . . . out," Marquita said hesitantly. "The police asked me a few questions and left."

"Did they ask you anything about me?"

"No," Marquita said nervously.

"Okay," Nola said, ignoring her daughter's anxiousness in favor of her own.

"I've got some things I need to handle," Nola said quickly, "and so do you."

Marquita didn't answer.

"I want you out of my house in an hour."

Nola disconnected the call and rushed to the taxi stand to take the trip home. She knew she didn't have much time.

On the other end of the line, Frank Nichols took the phone from Marquita. Then he took her outside and pushed her into a minivan for the trip to Center City.

———

As he turned the motorcycle onto Jefferson Street, Ishmael reached into his jacket pocket, extracted a remote control, and pointed it toward the garage on an awning-bedecked house in the quiet section of North Philadelphia known as Yorktown.

He pulled into the garage slowly, and parked the bike next to the old car that occupied the garage. Closing the door behind him and removing his helmet, he moved quickly through the garage and jogged up the stairs to the second-floor bathroom he'd used so many times before.

As he turned on the water in the bathtub and began to undress, he tried not to think of what the house meant to him. But he couldn't help remembering, because this house was a constant reminder of the one person who'd reached out to him and asked for nothing in return.

Two years ago, with no real family to turn to after his second upstate prison bid, he was about to return to the embrace of the streets before Anna Thornby stepped in.

The woman he came to know as Aunt Annie had seen something in him during her stints as a volunteer at the halfway house he was remanded to after two years in Albion State Correctional Institution. And so, when it was clear that he would have no place to go upon his release, she took him in.

A kindly old woman with a ready smile and stringent rules, she was everything to him: the mother he'd always wanted, the father he'd never known, and the confidante he'd always needed. It took him a while to open up and trust her enough to reveal his secrets. But once he began to talk, he couldn't stop. He told her about everything—the abuse he'd endured at the hands of his mother, his unsuccessful efforts to forge relationships with women, the atrocities he'd committed as an angry young man on the streets.

She listened to him carefully. And when he finished pouring

out his soul, she gently reminded him that nothing was an excuse for failure. No one was to blame for what he'd done. He could only control his here and now, because his past was already behind him. If he remembered those few truths and trusted God to reveal the rest, he would always be able to succeed.

He took her messages to heart, and used them to rebuild himself. First he found a job. Then he opened a bank account. He enrolled in a course to complete his GED. But on the day he passed the test and applied for admission to community college, he came home to find Aunt Annie stretched out on the floor, dead of a heart attack.

Her death made him bitter. He felt that she'd abandoned him, and he vowed to never love again. He couldn't live in the house she'd left him in her will, not with such anger in his heart. Because even in death, she'd see what he had become, and she would be ashamed.

But a funny thing happened when he returned to the streets to lose himself in the vicious rules of the drug game. He broke the only promise that he'd ever made to himself. He allowed his heart to feel.

He'd seen her for the first time walking past him as he shopped in Center City. She smiled at him, and something in him changed. It didn't matter that she was different from any woman he'd ever known. Nor did it matter that he was angry. He spoke to her, and she spoke back. They sat down on a bench on Market Street and talked until the sun went down, and there was no one left on the street but them.

She understood his pain, knew it like she'd experienced it for herself. He loved her because, in her empathy, she made that pain go away. Even now, as he prepared to return the favor, he marveled at the mark she'd left on his soul.

Turning on the bathroom light, he finished undressing, removed clippers and shaving cream from the cabinet, and examined himself in the mirror. His face was bruised slightly, and his locks were matted. But his body was sleek and hard, just like he needed it to be.

Before the day was out, he would have to do battle for her. And after the battle was over, she would take his hard, sleek body for herself.

Lieutenant Lynch left the Andersons to go to the third floor of police headquarters for a meeting with the mayor and Acting Commissioner Dilsheimer about the search for Jamal and the missing girl.

He didn't normally leave witnesses and complainants in his office while he tended to police matters. But this was no ordinary day.

News crews were stationed outside the building, getting hourly updates from public affairs officers. Rank-and-file police officers were on the streets, unleashing their rage on anyone who even remotely fit Jamal Nichols's description. And ordinary people like the Andersons were caught in the middle, trying desperately to make sense of it all.

After thirty minutes in Lynch's office, they'd come no closer to learning anything about their daughter's whereabouts. But they were sure of one thing: sitting in a closed room with their grief nestled between them wouldn't bring Keisha back.

"I'm ready to go," John Anderson said, getting up from his seat. "You coming?"

"For what?" Sarah said, staring absently into space. "What is there for me to go home to?"

John wanted to comfort his wife, but he didn't know how. "Look, Sarah—"

"No, *you* look," she said, whipping her head around to face him. "Don't try to preach to me, like you do to those people down at the church. I don't want to hear it."

"Why not?" he asked sarcastically. "Don't you believe in God anymore?"

"Yes," she said, nodding her head slowly. "I believe in God. I just don't believe in you."

"It's not about me," he said sorrowfully.

"Then who is it about, John? Me? Was I with Keisha when she disappeared? Was I the one who was supposed to be watching out for her?"

John was tired of the accusations. He was tired of the guilt. But most of all, he was tired of his wife.

"Yes, Sarah," he said, angrily. "You were supposed to be watching out for her. Not just this morning, but all her life. That's the only thing I ever asked you to do. Raise our daughter.

"But you didn't do that, did you? You were too busy feeling sorry for yourself. Our daughter needed you, and you weren't there to guide her."

Sarah sucked her teeth. "Look who's talking," she said bitterly.

"Yeah, Sarah, look who's talking! Take a real good look, and remember what I look like! Because you may not ever see me again."

John stood up and walked out the door, slamming it behind him.

As he walked down the hallway, a homicide detective was getting off the elevator, and called after him.

"Wait a minute, Reverend Anderson!" he shouted. "I can get somebody to give you a ride!"

"I don't want a ride," John said, calling over his shoulder. "I want my daughter."

Jamal dragged Keisha by the hand as they entered the back of the abandoned factory through a broken door. They ran to the front of the building and knelt by the tin-covered windows.

He pulled back the corner of one of the window tins, and daylight splashed across their faces as they watched a dozen police cars arrive on the scene.

"You ain't have to shoot him," Jamal whispered.

Keisha was in a state of shock, her back against the wall as she stared into the darkness. "I know."

"So why did you?" he asked.

She watched shadows and sunlight play against his sleek black skin.

"I did it for you," she answered, looking at him through a haze of tears.

He held out his hand. "Gimme the gun," he said.

"I dropped it in the alley," she whispered.

Jamal pulled his hand back slowly.

"They gon' find your prints on it," he said.

Keisha swallowed hard in an effort to calm herself. "Then I guess we can't stop now," she said resolutely.

"Yeah," he said, staring down at her with a mixture of anxiety and grief. "I guess we can't."

Keisha watched the conflict contorting his face. "What is it, Jamal? I thought this is what you wanted."

"It is," he said, taking her hand in his. "But I ain't want it like this."

"Like what?"

He rubbed his eyes with his thumb and forefinger.

"We killed people, Keisha," he said. "Ain't no turnin' back from that."

"Who said I wanted to turn back?" she said, staring at him defiantly.

He shook his head. "If it was just me, it wouldn't matter. I can take care o' myself. But when they find that gun in the alley and put the pieces together, your life will be over, just like mine. And I can't have that."

Keisha paused as she realized what he was saying. She wanted him to say it again. So she moved closer until their faces almost touched.

"Why can't you have that?" she asked, her voice low and husky.

Jamal felt his mouth begin to water as he looked down into her beautiful eyes.

"'Cause I love you," he said, almost in a whisper.

She touched his lips with her finger, and in that moment, they both knew the depths of the feelings that had been brewing since the long-ago summer when their love was kissed by sunsets.

It was real. More real than anything they'd ever felt.

"I love you, too," she said softly. "I always have."

Their lips touched, gently at first. Then their tongues danced with one another. But even as Keisha surrendered to the moment, Jamal's mind returned to the streets, and the net that was taking shape around them.

As much as he wanted to feel her softness against him, as much as he wanted to take her for himself, as much as he wanted to show her love in its physical form, he knew that they only had a few minutes to get out.

Just as he pulled away from her, they heard the sound of footsteps walking through the factory. Jamal held his finger to his lips, signaling for Keisha to remain quiet. He pushed the tin back into place, shrouding the factory in darkness.

And then he reached down for his gun.

The tall one wore a scarf to hide her matted hair. Her skin was dry, because the crack pipe had sucked the moisture from it. But even in the factory's dim light, one could see that her face had been beautiful once, back when her heart could feel something other than contempt.

In the days before cheap crack and pure heroin flooded the streets of Philadelphia's Badlands, she'd fetched a pretty penny for her services. Now she was just like the rest of them. Five dollars could buy almost anything, including what was left of her dignity.

The girl who crossed the factory floor behind her was slower, both physically and mentally. And she was young. Neither her face nor her body had ever been attractive. But she knew how to please a man. Only recently had she been taught how to please herself.

"You okay, baby?" the tall one asked as the shorter one followed her to a dark corner where the factory's long-dead machinery stood.

"I'm all right," said the girl, her high-pitched voice quivering in the darkness. "I just ain't never seen no bodies before. 'Specially no cop's."

The tall one reached down and held the shorter one like a man would hold a woman.

"That's why I be tryin' to tell you to watch yourself out here," she said, stroking her hair.

The short one began to tremble as she recalled the sight of the two dead men they'd seen in the alley. "That coulda been one of us out there dead like that," she said softly.

"But it wasn't," said the tall one. "Now just relax, baby. Let mommy make it better for you."

There was a flicking sound and a lighter's flame illuminated their faces as they lit their pipe. If they hadn't been engrossed in the hiss and crackle of the crack rock, perhaps they would have felt the eyes watching them. But as it was, they could only feel the high, and the hot rush that it brought to their loins.

As Jamal pointed his gun at them, Keisha looked on in disbelief at the two scantily clad prostitutes.

They were groping one another as they passed the crack pipe between them. Their moans rose along with the smoke as they were consumed by a passion that they never shared with their tricks.

While the crackling sound of the burning drug echoed softly through the room, their hands touched spots reserved for one another while their bodies writhed to the rhythm of searching fingers, lips, and tongues.

When they extinguished the lighter's flame and gave themselves totally to each other, Jamal crept across the factory's floor.

They heard the unmistakable double click as he chambered a round in the nine-millimeter. And then they heard his voice.

"Don't scream and you won't get hurt," he said. His tone was low and menacing.

The one who was holding the lighter dropped it. Her girlfriend gasped. They were more surprised than afraid. The Badlands, after all, was a place where the high was worth more than life itself. They'd just seen the evidence of it in the alley.

"We only got a couple rocks left," the tall one whispered quickly. "Just take 'em. We ain't got no money."

Jamal picked up the lighter that they'd dropped on the floor, flicked it, and held the flame between them.

"I don't want your dope," he said as Keisha watched from a few feet away.

He lowered the flame and pressed the gun against the tall one's head. "I want you to take off your clothes."

The crime scene was a flurry of activity. Fire Rescue vehicles and a van from the medical examiner's office were there, along with dozens of police cars, both marked and unmarked.

Only one of the officers on the scene sat still, on the steel bumper of a wagon.

"MacAleer!" the sergeant called out to him from across the street.

"Yeah, Sarge," MacAleer answered, while pulling a mask of grief over his fear.

"I'm sorry about Hickey," the sergeant said as he sat down next to him. "I know you two worked together for a couple of years."

"Yeah," the red-haired cop said, looking up into the sergeant's eyes. "He was a good cop."

They were quiet for a moment, reflecting on the deaths that had rocked the department in the last few hours.

"We ran the VIN on that Buick that was sitting near the alley," the sergeant said. "It came up registered to Joseph Barnes. Turns out he's done some work for Frank Nichols. Beat a murder case about two years ago when the witness had an accident."

MacAleer began to grow nervous. "Is that so?"

"Yeah. Crime Scene guys took a look at the scene and they're not sure Barnes was the shooter. Just looking at the car—you know, with the doors open and all—they're pretty sure somebody was with him."

"Well, I didn't see anyone else leaving the scene," MacAleer said.

The sergeant stood up. "Lieutenant Lynch is on his way

down from Homicide. You can run through the whole thing with him. Shouldn't take long."

MacAleer sighed and looked away from the sergeant to scan the faces in the crowd of prostitutes gathered at the edge of the crime scene.

There were two new faces that he didn't recognize. One was tall and dark, and like the other transvestites who turned tricks along with the women on the strip, his hair was tied back with a scarf. The other was short, with a smooth brown face, honey-colored eyes, and an outfit that barley covered her essentials.

Keisha began to back away from the crowd as the cop licked her body with his eyes. She was wearing the skimpy outfit that they'd taken from one of the prostitutes in the house, and her thick legs and round hips were bursting forth like ripened fruit. She was embarrassed. And Jamal was afraid.

He'd wrapped one of the prostitute's scarves around his head, to hide his dreadlocks. He'd buttoned down his shirt and tied it at the bottom to reveal his flat, hard stomach. The pocketbook he'd taken from the prostitute contained his gun. The jeans he wore were his own.

The outfit wouldn't hide his identity for long, even in a crowd. And the prostitutes they'd left in the house would soon break the makeshift bonds that Jamal had tied around their hands, mouths, and feet.

"Don't look back," Jamal said as the two of them moved away from the crowd and walked toward the corner of the block. "Just follow me."

Keisha couldn't have looked back if she'd wanted to. She was filled with a fear she'd never known, and an uncertainty that

left her almost completely crippled. That is, until she glanced at
Jamal.

The tied-up shirt fit awkwardly on his lean, tight physique.
And the head scarf gave him the theatrical look of a drag queen.

"You know you look crazy, right?" she asked, grinning nervously as they turned the corner.

"Not as crazy as I'd look in prison," he said, absently scanning the street. "Or dead."

His words were sobering, and her grin rapidly disappeared.

"You see that car?" he asked as he spotted a blue Dodge Neon
riding slowly down the block.

"Yeah," Keisha said, watching the middle-aged driver trying
to wave her over to his car.

"Go over there and talk to him," Jamal said. "Get him to
open the door."

Keisha looked at Jamal as if she didn't want to do it.

"Just say, 'What's up?'" Jamal said quickly. "He'll do the rest.
Now hurry up 'fore he drive away."

Jamal crossed the street, leaving Keisha to her own devices.

The car slowed down and stopped as Keisha approached. She
was luscious, even in a soiled miniskirt and halter top. And with
her ample cleavage on display, she was downright irresistible.

"What's up?" she said as the driver pulled up and stopped in
front of her.

The man was heavy, and his face was covered with sweat. His
beady eyes darting to and fro, it was clear that he was uneasy. He
knew that she was too beautiful for these streets. And with an incident around the corner drawing so many police to the area, he
wondered if she was part of some sort of sting.

"You ain't no cop, is you?" he said, stammering slightly.

She shook her head and tried to give him a reassuring smile.

The man watched her for a few seconds more. And though it

was clear that he still had lingering doubts about her, lust overcame sound judgment, and he reached over to unlock his door.

"Get in," he said gruffly.

Before the words were even out of his mouth, Jamal, who had
crept over to the side of the car, leaped into the front seat holding
the gun.

"Hey, what are you—"

"Shut up," Jamal said, pulling the bucket seat forward to allow Keisha to get in the back.

The driver's beady eyes looked from one of them to the other,
and his face began to tremble as Jamal shut the door and locked it.

"Don't hurt me," he said, holding his hands up in the air.

"Put your hands down and drive," Jamal said calmly.

The man hesitated for a moment, and Jamal jammed the gun
into his ribs.

"Now," he said, his voice barely audible. "Go straight 'til I tell
you to turn. Not too fast."

The man did as he was told while looking back at Keisha.

She refused to look at him. But as the driver rode past the
block where a throng of police were gathered at the crime scene,
she couldn't help stealing a glance at Jamal.

When the cab Nola had taken from the Thirtieth Street Station pulled onto her block, there were police cars lined up outside her brownstone, plainclothes and uniformed officers were trotting up and down her steps, and her neighbors were peering out their windows, shaking their heads at the spectacle of it all.

The driver stopped, and Nola tipped him generously before getting out of the taxi. Then she crossed the small street with her head held high, as everyone—police and neighbors alike—stopped what they were doing to watch her.

They couldn't help it. Nola was polished femininity, dressed provocatively yet tastefully, with a beauty that shone like sunlight, and a raw sexuality that lingered just beneath.

With a hint of perfume trailing behind her, she nodded politely as she passed the officers on her steps and stepped into her house.

She walked through her vast living room and the ornate dining room and entered the state-of-the-art kitchen. She dropped her purse on the counter, and there was the crunch of glass under her feet as she stepped on the windowpane the police had broken when they'd entered her home.

The sound of it was a reminder of what had happened there this morning. It made her angry.

"Marquita!" she called out, then turned around to unleash her wrath. "Marquita, are you—"

"Who's Marquita?" Lynch said, startling her as he walked into the kitchen.

Nola jumped. "Who the hell are you?"

"I'm Lieutenant Lynch," he said, handing her a folded piece of paper. "And this is my warrant. It allows us to search the premises for any weapons that may have been used in, or documents pertaining to, the murder of Commissioner Darrell Freeman."

Nola skimmed the warrant and handed it back to him.

"And what does any of that have to do with me?"

"Frank Nichols is wanted in connection with the police commissioner's murder," Lynch said with a shrug. "He was spotted here this morning. Now, can I ask you a question?"

"You're the one with the warrant," she said, folding her arms.

"Who's Marquita?"

"My daughter. She lives here with me."

"I see," he said, almost to himself. "I guess that explains it."

"Explains what?"

"There were, um, signs that Mr. Nichols wasn't alone."

"If you're trying to tell me that my daughter slept with him, I already know that," she said, her eyes flashing anger as she fell into a nearby chair and crossed her legs.

"She called me this morning and told me what she had done. I guess she figured I'd find out sooner or later, since the police had come here looking for Frank."

"Was she here when we arrived this morning?"

"I don't know," Nola said. "I was on my way in from New York when she called. But she did tell me that the police had been here."

"Well," Lynch said, thinking aloud. "Until we find out different, we're going to have to operate under the assumption that she was here, and that she went with him when he ran. Depending on how things turn out, that could make her an accessory to murder."

Nola's eyes welled up with tears. Embarrassed, she wiped them away quickly. "I'm sorry," she said, sniffling. "I just don't want to see my daughter caught up in this."

"Then maybe you need to start talking."

"If I had something to tell, Lieutenant," she said, wiping her eyes. "I would tell it. But I don't."

"So instead of talking, you're going to allow yourself to be dragged into this?"

A cloud of anxiety passed over her face. But just like the anger that had appeared in her eyes a few minutes before, it vanished as quickly as it had appeared.

"I'm not going to be dragged into anything," she said, growing more agitated. "I don't know anything about Frank's business, I certainly don't know anything about any murder, and I've never committed a crime in my life. The only thing I'm guilty of is choosing badly when it comes to men."

Lynch looked her up and down. Then he made a great show of looking around at the trappings of her wealth before resting his gaze on her again.

"Looks to me like you can have any man you want," he said, looking at her through narrowed eyes. "Why Frank Nichols?"

"Isn't it obvious?" she said with a disingenuous smile. "That *is* who I want."

Both she and Lynch knew that there was more to it than that. But Nola wasn't about to talk.

As Lynch stared at her in hopes of breaking the stalemate, Detective Ron Hubert, a curly-haired homicide veteran, approached Lynch from behind.

"We're wrapping it up, Lieutenant," he said, looking from Lynch to Nola and sensing the tension. "There's nothing here."

Lynch looked back at the detective, then at Nola. "I find that hard to believe," he said. "But then, I find a lot of things hard to believe."

The message wasn't lost on Nola. She got up from her seat, snatched her purse off the counter, and reached inside for a business card.

"I find it hard to believe that you're here harassing me when there's a murderer out there someplace," she said while scribbling a number on the back of the card.

She stopped to look at her watch. "If you hear anything about Frank or my daughter, please call me. Now, if we're finished here, I've got a pressing business appointment. Do me a favor and lock the door when you leave."

Nola handed Lynch the card and started to walk out.

"Ms. Langston," Lynch called after her.

Nola turned around. "Yes, Lieutenant?"

"Don't go too far," he said, locking eyes with her.

"I wouldn't dream of it," she said with a quick grin. "Good day."

As she walked away, Hubert turned around to admire her extensive attributes. Lynch looked at her business card.

"Says here she's a buyer for Strawbridge's and Lord & Taylor," he said, shaking his head slowly in disbelief. "A nine-to-five couldn't support a woman like that."

He turned to the detective. "I want her followed. I want to know where she goes, who she's with, and what she does."

"Okay, Lieutenant."

As the detective rushed out to catch Nola, Lynch's cell phone began to ring.

He answered it, and after listening to the officer on the other end for a few seconds, he disconnected the call while staring across the room in shock.

There'd been another police shooting in the Twenty-fifth District. And it looked like Jamal Nichols was involved.

The sounds of clanging pots and sizzling oil emanated from the Andersons' kitchen. But even as the sisters from the pastor's aid committee prepared him a meal, John sat sullenly on the couch, trying desperately not to think of what the Nichols boy was doing to his daughter.

A white-haired deacon sat to John's right. A younger deacon in a wrinkled black suit sat to his left. Both men had tried to speak words of comfort to their pastor. But John couldn't hear them. Because the sisters and the deacons, while they meant well, were reminders of what had filled his family with bitterness.

John had given his all to his parishioners, just as they were now giving their all to him. But over the years, he had forgotten that his family should be his first ministry. And now he was paying the price.

When Sarah walked in, having accepted the ride home that the detective had offered to her husband, she was even angrier than she'd been when they'd argued back at police headquarters.

"How you doin', Sister Sarah?" the white-haired deacon asked as she crossed the room.

"Not good, Deacon Burrows," she said as she shot a malevolent glance at her husband. "Not good at all."

John could feel her eyes, but he didn't look up, because he didn't want to argue with her anymore.

Deacon Burrows saw the tension between them and stood up. The other deacon followed his lead.

Walking over to the pastor's wife, Burrows spoke quietly. "Just remember, Sister Sarah, God knows what you goin' through and He gon' move in His own time," he said reassuringly. "And when He move, He gon' move in a mighty way."

Sarah didn't respond. Neither did John.

Seeing their lack of faith, the old deacon shook his head disappointedly. "We'll be in the kitchen if you need us," he said as he and the younger man shuffled out of the room.

Sarah put down her purse and crossed to the mantelpiece. While John sat quietly on their battered couch, she looked around the room, and shook her head. She saw the dull red rug in the middle of their worn hardwood floor, the sparse furnishings that were scattered about, and the Christian study books lining the bookshelf along the far wall.

Seeing what little they had made Sarah question the sacrifice they'd made for the ministry.

She glanced across the room through watery eyes while her husband mouthed something that looked like a prayer.

Thoughts of her husband crowded thoughts of her daughter, and she grew angry. She stomped across the room and brushed against the bookshelf. Several books tumbled down onto the floor, and she was furious.

She screamed out of frustration. It was a sound that brought John leaping from the couch and the deacons and the sisters running in from the kitchen. John knelt down next to his weeping wife as the church members looked at each other worriedly.

When John reached out gingerly to touch Sarah, to wrap his arm around her shoulders, she flinched and he retreated. He reached out again, this time more firmly. She melted into him as he held her in his long, powerful arms.

"Why?" she asked, her mouth quivering as the tears streaked her face. "Why did God do this to us?"

John's mind raced through all the things he'd done to people in his past. And as the bloody memories overtook him, he couldn't help but think of the Bible verse that talked about sowing to the wind and reaping the whirlwind.

"God doesn't do everything to us, Sarah," he said solemnly. "Some things we do to ourselves."

The two of them sat in the middle of the floor, sobbing and holding one another, as they swayed to the rhythm of their grief. Instinctively, the deacons and the sisters surrounded them, joined hands, and began to pray.

John and Sarah sat there within the circle of prayer. Things were almost as they used to be. John and his wife were close to one another and sharing each other's burdens. But something was missing. Something they'd stopped looking for long ago.

John bowed his head and joined the others in silent prayer as Sarah slowly lifted her head from his shoulder and stared straight ahead. Her eyes were red, not from the tears, but from the fiery anger that burned in her heart.

"I've got to get out of here," Sarah said, pulling away from him. "I need some air."

One of the sisters started to take off her apron and go after her, but Deacon Burrows put out his arm to stop her. This was a family matter, he said with his eyes. Reluctantly, the woman stood still.

John watched his wife fetch her purse from the armchair and

walk out the door, and he knew that his prayers would not be enough this time.

The moment he arrived at the crime scene, Kevin Lynch knew that he'd been there before. It was an area that had long been a hotbed of prostitution, and as such, it had played host to its share of murders.

This time was different, however, because one of the victims was a cop, the second to die in one day. Lynch couldn't remember anything like that ever happening before.

Parking his car behind a paddy wagon, Lynch walked past a throng of police and approached the slain officer's partner.

"You MacAleer?" he asked the red-haired cop who was leaning against a district car.

"Yeah," he said, his eyes downcast in grief.

"I'm Lieutenant Lynch—Homicide. You want to tell me what happened here?"

MacAleer sighed. "My partner got outta the wagon to take a piss. He walked up on some people in the alley. There were gunshots. By the time I got out and made it over to him, he was dead and so was the shooter."

Lynch nodded. "You and your partner always piss in alleys where prostitutes hang out?"

MacAleer shrugged. "It's a tough neighborhood. Guy's gotta piss somewhere."

"And hookers have to do business somewhere, right?" Lynch asked, looking down at MacAleer's zipper, which was still undone.

MacAleer followed Lynch's eyes to his crotch and zipped his pants.

Lynch moved closer to MacAleer and pointed toward the alley. "Your partner walked right past that Buick over there. Any cop who's worth a damn checks out an empty car with its doors open on a street like this. But I get the feeling neither one of you ever checked out anything. What do you do, take a cut of the hookers' money to let them work the strip?"

Lynch looked down at a crusty white stain on MacAleer's uniform pants. "Or do they give you something else besides money?"

"Lieutenant, you've got it all wrong. I wouldn't—"

"Internal Affairs is gonna be giving you a call, Officer MacAleer. And then they're gonna be giving me a call. If I find out you were screwing some hooker while your partner was being shot, it won't just be your badge. You're going to jail."

As a stunned MacAleer stumbled for a response, Lynch turned and walked over to the crime scene.

Passing by the yellow tape that stretched across the end of the alley, he knelt down and pulled back the sheet that covered the slain police officer's body. His brow furled as he examined the exit wound in back of the officer's head, and the gun that sat just a few inches from his outstretched hand.

There were two bullet casings nearby. They'd already been circled in chalk by officers from the Crime Scene Unit.

Putting the blanket back in place, Lynch moved further down the alley to take a look at the other dead man. But before he could do that, he saw something that piqued his curiosity. There was a smear of blood on the brick wall, and what appeared to be pieces of rolled-up skin. It looked like someone had scraped against the wall and gotten an abrasion.

"Come here for a minute, Sergeant," he said, calling out to one of the Crime Scene officers.

The sergeant put away the tape measure he was using to

measure the space between bullet casings. "Yeah, Lieutenant, what's up?"

"Did anybody get this?" he asked, pointing to the skin and blood against the wall.

The sergeant moved in to get a closer look. "No, but I'll get somebody on it."

"Thanks," Lynch said, already looking down the alley at a freshly broken branch on one of the overgrown weeds.

As the sergeant waved one of his men over to bag the blood and skin sample, Lynch took a quick look at the other body. Then he walked past it to finger the broken branch.

He removed his gun from its holster and walked through the weeds, following the trail of trampled trash and leaning weeds until he came to the broken back door of the factory.

Something inside him pulled him toward that door. He walked inside, and when he heard the muffled grunts from across the factory floor, he knew that his hunch was right.

The naked prostitutes were huddled in the corner with their bonds tied tightly around their hands, feet, and mouths. They looked up at him with eyes stretched wide as he approached them through the dim light.

He reached out and removed the strip of cloth around the tall one's mouth.

"Who did this to you?" he asked.

"It was a guy and a girl," she said. "He had dreadlocks and a gun."

Lynch bent down to untie the rest of her makeshift bonds as the sergeant from the Crime Scene Unit walked in through the broken factory door.

"What about the girl?" Lynch asked, reaching over to untie the shorter one.

"It was hard to see. But she looked young."

"Did it look like he was forcing her to do anything?"

The shorter one rubbed her wrists when he undid her bonds. "He ain't force her to do shit," she said bitterly. "She was with him 'cause she wanted to be."

"It must've been Keisha Anderson," the sergeant said as he walked up and stood behind Lynch.

"Maybe not," Lynch said hopefully.

"There's no maybe about it," the sergeant said, handing a plastic bag to Lynch.

Lynch looked inside and saw a photograph encased in plastic, with a string attached to it so that it could be worn like a necklace.

"That was in the Buick that was parked by the alley," the sergeant said. "It's her work ID from Strawbridge's. It must've fallen out of her pocket when she got out of the car."

9

Frank and Marquita, dressed in the jeans and hoodies that Frank's men had provided, were safely hidden behind the tinted windows of a Mazda MPV.

They'd been sitting there, in a parking space on Market Street near Fifteenth, for the better part of a half-hour.

Marquita didn't know why they were sitting there, in the shadow of City Hall. She only knew that her dream of making love to Frank Nichols had rapidly disintegrated into a nightmare.

She'd gone from savoring his passion to tasting his wrath. And now, rather than lying down with him in pleasure, she was sitting up with him in pain, and reflecting on how it had come to this.

She remembered the way Frank had looked at her when her mother introduced them over a year ago. It had intrigued her. But when she went back to her college dormitory in upstate Pennsylvania, she forgot all about it.

Two days later, when she returned to the dorms from class, her room was filled with roses. The card contained two words: "Look outside."

When she did, she saw Frank Nichols, standing next to a black Mercedes, beckoning for her to come down. She did, and that was the beginning of the end.

For months Frank played the patient suitor, never pushing her to do anything she didn't want to. And as her feelings for him developed, the fact that he was her mother's man became less significant.

As time wore on, their secret meetings grew increasingly sexual. Marquita knew that she would eventually relinquish her virginity to him. What she didn't know was that in doing so, she could end up giving up her life as well.

Marquita glanced over at Frank. Now, instead of holding her body, he was holding a gun. And in between his frequent glances out the van's windows and mirrors, he kept looking at his cell phone, as if he could will it to ring.

He hadn't told her who he was waiting for, but she knew in her heart that it was her mother. She also knew that whatever Nola had, it was something that Frank wanted very badly.

She shook her head and sighed at her own stupidity. After all the time she'd spent wanting Frank Nichols, the only thing she wanted now was to escape from him.

Looking out the tinted windows at the throngs of people passing outside on the city's busiest streets, she contemplated screaming or running away. Then she thought better of it, knowing that Frank wouldn't hesitate to use the gun.

But while the gun could control her movements, it couldn't control her heart. And in her heart, she hated him for the way he'd abused her body and her mind.

The question now was, what could she do about it?

"Frank," she said softly. "Can I ask you something?"

He turned his intense stare on her, and waited for her to speak.

"Why don't you just turn yourself in? I mean, you couldn't have done what they think you did, because you were with me when it happened."

Frank laughed. "That's the problem with you," he said, smiling at her naïveté. "All you see is what you see. You don't take the time to look underneath it, and see the truth."

He became deadly serious. "Ain't none o' this about what I did or didn't do," he said. "If it was, I would do what I always do—beat the case."

"What's it about, then?" she asked, though she was afraid to know the answer.

Frank bored his eyes into her. "Same thing everything else in life is about—money."

Lynch returned to police headquarters, knowing that it would take a while to sort through the evidence they'd found at the scene of the latest shooting.

He headed to the third floor carrying the file he was compiling. The murders of a commissioner and an officer in a single day had made the case the most high-profile he had ever handled.

Walking briskly through the halls and into the department's executive offices, Lynch smiled sadly as Commissioner Freeman's longtime secretary waved him inside.

He slowed down and looked at pictures from a career that spanned decades, trinkets from a life that had touched many, and an aura in the room that would not soon disappear.

After seeing and feeling all those things, Lynch walked into Freeman's old office with a forlorn expression and sat down opposite Acting Commissioner Dilsheimer.

"It's not easy, is it?" Dilsheimer said, leaning back in his chair as he watched the lieutenant.

"What's not easy, Commissioner?"

"Losing a man like Freeman," Dilsheimer said, rounding the desk and sitting down next to Lynch.

"I worked with him for a lot of years, and I'm going to miss him," he added in a melancholy voice. "But I know he understood the risks we take as cops. And I know he would've wanted us to do our jobs, no matter what."

"I understand that, sir," Lynch said while fingering the file in his lap.

"Good," Dilsheimer said, settling back into his chair. "What've we got so far?"

"We're still running ballistics on the bullets from all the shootings, and waiting to see what that tells us," Lynch said. "In terms of what we know, Reverend Anderson and Nichols apparently had a long-running feud that blew up when Keisha Anderson was assaulted.

"Now, we've got three bodies, including the old woman, the commissioner, and a Twenty-fifth District officer."

"Do we have anything connecting Frank Nichols to any of this?" Dilsheimer asked.

"Other than the fact that he ran when we caught him at his girlfriend's house this morning? No."

"What's this girlfriend's name?"

"Nola Langston."

"Was she there when he escaped?"

"No, sir. Nichols was there with the girlfriend's daughter.

When he ran, she did, too. We haven't seen either one of them since. But we're still looking."

Dilsheimer nodded. "And this Nola Langston, she's not talking, even after Nichols got caught with her daughter?"

"No, sir. She claims she's worried about her daughter, and that she doesn't know anything about Frank Nichols's business. But there's something fake about her. She knows more than what she's saying."

"And where is Ms. Langston now?" Dilsheimer asked.

"I've got a tail on her," Lynch said. "He checked in with me a few minutes ago and she's still in the Center City area. It's just a hunch, but I'm thinking she's gonna lead us to something we couldn't get just by asking."

Dilsheimer looked thoughtful.

"Okay," he said. "I'll trust your judgment on that for now. But if we don't get anything soon, I want you to bring her in for questioning."

"Yes, sir."

"And keep me posted on Nichols, too," the commissioner said, standing up to pace the floor. "If his son is the one who kidnapped Keisha Anderson, I'm willing to bet Frank Nichols is behind it."

"There's just one problem with that, Commissioner," Lynch said, his tone grave. "Keisha Anderson may not have been kidnapped."

Dilsheimer was confused. "What are you talking about?"

"After that last shooting, Keisha and Jamal took some clothes from a couple of prostitutes, tied them up, and walked away together."

"How do we know Nichols didn't force her to go with him?" Dilsheimer asked.

"We don't. But if you believe the hookers, Jamal didn't force Keisha to do anything. And I've gotta believe that by the time they left, there were enough cops around that if she wanted to call for help, she could've."

"But why would she go with him?" Dilsheimer asked, his tone dubious.

"I don't know," Lynch said with a weary sigh. "But if I were a betting man, Commissioner, I'd say this thing is probably a little more complicated than it looks."

Ishmael ran the razor across his scalp, dipped it into the water-filled basin, and swiped it over his head again. Then he scooped out a handful of water, splashed it against his face, and looked at his reflection.

He didn't recognize the bald man who stared back at him from Aunt Annie's bathroom mirror. His smooth face and head gave him an almost angelic look that he found amusing.

Reaching up toward the door, he dressed quickly in the suit that had been there, at the house, since the day he'd come there from the halfway house two years before.

After tightening the knot on his red tie, he donned reading glasses and looked into the mirror again. The transformation was unbelievable. He looked like more like a preacher than a killer. And that would serve him well.

He knew that he wouldn't get many more opportunities to do what his lover had asked him to do. And he knew that she would leave him if he didn't accomplish the mission.

The thought of living without her was painful enough. But nothing could be worse than disappointing her, and watching tears stain her beautiful face.

He'd seen her cry only once. And that was when she'd told him of all the things she'd endured at the hands of her tormentor.

She told him of rapes and beatings, humiliation and torture. She recounted the time he'd branded her like an animal with a hot poker, then bound her and held her captive for days on end. And then she told him that he'd threatened to kill her if she ever told anyone.

The moment she shared that with him, the thought of her death flashed before his eyes. The sight of it, even in his imagination, was unbearable. So he offered to kill him for her.

At first she told him that he couldn't, that he shouldn't. But he would hear none of it. The man who'd done these things would have to pay with his life. And Ishmael would be the one to take it from him.

Picking up the briefcase that carried his pistol, he went down the steps and into the garage.

He walked past the motorcycle, took a set of keys from the wall, and got behind the wheel of the old Chrysler.

The plan she'd given him was perfect, he thought as he pulled out into the bright sunshine. But now it would have to be altered.

Nola Langston watched the gray Mercury pass by her as she walked on Walnut Street. It turned onto Eighteenth and parked illegally, in a handicapped space.

A minute later, as she traversed Rittenhouse Square's high-end retail and restaurant district, stopping occasionally to look in store windows, she saw the car's occupant—the curly-haired detective she'd seen at her house—trailing her on foot.

Nola knew that she was being followed. And she knew that she had to elude him if she was going to do what she'd planned.

Walking into the jewelry store on the corner of Fifteenth and Walnut, she browsed for a few minutes before trying on a diamond necklace. Bending down at the small mirror on the counter, she looked over her shoulder and saw the detective waiting across the street, in the doorway of the cigar store.

Nola took the necklace off and handed it to the salesman. "I'd like to put this on my American Express card and have it delivered to the usual address," she told him.

"No problem, Ms. Langston."

Nola wandered around the store while the salesman ran the card. Then she nodded to the guard, who buzzed her out.

She left the store and walked leisurely toward Broad Street. From the corner of her eye she could see the cop across the street, following her.

She crossed to the other side so she could be closer to him. As she did so, the salesman came running out of the store.

"Ms. Langston!" he shouted. "You forgot to sign your receipt!"

Nola screamed and pointed at the plainclothes detective. "He's got my purse!"

The guard from the jewelry store ran outside, drawing his weapon and aiming at the cop. The cop pulled his as well.

"Police!" he shouted. "Put it down!"

"I don't see a badge!" the guard yelled back. "You put yours down!"

Two women screamed when they saw the guns, and people on the crowded street began to panic. Shoppers dived for cover. A bus was rear-ended by a car. Commuters pushed against one another in an effort to get out of the way.

And Nola Langston ran as fast as she could toward Broad and Walnut. There she disappeared down the subway steps and melted into the network of walkways that ran beneath the city's center.

As she walked north in the passage underneath Broad Street, she looked behind her to make sure she hadn't been followed, and moved quickly until she was beneath City Hall.

She walked in the open passages under the courtyard, past the manmade waterfalls, and crossed into the tunnels that led to Market Street. By the time she emerged from the stairway at Thirteenth and Market, she knew that she'd lost the tail.

Crossing Market Street, she strolled into Lord & Taylor, hoping to go unnoticed. But Nola wasn't the type of woman whom people didn't see.

"Hi, Nola," said a floor manager from men's clothing. "How was the trip to New York?"

"Fine," she said without breaking stride.

When she reached the steps that led to her office, she was almost running. Making her way to the second floor, she walked into the executive offices and smiled pleasantly at the receptionist.

"Good morning, Ms. Langston," she said as Nola walked past.

"Good morning," Nola said, strolling into her office and locking the door.

She opened the closet and began to move the boxes that littered the floor. Most contained pictures and samples from the upcoming fall lines for various designers. When she got to the final box, however, she found what she was looking for.

Opening it carefully, she removed a diamond necklace and a three-carat ring. And then she removed a binder that was worth far more than both of them combined.

Nola flipped through the documents that the binder contained, and took out the paperwork she'd need. She put on the necklace and the ring, then stripped out of her clothes and extracted a strapless linen dress from the closet.

She left her office wearing sunglasses and the dress, with nothing beneath it but perfume. The papers she needed were neatly folded in a small black purse as she stepped out into the summer air for the three-block walk to the Center Square building.

She needed the walk to clear her mind, because she knew that what she was about to do could literally cost her life.

But she would have to make her move now. There was really no other choice.

She was going to get the money, just as she'd always planned to do. And then she would be rid of Frank Nichols forever.

Jamal untied his shirt and removed the scarf from his head with one hand. With the other, he pointed the gun at the man they'd forced to drive them from the scene of the shooting.

"Turn over there and go underneath the highway," Jamal said as they approached I-95 from a side street.

The beady-eyed man looked at him, then glanced down at the gun. "Look, I got some money, if that's what you want."

"Shut up, and pull over there!"

Keisha, sitting silently in the back seat, watched as the man pulled beneath the overpass and stopped the car between a pile of old tires and a stack of discarded furniture.

"Get out," Jamal said, trying not to acknowledge the quickening double thump of his heart.

The man looked at him in disbelief.

"I said, 'Get out!'" Jamal shouted, raising the gun.

The man scurried to leave the car.

"Wait a minute," Jamal said quickly. "Pull your pants off."

126

The man looked back at Keisha in embarrassment, then at Jamal, as if to ask why.

"Pull 'em off!" Jamal shouted. "Your shirt, too!"

Keisha watched nervously as Jamal snatched the keys from the ignition, pushed the pudgy man from the car, and got out behind him.

"Open the trunk," he said to Keisha, tossing her the keys and pointing the gun at the man.

Keisha got out, walked to the trunk, and unlocked it. Then she watched the man standing at the trunk with Jamal pressing the gun to his temple.

"Get that shit outta there," Jamal said, pointing to the spare tire and other supplies in the trunk of the car.

The man's eyes begged Jamal to stop. When it was clear that he wouldn't, the man emptied the trunk and waited for the inevitable.

"Get in," Jamal said.

The man climbed in, bending and twisting until his girth fit inside the cramped space.

Jamal closed the trunk as Keisha watched. Then he walked around to the front of the car and got in.

"Get up front," he told Keisha.

She did as she was told. But as Jamal drove from beneath the overpass with his head on a swivel and merged onto I-95 North, Keisha looked back at the trunk, hoping that the man inside wouldn't become another body.

The gray-haired, leather-faced cop in car X2 had been a police officer for most of his adult life. He'd seen everything there was to see—from Black Panthers stripped naked on Cecil B. Moore Avenue to police officers arrested in drug-dealing scandals.

Still, the news of the commissioner's death shocked him. And as he listened to the dispatcher's voice reading a description of the black man with dreadlocks who'd allegedly murdered the commissioner, he was reminded of his own mortality.

Reaching down to adjust the volume on the radio, he glanced at the traffic about a block ahead and to his right, and watched as a blue Neon merged onto I-95 at the Bridge Street entrance.

The car swerved slightly as it cut off a minivan and burst into traffic. That wouldn't have been enough to draw the attention of the officer, who often saw aggressive drivers on this stretch of the interstate.

But as he sped up slightly and pulled closer, he noticed that the back of the car was resting almost entirely on its rear wheels, even though there was no one sitting in the back seat.

As he reached for his radio to call in the tag, he hoped that there was a reasonable explanation for the extra weight in the trunk.

In case there wasn't, he unsnapped the holster on his gun.

Jamal glanced at Keisha, then looked in the rearview mirror and watched the police car lingering two cars back.

"It's a cop behind us," he said, gripping the steering wheel tightly as he sped up to fifty-five.

Keisha followed his eyes as he looked in the mirror again. When she saw the police car, her breath came fast and heavy.

Jamal switched to the far left lane. Keisha looked back and saw the cop do the same.

"Don't worry, baby," Jamal said, looking in the mirror. "We gettin' outta this."

He looked in her eyes and saw that she wanted to believe him.

She was, despite her womanly facade, a little girl who'd been waiting all her life for a knight in shining armor.

He wondered if he was the one.

Jamal nodded toward the mirror. "If he try to stop us, I'm jettin'. I can't shoot and drive at the same time, so take this."

He reached into his waistband and handed her his gun.

"You ain't scared, is you?" he asked as she took it.

"No," she said, turning it over in her hands.

"Why not?"

Keisha paused to think for a moment. "I always did what I was supposed to do," she said, chambering a round as she'd seen him do. "Now I wanna see what it's like not to."

Just then the cop pulled directly behind them and blasted his siren once.

Jamal kept going.

He blasted it again, this time accompanying the siren with the whirl of his dome lights.

Jamal maintained his speed.

The cop pulled up to their rear and bumped it slightly.

That's when Jamal bolted. Skidding into the middle lanes as nearby cars braked and swerved to avoid them, Jamal pushed the car as hard as he could, but the cop switched lanes and pulled up beside the fleeing vehicle.

Jamal and the cop looked at one another as they rode side by side. But only for a split second.

Jamal braked suddenly and jerked to the right, cutting off a tractor trailer. A second later, he switched lanes again, moving to the right and falling in beside the truck.

The cop tried to follow, but he was going too fast, and shot past as the truck exited at Academy Road. While Jamal raced to get in front of the truck, the cop braked and skidded to a stop, backed up, and turned onto the exit ramp. But as he sped around the arcing exit in an effort to catch up to Jamal, he was trapped behind the slow-moving tractor trailer.

Meanwhile, Jamal sped to the top of the ramp, made a hard left, and skidded onto Frankford Avenue.

By the time the time the cop caught up, the empty car had been left running on Frankford Avenue. Jamal and Keisha were headed for a nearby housing project, running for their lives.

10

Sarah Anderson had spent the last fifteen minutes walking through the neighborhood, trying to clear her thoughts. But the walk hadn't worked for her. She was still angry, still filled with guilt over her daughter's disappearance, and still lost as to what to do next.

She walked into the church hoping that the Senior Women's Ministry that met there on Thursday afternoons hadn't canceled in the wake of everything that had happened.

When she heard the chorus of amens that always accompanied the prayers of Mother Wallace, she knew that the women were there. And she was grateful, because she needed them now more than ever.

Walking slowly up the steps toward the sanctuary, she could hear bits of the prayer floating out toward her.

"And bless Sister Sarah," Mother Wallace said, her strong voice pounding each consonant and stretching each vowel until the words sounded more like a sermon than a prayer. "Bless her like you blessed her namesake in the Bible. Bless Keisha, the fruit of her womb, as you blessed Jacob. Bring her back safe, so the world can see the glory of the Lord."

Sarah could hear the smattering of hallelujahs that followed every word. And as she walked into the back door of the sanctuary, watching the women holding hands as they reached over pews in a circle of prayer, they sensed her presence. And one by one, their voices went silent as they watched her walk down the very aisle that Keisha had walked the night before.

Mother Wallace opened her eyes to see who had joined them. When she saw that it was Sarah, she stopped her prayer in midsentence and said, "Amen."

"Come over here and join us, Sister Sarah," she said, standing up with a sympathetic smile.

The two women sitting with Mother Wallace stood also. They made their way to the edge of the pews and reached out, silently inviting Sarah into their midst.

She stumbled down the aisle and fell into their arms as the effects of her sleepless night showed through. Her red-rimmed eyes were filled with tears. But none of them fell.

Mother Wallace saw the pain in her face. "It's all right, honey," she said as if she were talking to a wounded child. "You with us, now. Go ahead and let it out."

The tears still refused to come. Instead Sarah smiled weakly and responded as her husband would have. She was still the first lady of the church. And no matter what she was going through, she still had to minister to others.

"I see you saved a seat for Mother Johnson," she said, nodding toward the empty space in the middle of the pew. "We're going to miss her. Especially at times like this, when God's prayer warriors need to be out on the battlefield."

"She ain't gotta worry 'bout none o' this now," Mother Green said, lifting her chocolate face toward the heavens. "It's sad, what happened, but God knows best."

"Yes, He does," said Mother Wallace as she took Sarah's elbow and gently led her to a seat. "How's Pastor?"

"He's fine," Sarah said, knowing, just as they all did, that this was a lie.

"Any news about Keisha?" Mother Wallace asked sheepishly.

"I heard they think that Nichols boy took her," said Mother Jones. "I just hope he didn't . . ."

The other women cast disapproving stares in Mother Jones's direction and she allowed her words to trail off. But everyone knew what she was going to say. She hoped that Jamal hadn't hurt Keisha.

Sarah chose not to look at Mother Jones. Instead, she looked inward and stood face-to-face with the reality that she might never see her daughter again.

That sobering thought caused tears to slide down Sarah's cheeks as Mother Wallace stepped forward and folded her in her arms. Sarah's weeping gave way to sobbing as she rested her moist face against Mother Wallace's ample bosom.

Sarah found comfort in Mother Wallace's arms. It was the kind of comfort that her husband couldn't give, because only another woman can truly understand the loss of a mother's child.

"It's all right, baby," Mother Wallace whispered, slowly rubbing Sarah's back as the tears flowed. "God is gonna fix this. He's gonna fix all o' this."

Sarah closed her eyes and listened to Mother Wallace's soothing voice. She thought of the rocky relationship she had with her daughter and the contentious marriage she shared with John. And as she did so, she felt herself hurtling down an emotional sliding board and landing in the sands of regret.

"I just wish I would've done something differently," Sarah said between sobs. "I wish I would've—"

"Sshh," Mother Wallace said while continuing to rub Sarah's back. "Ain't nothin' you coulda done."

Mother Green chimed in. "Just do what you can right now," she said softly.

"But first, let them tears go," Mother Jones added empathetically. "Let 'em come down, baby. That's God's way o' washin' away the pain."

They stood there for the next few moments, comforting her as she cried. When the sobbing eased, Mother Wallace released Sarah from her arms and stared compassionately into her eyes.

"Go home, Sister Sarah," she said with conviction. "Your husband needs you now more than he ever has before. No matter what happens, he's gon' need to know that you there for him. Besides the Lord, you might be the best thing he's got left."

Sarah looked up into Mother Wallace's eyes and mouthed a silent *thank you*. Then she wiped away the last of her tears, turned on her heel, and walked out of the sanctuary doors to do what she must.

Having convinced the deacons and the sisters to go home after assuring them that he was okay, John Anderson wandered aimlessly through his house. He tried to ignore the sick feeling in the pit of his stomach while watching and waiting for Sarah to return.

He knew when he walked back into the living room and glanced toward the pictures on the mantelpiece that the time for wandering had ended.

Slowly, he crossed the room and took their wedding picture in his hand. He held it up and blew the dust from the glass pane, then lifted it to his eyes and gently touched it with his fingertips.

He examined the smile on his wife's face, and tried to remember the last time she'd looked that way. He couldn't. In fact, he couldn't remember the last time she'd smiled at all.

He put down the picture and sighed, then looked toward the heavens and prayed that God would forgive him for what he was about to do.

Walking up the stairs to the bedroom he shared with Sarah, he opened the closet, reached up to the top shelf, and felt among the dust bunnies. His fingers closed around a familiar shape.

When he pulled down the sawed-off shotgun and looked at it in his hands, he was almost sorry that he still had it. He didn't want to revert back to the man he'd been so long ago, a man who'd done terrible things.

He still remembered every detail of the last job he'd done with a shotgun like the one he was holding. It was one of the last jobs he had done for the family, just prior to his father's murder. And though he'd convinced himself that John Senior's death was the thing that prompted him to leave the family business, he knew that was a lie. He left the business because he'd found out the hard way that he could never kill for a living.

It had happened thirty-five years before, on a summer day that bathed North Philly in a quiet too complete for city streets. John had received an order from his father. And just as he was instructed, he had told no one.

When dusk turned to evening and evening turned to night, he had gotten into the car that his father had left parked for him on Susquehanna Avenue, near Don's Doo Shop. He drove one block south on Fifteenth Street, and made a slow right turn onto Diamond. As he cruised toward the pale moon that hung like a giant clock in the midnight sky, he saw his target, and his heart began to beat faster.

The Cadillac Eldorado he drove crept slowly alongside a

small-time dealer who'd had the audacity to challenge John Senior. He rolled down the windows and stopped the car. Then he
leaned over and aimed the sawed-off shotgun. The man's horri-
fied face turned toward him just as the gun belched fire. The
buckshot slammed into his flesh, and the impact threw him back
into one of Diamond Street's massive brownstones.

When it was done, the man lay bleeding on the sidewalk, his
shocked eyes staring up into a star-speckled, purple summer sky.
John only saw that look for a second before he peeled out and
drove the car to a South Philly chop shop.

But he never forgot that look. And though few people ever
knew what he had done, John was left to deal with the guilt long
after his father went to his grave.

It was the guilt that had driven him to the ministry. He believed that if God could forgive him, then perhaps he could forgive himself. But it had never worked that way for John. Not
completely, anyway. He still carried the memory of his victim's
lifeless eyes, staring into the sky as if to ask God why.

As he stood there in front of his closet, packing the gun into a
small black gym bag, John thought of the other secrets that drove
him to his knees every day to seek forgiveness, secrets that were
born of his lusts.

Nola walked past the giant clothespin outside Center Square,
careful to survey the area for the detective she'd elduded earlier.

Though she didn't see him, she still had the uneasy feeling
that she was being watched. The sensation made her walk faster.

Nola pranced into Center Square's cavernous lobby, and
through the glass doors leading to the bank, ignoring the lustful
stares that she normally thrived upon.

There was business to handle. And if she'd learned anything from Frank Nichols, it was that business was the most important thing in life, and everything in life was business.

She walked over to the counter near the door, removed a fountain pen and a piece of paper from her purse, and filled out a withdrawal slip for a million dollars.

As second signer on the checking account for Alon Enterprises, the business through which Frank had begun laundering money at her suggestion, Nola was the only person other than Frank who was authorized to access the account.

She'd never touched the money before. Frank would have killed her if she did. But now, things would be different.

Nola smiled as she took the slip, crossed the lobby, and walked past the couch where new customers waited nervously for loans that would never come.

As she rounded the glass partition and headed toward the rear offices, a secretary tried to stop her, but Nola pranced past the woman as if she didn't exist.

By the time the secretary caught up with her, she'd already opened the regional vice president's door.

"Mr. Johannsen?" she said with a radiant smile. "Do you have a moment?"

She walked over to the red-faced man whose receding blond hair was arranged in a stiff comb-over.

"I always have time for you, Ms. Langston," he said, waving away the secretary as he got up to embrace her and kiss her hand.

The secretary backed out of the office and closed the door. Nola sat down and watched Johanssen spin fantasies while staring at her across his desk.

"I've got a little problem," she said, putting her forefinger between her teeth, as if she were nervous about something.

He watched her mouth on her finger, and his face turned redder by the second.

"I can't imagine you ever having a problem," he said with a sly smile.

"I need to make a withdrawal from my business account, and I need it in half an hour," she said in her best damsel-in-distress voice.

"That shouldn't be a problem, Ms. Langston."

He got up from his chair and walked around to the front of the desk. "Do you have a withdrawal slip?"

"Yes," she said, reaching into her purse and handing it to him. "It's for a million dollars."

Johanssen licked his lips nervously, knowing that he'd have to overstep his authority to complete such a huge transaction. The FDIC would have to be contacted, and so would company headquarters. It could cost him his job.

"Can you help me, Mr. Johanssen?" she asked, looking up at him with her eyes stretched wide and her mouth slightly open.

He looked at her ample lips and supple legs until desire overcame good sense.

"Maybe we can help each other," he said, walking over to his office door and locking it.

"I think that can be arranged," she said, stepping out of the dress she was wearing.

When Johanssen turned around and saw her delicious body standing naked before him, he began to tremble with desire.

And as he prepared to take her, Frank Nichols was exiting the minivan with Marquita in tow, getting ready to take back what was his.

———

Ishmael had been circling the block for a half-hour. It didn't matter to him that the police were nearby, knocking on doors and questioning tight-lipped neighbors about the commissioner's murder. They weren't looking for him, and even if they were, he was a different man now, both inside and out.

Not only did his conservative suit allow him to elude his pursuers, but he was filled with a righteous indignation that fueled his every move. He was right. His victims were wrong. And for their wrongs, they deserved to die.

Bespectacled and bald, he leaned back in the driver's seat of the blue Chrysler, turned left onto York Street, and rode slowly down the Andersons' block. He did so with the full knowledge that he was virtually unrecognizable.

Glancing in his rearview mirror, he saw a woman walk down the steps of the church at the opposite corner. She was carrying a Bible and a purse, and walking slowly.

She wore a white, round hat that covered almost every strand of her hair, large glasses that hid most of her face, and a long, loose dress that covered every inch of her femininity. She looked as if she could be beautiful beneath the trappings of her religious fervor. But there was something sad about her, something that shone through in her dour expression.

Curious, he pulled into a nearby parking space and watched her. As she came closer, her features became clearer, and it was easier for him to see the beauty she hid so well.

A wisp of hair hung from the side of the hat she wore, and dangled about three inches past her shoulder. Her mouth bore a certain sensuality that was evident even as she appeared to wear the weight of the world on her shoulders. She seemed to think of something that broke through that sadness for just a moment, and her face creased in a slight smile.

For half a second the rhythm to her gait and the swing of her hips were alluring, even beneath her long, dowdy dress.

But a second later, her demeanor changed. The swing in her hips stiffened. The rhythm of her movement disappeared.

As she drew closer to the car, he reached down, pulled the handle on the side of his seat, and leaned back slowly to avoid being noticed.

She started up the front steps of a nearby house, dragging her feet as if she dreaded going inside.

As she reached out to open the door, a tall man with a black gym bag came charging out and almost knocked her down. His back to Ishmael, the man tried to walk past the woman, but she stopped him, and Ishmael watched her dour expression turn to an enraged scowl.

"Where are you going, John?" the woman said, her tone short. Something about her voice made Ishmael listen more closely.

"I'm going to find our daughter," the man answered impatiently.

"No you're not!" she said sharply. "You see what happened the last time you did that."

"Get out of my way, Sarah," the man said in a low voice.

Ishmael watched the woman cast a venomous stare in the man's direction before she grudgingly stood aside.

The man turned to look up the block, and Ishmael saw his face. A chill ran through his body as he saw his target close up for the first time.

Reverend John Anderson, the man who had violated the woman of his dreams; the hypocrite who had led so many of his followers astray; the prey that he would hunt down like an animal.

Ishmael smiled as he watched the preacher stalk down York Street and get into a black Ford at the other end of the one-way street. When John started the car and rode past him, Ishmael pulled out of the space and followed him.

John Anderson was going to die for his sins. And not even his children would be able to escape the consequences.

Keisha and Jamal had barely crossed the street before the highway patrolman pulled up behind the blue Dodge Neon. He didn't see them disappear into the maze of two-story houses that comprised the housing project behind Frankford Avenue.

Now, as they ran down one of the driveways, Keisha couldn't shake the feeling that she'd been there before.

Glancing at the dull brick facades of the houses in the development, she tried to remember where she had seen them, but her memory betrayed her.

Looking back over her shoulder, she could see other police cars pulling in behind the first. Their swirling lights shone against the buildings, and Jamal's description was read repeatedly over their radios.

But even as they ran and ducked through the small concrete backyards of the houses, moving ever deeper into the projects, it was the past, rather than the present, that gnawed at her.

Jamal grabbed her hand and led her to a space between two houses. Crouching down, he signaled for her to remain still as he tried desperately to think of a way out.

Kneeling there, she listened to the sound of traffic on I-95, speeding by in waves from two blocks away, and the sounds of everyday life emanating from the nearby houses in the projects.

She heard the sound of soap opera drama, talk show mayhem, and television news. She heard babies crying, women on telephones, and children playing rope. And that's when it hit her. She had, indeed, been there before.

"Jamal," she said, pointing to the back of a nearby house. "This way."

Staying low to the ground, she jogged across the driveway to the backyard of the house she remembered.

Jamal hesitated. But when he glanced through a crack between the houses and saw ten police cars surrounding the Neon they'd abandoned five minutes before, he knew that he had to move, because Keisha still had the gun he'd handed her in the car.

He got up and followed her path across the driveway, and knelt next to her at the back door of the house. She looked at him, saw apprehension in his eyes, and knew that he didn't trust her completely. Keisha didn't blame him. But neither of them had much choice now. They needed each other to survive.

Keisha tapped on the door three times. When there was no answer, she knocked harder.

The ensuing pause seemed to last an eternity, especially after they saw a police car turn onto the driveway's cracked concrete.

Keisha knocked again.

"Who is it?" an old woman answered in a frail voice.

"It's John's daughter," Keisha said, just loud enough for the woman to hear.

Footsteps shuffled toward the door as the two of them watched the slow-moving police car riding down the driveway.

"Just a minute, honey," the old woman said sweetly.

Keisha and Jamal tried to hunker down further, but there was nothing in the small yard to hide them.

Jamal looked down at Keisha's purse and the gun that it contained. The police car, now just ten houses away, drew even closer. Jamal was about to reach for the gun when the door creaked open.

"Keisha?" the old woman said while looking aimlessly over their heads.

"Aunt Margaret," a relieved Keisha answered while she and Jamal moved past her and into the kitchen.

The old woman closed the door behind them and turned around unsteadily.

"Who's that with you?" she asked, her eyes sweeping the room, but focusing on nothing.

"This is my friend André," Keisha lied. "We were in the neighborhood, so I wanted to stop by, since I haven't seen you in a while."

"I don't know why you stoppin' by now," the old woman said sarcastically. "You don't stop by no other time. I coulda been layin' up in here dead or somethin', and y'all wouldn't even know."

"I'm sorry, Aunt Margaret. I'll try to do better."

"What you say your friend's name was?"

"André."

"Nice to meet you, André," the old woman said as she felt along the back of a chair, pulled it out from under the table, and sat down.

"Nice to meet you, too," Jamal answered uneasily.

"Keisha," the old woman said. "I don't think I've seen you since your Uncle William passed away last year. 'Fraid my cataracts is a lot worse since then. Can't see like I used to."

"I'm sorry to hear that," Keisha said.

"Oh, don't feel sorry for me," Aunt Margaret said with a wave of her hand. "Sometimes, when you lose your sight, you see things a lot clearer. Now, come on over here and give your aunt a hug."

Keisha approached hesitantly and reached down to hug her grandfather's oldest sister, who was still spry, independent, and sharp, even at the age of ninety.

The old woman wrapped her arms around her great-niece and squeezed with a strength that belied her age. She felt the warmth of Keisha's nearly bare breasts against her neck, and smelled the mingled odors of sweat and drugs in her clothing.

A frown creased Aunt Margaret's forehead as Keisha moved past the walker that stood folded in the corner of the kitchen and sat down in a nearby chair. The house was silent except for the sound of the television in the living room, until Aunt Margaret spoke.

"You sure have changed since the last time I saw you, Keisha," she said sternly.

"What do you mean, Aunt Margaret?" Keisha asked nervously.

The old woman leaned back in her chair and pursed her lips in a look of disappointment.

"I'm old, but I ain't stupid, honey," the old woman said. "And I ain't much for games, either. So I'ma give it to you straight. I been hearin' your name on the news all mornin'. You and your friend Jamal here. I know they lookin' for him for shootin' Commissioner Freeman, and they said he kidnapped you, too."

Keisha and Jamal exchanged a worried look as the old woman leaned forward in her seat and placed both hands on her kitchen table.

"Now, I guess the news musta got somethin' wrong," she said, "since y'all came in here together like you did. But I heard the sirens on Frankford Avenue a few minutes before you got here. So I know they gon' come knockin' pretty soon."

"Aunt Margaret, let me explain," Keisha began.

"Ain't nothin' to explain," the old woman said, cutting her off. " 'Cause evidently, if you runnin' with him, you musta did somethin', too. But lemme tell you somethin', Keisha. Your grandfather got swallowed up in these streets, and so did your father.

"So before the police come to my door lookin' for you, I want you to tell me somethin'," she said, folding her arms defiantly. "Why the hell would you wanna get swallowed up, too?"

Jamal watched them sitting there, and for the first time, he saw the resemblance between them. It wasn't purely physical, though their faces held some similarities. Their likeness was in their fire.

Jamal wanted to extinguish it, to snatch the gun from Keisha and force the old woman into a closet. He needed Keisha to believe that they could make the impossible escape. In truth, he needed to believe it, too.

"Answer me, Keisha!" the old woman said, interrupting Jamal's racing thoughts.

Keisha began to weep. It was a sound that tore through Jamal like a jagged blade. Thankfully, her tears stopped as quickly as they had begun. And when she finally spoke, she spat her words like venom.

"Aunt Margaret, the streets can't swallow me up, 'cause my family already did that," she said bitterly. "All my life, y'all wanted me to be the perfect little girl—the good reverend's faithful daughter. But I can't be that, and I'm tired of trying.

"I don't know why things happened the way they did in the past. And I don't want to know. But I *do* know this. I love Jamal. I've loved him since the first time I met him five years ago. He was the first boy I kissed, the first boy I dreamed about, the first boy I wanted. And I'm gonna be with him, no matter what you or anybody else in the family thinks."

"And what about his father?" Aunt Margaret said.

"What about him?" Jamal said angrily.

"You shut up, boy! I'm not talkin' to you!"

Jamal moved toward the old woman, but Keisha held up her hand and stopped him.

"Whatever happened between Frank Nichols and my father is between them," she said defiantly. "And whatever happens with me and Jamal is between us."

The old woman grunted in response. Then she slowly stood up and walked toward the front of the house, lightly touching furniture to guide her from one room to the other, as Keisha and Jamal watched silently.

"What about your grandfather, Keisha?" the old woman said, speaking over her shoulder as she sat down in a chair in the living room. "Does what Jamal's father did to him have anything to do with you? Or don't that matter, either?"

The question floated in the air between them like a poisoned mist, threatening to take their breath away.

But before Keisha could answer, there was a hard knock on the front door. The old woman turned her blind eyes in the direction of the noise and, without a word, got up to answer it.

Flattening themselves against the wall that separated the living room from the kitchen, Keisha and Jamal stood stock-still, holding their collective breath and waiting nervously for the inevitable.

11

Lieutenant Kevin Lynch was leaving the commissioner's office when he got another call. A Highway Patrol officer had spotted Jamal and Keisha in a car on I-95 and lost them on Frankford Avenue.

From the sketchy information he'd received over the radio, it seemed that the prostitutes back at the abandoned factory were correct in their assertion. Jamal and Keisha were working together.

But as he rode north on I-95 to meet his detectives at Keisha and Jamal's last known location, Lynch still couldn't understand why.

"Dan two-five," the dispatcher's voice came over the radio.

Lynch picked up the handset. "This is Dan two-five."

"Meet Fifteen Command at Frankford and Academy."

"I'm at the Academy exit now. I'll be there in a second."

Putting down the handset, Lynch rounded the arcing exit

and made the left onto Frankford Avenue. He spotted the blue Dodge Neon, surrounded by officers from Highway Patrol and the Fifteenth District.

Parking in back of the other cars, Lynch walked over to the dark-haired lieutenant from the Fifteenth District who'd called for him on the radio.

"Any sign of our suspects?" Lynch asked.

"Not yet," he said. "But we've got officers checking all the stores, and three teams in the projects going door-to-door."

"Good," Lynch said. "I've got some detectives en route, too. In the meantime, I need to talk to the guy they carjacked."

"He's pretty shaken up," the lieutenant said, pointing to a man sitting in the back of a Highway Patrol vehicle. "But he's right over there."

"Thanks," Lynch said, walking over to the car and opening the back door.

"I'm Lieutenant Lynch, Homicide," he said to the rotund man with the blanket over his shoulders. "How are you?"

The man looked up at him with a sad smile. "I've been better."

"That's understandable," he said. "I've only got a couple of questions."

"Sure," the man said. "Go ahead."

"We were under the impression that the girl had been kidnapped by the guy," Lynch said. "But apparently they were working together. And I'm trying to understand why."

The man shivered, though the temperature outside was approaching ninety.

"It's funny you should ask that," he said. "Because I heard the guy ask the girl if she was scared."

Lynch took out his notepad and pencil. "And what did the girl say?" he said, with his pencil poised over the page.

The man sat there for a few moments, trying to recall the words that had filtered into the closed-in space as he lay curled up and sweating in the trunk.

"She said, 'I always did what I was supposed to do. Now I wanna see what it's like not to.'"

Lynch was aghast. Even after all he'd seen over the years, it was hard for him to believe that the frightened, beautiful woman-child he'd seen at that morning's protest could be that heartless.

"Could the voices you heard have been the radio or something?" Lynch asked.

The man looked over at Lynch with a certainty that was born of fear.

"I know it was them, I know what they said, and I'll never forget it," he whispered. "Because it made me think I'd never see daylight again."

Lynch nodded and slowly put his notepad and pencil back into his pocket.

Closing the door of the car, he waved over two homicide detectives who'd just arrived on the scene.

Moments later, as the three of them walked together into the projects, Lynch found that he had yet another death to mourn: the death of Keisha Anderson's innocence.

The old woman wore a bewildered expression as she opened the door for the white, uniformed police officers. It was the look she always wore when she wanted people to believe that she was fragile.

"Can I help you, officers?"

"There's a murder suspect on the loose in this area," one of them said.

She responded with a blank stare.

"His name is Jamal Nichols," the other officer said, holding up an old mug shot. "Have you seen him?"

The old woman smiled. "I ain't seen nothin' in a long while. I'm blind."

"Oh," the officer said, looking into her eyes for the first time. "I'm sorry."

"That's okay," she said as she imagined what must be going through Keisha and Jamal's minds while they hid in the kitchen.

"Maybe we should take a look around," one of the cops said. "Just in case."

"That won't be necessary. But if I hear somethin', I'll be sure to call 911."

The officers nodded and walked away as she shut the door, returned to her seat, turned off her television, and listened.

A minute later, Jamal and Keisha meekly came out of hiding, and she held out her withered hand.

"Y'all come here," she said quietly.

Hesitantly, they both walked over to the chair. The old woman reached up and ran her hand over Keisha's face.

"You see what I just did, child?" she asked softly. "That's what you do when you love somebody. You look out for 'em."

She turned her head toward Jamal, and though he knew she couldn't see him, he could feel her looking through him with something that went far beyond sight.

"Your grandfather looked out for this boy's father," she said, pointing an accusing finger in his direction. "Looked out for him when he ain't have noplace else to go. Treated him like a son. Three years later, Frank set him up. Killed your grandfather and took over what he built."

Jamal and Keisha looked at one another uneasily. Neither of

150

them had ever heard the history that had put their families at odds. And both of them were sorry to hear it now.

"You say you don't care why your father feel the way he do about Frank Nichols, Keisha. But you should. 'Cause wise folks learn from other people mistakes, and fools don't even learn from their own."

The room was deadly still as the old woman sat back in her chair and pursed her lips, satisfied that she'd done what was right. She'd warned Keisha. The rest was up to her.

Keisha looked at Jamal, her eyes filled with the same uncertainty that she'd felt in the moments after saving his life. Only now her fear was anchored by the reality that had split their families all those years before.

Jamal saw the look in her eyes. And he knew that he couldn't allow it to remain there. So he turned to the old woman and spoke from his heart.

"I ain't my pop," he said with conviction. "And she ain't her grandfather. This ain't forty years ago, either. This is now. And right here, right now, it's only two things in this world I know. I know I wouldn't be alive without Keisha. And I know I wouldn't want to."

He looked at Keisha.

"You rollin' with me or not?" he said, holding out his hand.

She looked down at her great-aunt, then turned her gaze on Jamal. Releasing the old woman's tired grip, she gave her hand to him. And she gave him her heart as well.

"Ride or die," Keisha whispered.

It was a line from a song she'd heard in passing—one that she'd never fully understood until that moment. As she stood there looking into Jamal's eyes, she pledged her loyalty and her life to him. She was going to ride with him until the end of their journey, or she was going to die trying.

Aunt Margaret felt the message in their silence, and leaned back in her chair. If she'd learned anything in her ninety years, it was that you can't tell a person whom to love. You can only try to soften the hurt that love inevitably brings.

"Well, Keisha," she said softly. "If you willin' to live with that decision, I guess I am, too. It's only one thing I wanna know. Did Jamal really kill Commissioner Freeman?"

Keisha opened her mouth and was about to answer.

"I can speak for myself," Jamal said. "The answer is no."

There was a long silence as Aunt Margaret contemplated his answer.

"Okay, then," the old woman said, getting up from her chair and walking into the kitchen.

"Only thing I can tell you is, don't get caught," she said, speaking over her shoulder. " 'Cause if you do, they gon' kill you. And ain't no comin' back from that."

She opened a kitchen drawer, pulled out a pair of scissors, and walked back to the living room.

"First thing they talk about on the news is them dreadlocks, or whatever you call 'em," she said, handing the scissors to Jamal. "Cut 'em off."

Keisha glanced at Jamal, who didn't hesitate before taking the old woman's advice. He held his locks up, three or four at a time, and cut as close to the roots as possible. He would have done more, but he knew that they didn't have time.

The old woman turned toward Keisha.

"You know you gotta find the truth, don't you?" she asked.

"The truth about what?"

"Who killed the commissioner, and why."

"We're just trying to make it to another day, Aunt Margaret," Keisha said. "We don't have time to find the truth."

"If you ever wanna live your life without lookin' over your

shoulder, you *better* find it," she said, reaching back for her chair and sitting down.

"You can only spend so much time runnin'. After a while, you gotta stop, turn around, and fight."

Aunt Margaret's words reverberated in Keisha's ears as the last of Jamal's dreadlocks fell to the floor.

Keisha turned and looked at him. He was even more handsome without the hair spilling against his cheeks. As she stared into his eyes, she found herself imagining him with all his other coverings removed.

Jamal saw the lust in her eyes, and fought to keep it out of his own.

"I got a friend 'cross town who can help us," he said, looking around. "I just don't know how we gon' get to him."

"First, you gotta get outta here," the old woman said. "But you gotta change first. Go upstairs and get you some fresh clothes out the closet. Your uncle's clothes still up there, Keisha, so it should be somethin' up there to fit Jamal. You can put on one o' my Sunday dresses and a hat or somethin'.'"

"Then what?" Keisha asked.

"Then the two o' y'all gon' take a walk."

Lynch had his detectives do a second sweep of the projects. But he did so knowing that they'd be hard-pressed to find anything in such a place.

These projects, with their neat, two-story houses and quiet walks and driveways, looked nothing like the high-rise buildings he knew. But Lynch had the eerie feeling that its brick walls and pothole-ridden asphalt held the same kinds of secrets that had destroyed generations in his old housing project.

As detectives and uniformed police went door-to-door with

pictures of Jamal Nichols, Lynch went to the management office and knocked.

A frightened-looking older woman cracked the door.

"What do you want?" she said with an attitude.

Lynch pulled his badge. "A little touchy, aren't we, Miss . . ."

"Bagwell," the woman said, exhaling and opening the door as she stepped back to allow Lynch inside. "My name is Miss Bagwell."

"Lieutenant Kevin Lynch, Homicide."

The woman's face twitched as she smiled nervously. "I'm sorry I was a little rude. I guess I'm just used to residents coming here and harassing me."

She shook her head. "Their rent is a couple dollars a month, and they won't pay it. Then when they get an eviction notice, they wanna come here and curse me out. I guess I should expect that, though. They're all that way."

Lynch looked at her for a long moment.

"I grew up in the projects, Ms. Bagwell," he said with an edge to his voice. "Some people are like that, some aren't. But if I've learned anything over the years, it's that it takes a lot to survive when you've got everybody looking down on you."

Ms. Bagwell started to respond, but thought better of it. Instead, she put on her glasses, in the hope that he couldn't see the embarrassment in her eyes.

"So I see you've got officers going door-to-door," she said, changing the subject. "What's going on?"

"There's a murder suspect on the loose," Lynch said. "We think he may be hiding somewhere nearby."

"Well, he's not in my office, if that's what you wanted to know," she said, going to her desk and shuffling through papers as if to dismiss him.

"Actually, I wanted to look through the names of the residents. I was thinking he might have come here because he knows someone who lives here."

"I'd have to call down to the main office to get permission," she said without looking up.

"Ms. Bagwell," Lynch said, moving a step closer to her. "You've made it clear that you don't care about these people. But I do. Now, there's a murderer on the loose, and I'm not gonna sit here and let him kill somebody else because you wanted to put me through a bunch of red tape. Give me the list of residents. Now."

The woman swallowed hard, reached into her desk, and gave it to him.

Lynch snatched it and began going down the list of names.

"Were there any names in particular you were looking for?" Ms. Bagwell asked timidly.

"Nichols," he said, while continuing to scan the list. "People with the last name of Nichols."

The woman thought for a moment. "There isn't anyone here by that name."

He finished scanning the list and sighed in frustration. Then he thought of the strange relationship between Keisha and Jamal, and turned to Ms. Bagwell.

"How about Anderson?" he said.

She shook her head no.

"Okay," he said, handing the list to her and walking toward the door.

She stood at the desk and ran down the list once more, then spotted a name that she recognized.

"Lieutenant?" she said.

Lynch turned around.

"There's a Margaret Jackson on this list. Really nice old

woman I check up on every now and again. She has a nephew named Anderson. John Anderson, I think. She talks about him all the time."

Lynch's eyes lit up. "What unit is she in?"

"Twelve-C," she said, pointing out the window. "It's up that first walkway on your left."

The stooped old man leaned heavily on his aluminum walker as he plodded toward Frankford Avenue from the projects. With a canvas shopping bag dangling from one of the walker's handles, he looked as if he was on his way to the nearby supermarket.

This was the time of day when the neighborhood's seniors normally made such trips. The time of day when the streets were less crowded, and the pace a little slower. But today was different. With police cars lined up on the avenue and officers going door-to-door, there was obviously something going on.

It was even more obvious that whatever it was had little or nothing to do with the old man.

He shuffled closer to Frankford Avenue, looking through the gap between the top of his reading glasses and the brim of his fedora. He paused for a moment to catch his breath. Then he wiped his brow, looked up into the noonday sun, and decided against crossing the avenue.

Instead, he turned left, past the police cars, and walked toward a nearby Kentucky Fried Chicken. There would be air conditioning there, and he could rest before continuing his trek to the market.

An old woman in a flower-print dress and straw sun hat had already made her way from the projects to the KFC. She was sitting inside, with a soda on the table, when he made his way over to her.

The two of them sat there for a few minutes. Then they walked slowly out of the restaurant and toward the drive-through. A few minutes later, they got into the back seat of a green Ford.

The man who was driving turned left onto Frankford Avenue, looked anxiously at the people in his back seat, and cursed himself for lowering the window when they'd asked him a question.

"Don't worry," Keisha said as she removed her sun hat and pointed the gun at the driver's head. "We won't hurt you if you do what we say."

Jamal took off the reading glasses he was wearing so that he could see clearly as he looked out the rear window at the police cars still gathered on Frankford Avenue.

"What do you want us to do?" asked the woman in the passenger seat.

"Keep drivin'," Jamal said. "Keep drivin' 'til we tell you to stop."

Lynch left the management office with walkie-talkie in hand, screaming into the handset as he half-ran toward Margaret Jackson's unit.

"Dan two-five to Fifteen Command, seal off all entrances to this development, and get me some uniformed officers to Unit Twelve-C!"

After a few seconds of static, the lieutenant responded.

"Fifteen Command, okay."

The district cars on Frankford Avenue moved out of the tight circle they'd formed around the carjacked Dodge Neon. Engines hummed and spinning lights filled the air as they raced to the various entrances of the development.

Officers ran in from every direction, converging on Unit 12C with their weapons drawn and their resolve evident. They were going to catch the commissioner's killer, no matter what the cost.

Lynch could see them as he ran up the walkway. He knew that he only had a few minutes to gain control of the situation. If he didn't, there would be bloodshed. And there'd been enough of that already.

He signaled to two of his detectives who'd entered the projects with him, and ordered them to take four officers each and post them in the driveway and at the back door of the woman's home. He took four more officers with him, and approached the front of the house.

"Fifteen Command," he said into his radio. "I need officers in position at both ends of that driveway behind this unit."

"Fifteen Command, okay."

Lynch watched as the officers moved into position, then he drew his weapon and signaled to three officers to take the right side of the door. He and the other officer took the left side.

Taking a deep breath, Lynch knocked on the door. There was no answer, so he knocked again. When there was no response, he took out his radio.

"Dan two-five to Dan two-six," he said to the detective posted at the back door. "Send two guys upstairs. Have two check the kitchen. You meet me in the living room. We go on three."

"Dan two-six, okay."

Lynch held his gun aloft in his right hand, counted down three seconds with his left, and stood back as one of the cops kicked the door open.

The five of them rushed into the darkened living room with their weapons held out in front of them. As they did so, the kitchen door burst open, and five more officers rushed in through the back.

There was shouting and rumbling footsteps as the cops fanned out through the house, checking every room for Keisha and Jamal.

The detective from the back door met Lynch in the living room. The two of them checked every corner of the room before their eyes came to rest on a frail, dark figure in a chair.

It took a few moments for Lynch's eyes to adjust. But when they did, he saw that it was the old woman.

"Mrs. Jackson?" Lynch said, sounding perplexed.

"That's right."

The officers upstairs sounded the all-clear, and Lynch and the detective lowered their weapons.

Lynch went to the windows and raised the shades, then reached over to the wall and flipped the light switch so he could get a better look.

"I'm Detective Kevin Lynch, Homicide," he said, walking toward her.

He stopped at the severed dreadlocks arranged in a pile in the middle of the floor. Bending down, he picked one of them up.

"I guess I don't need to ask whose hair this is," he said, dropping it into her lap.

The old woman felt the lock of hair and smiled. "I suspect you don't have to ask me nothin'. The way y'all came bustin' in here, you must have it all figured out."

Lynch bent down in front of her, looked into her eyes, and saw that she was blind. But in spite of her blindness, her stare was far from vacant.

"The only thing I know is that Keisha came here because she knew you would protect her," Lynch said.

"Protect her from what?"

"Herself. She's obviously not thinking rationally. If she was, she wouldn't be running with a murderer."

The old woman folded her arms. "She ain't did nothin' wrong."

"You don't know that! You only know what she told you. And if, by chance, she is charged with something, then you'll be the one who protected her. You know what they call that, don't you?"

The old woman didn't answer.

"They call it obstruction of justice. And it's a crime."

"All I know is, she ain't did nothin' wrong, and she ain't here."

"But she *was* here, and so was Jamal Nichols," Lynch said.

Margaret Jackson sat back in her chair, and it was clear that she wasn't intimidated. So Lynch tried to appeal to her sense of reason.

"Look, just tell me where they are now. If you do that, we can avoid any charges that could be filed against you."

Keisha's great-aunt pursed her lips. "Honey, I'm ninety years old. You think a judge gon' put me in jail?"

"It doesn't matter what I think."

"Now that's the smartest you done said yet. It don't matter what you think. I ain't sayin' nothin' about my great-niece, no matter what you think, no matter what you say, no matter how you feel. So if you call yourself ready to lock me up, go 'head and do it now, 'cause I ain't tellin' you nothin'."

Before Lynch could respond, an officer walked down the steps with Keisha and Jamal's clothing in his hand.

"Lieutenant Lynch, I found these in the bathroom," he said as he handed over the clothes. "There was a big mess in the bedroom, too, clothes all over the place. Looks like they might have changed before they left."

160

Lynch quickly examined the clothes and saw that they were the outfits that had been taken from the prostitutes in Kensington.

He turned to one of his detectives. "Have Housing Police secure this place, and take Mrs. Jackson down to headquarters. Have someone call Keisha Anderson's parents, too, and get them down to Homicide. Maybe they can get the old woman to talk."

Lynch got on the radio and relayed the message that Keisha and Jamal had last been seen in Frankford, that they were clothed differently, and that Jamal had cut his hair.

The police would have to depend on their facial features and body types to describe them, which meant that the chances of catching them had just grown that much slimmer.

Sarah Anderson sat stoically on her couch, listening to life go on around her.

The sounds of little girls outside, playing double Dutch on the sidewalk, crept in through her living room windows and reminded her of both the little girls she'd lost: her daughter, and herself.

Sarah sat and wondered what it would be like to know the joy she should have as a daughter, wife, and mother.

She'd never experienced it. And she often wondered if she ever would. Was there more to life than striving for goals that one could never reach?

Sarah didn't know anymore. All she knew was that the very things that should have brought her joy brought her misery. And the very people she loved were the ones who hurt her the most. The pattern extended back to her childhood, and the man whom she idolized above anyone else—her father.

She'd spent most of her days running from the legacy of her father—the preacher who'd raised her to seek perfection.

."Who can find a virtuous woman?" she whispered to herself, recalling the Bible verse that her father often read to her as a child.

As she thought of the rest of the passage, and the value of such a woman being greater than that of precious gems, she overheard the little girls outside, shouting vulgarities within earshot of the church. And she answered the question for herself.

"No one can find a virtuous woman," she said while shaking her head sadly. "Not even me."

As she got up to lower the window, to drown out the sounds filtering in from the street, Sarah reflected on how much the world had changed since her youth.

She could still remember little girls wearing lace gloves and white dresses to church, children respecting the presence of adults, and cleanliness being next to godliness.

Now there was no respect, for self or for others. People lived in filth. And children ran amok with little regard for any adult, including their own parents.

Yes, things had changed. But Sarah wasn't ready to criticize the world for what it had become. In truth, she had changed, too. And she wasn't about to apologize for the transformation.

Like her own daughter, she had grown up as the only child of a pastor and his wife. Reverend Henry Fuller was a dynamic preacher whose life revolved around his ministry. Sarah's mother, Ruth Fuller, had given her life to the ministry as well. But her personality wasn't as strong as her husband's. She tended to fade into the background. As beautiful and intelligent as she was, she somehow seemed plain next to her husband. More than anything, she was his servant—a woman to be pitied rather than revered.

Still, their West Philadelphia church was the center of a community—the place where people went to be healed and energized, rebuilt and refocused. And Sarah had been an integral part of the culture there.

She was a junior usher, a member of the youth choir, a junior trustee, and a pastor's aide. She was Reverend Fuller's little girl, and she was willing to do anything to win the approval of the man whose approval was sought by everyone. Some days she thought she'd won it. But on most days, she knew that she hadn't.

Growing up listening to fiery sermons in which her father chastised his parishioners for their shortcomings while urging them to repent for their sins, she lived her childhood walking on eggshells in an attempt to live up to every word she'd ever heard her father preach. By the time she reached adolescence, she believed that her life should be perfect. And she believed that his should, too.

She quickly realized that she could never achieve the perfection that she so desperately sought. So she stopped trying, and her life went into a tailspin.

By the time she reached high school, Sarah had quietly become the opposite of everything she'd ever tried to be. From Monday through Saturday, she drank and smoked, used profanity, and dated men. But on Sunday morning, she was the innocent little girl her father had always imagined her to be. She brought him water after his sermons, and sang solos on second Sundays. And regardless of the things that happened to her while she walked the fine line between the church and the world, she always hid her dark side, out of respect for her father.

But late one Sunday evening, after the parishioners had gone, she walked into his office to ask him a question about the passage he'd preached from that morning, and saw him in the throes of passion with a woman she didn't know. She was devastated at learning that her father was human, just like the people to whom he preached. She carried that hurt for years.

Through every triumph and every defeat, through every hurt and every joy, she always remembered that the man she'd trusted the most, the man she'd always idolized, had disappointed her in a way that she could never quite forgive.

But in spite of the terrible pain her father had inflicted, she married a man much like him, because her father was the only example of manhood she'd ever seen up close. She didn't know of any other type of man. And so she didn't know what else to look for in a man.

A fiery orator whose public life reflected the words he preached, her husband was a good man. Or at least as good as a man could be, in Sarah's eyes. Still, she could never quite put her faith in him completely.

Even now, as he combed the streets in an effort to find their daughter, Sarah didn't trust him to do as he'd said he would. He'd already proved, time and time again, that he was incapable of loving his family in the way that the Bible commanded him to do—sacrificing for them, and putting them before himself.

But perhaps Keisha's disappearance had changed him. Maybe it had taught him to love in such a way that he was willing to sacrifice himself for his wife and daughter, just as Christ had sacrificed himself for the church.

In Sarah's mind, it was already too late for such heroics. And when the phone rang, echoing through the room like a voice from the distant past, she believed that it was a message from God, a message that would confirm that it was already too late to save Keisha.

She got up from the couch slowly and walked to the end table, listening to the sound of the phone growing louder with each ring.

Standing over it for a moment, she tried to prepare herself for the news the call would bring. But she realized that there was nothing to prepare her. So she picked up the phone and summoned the strength to speak.

"Hello?" she said, and held her breath for the voice on the other end.

"Mrs. Anderson, this is Detective Glenn from the Philadelphia Police Department. Lieutenant Lynch asked me to call you."

"Is Keisha all right?"

"As far as we know, ma'am, yes, she is."

"What do you mean, 'as far as you know'?"

There was a long pause on the phone.

"Mrs. Anderson," the detective said, "we want to ask you and your husband a few questions about your daughter. We think she may be working with Jamal Nichols."

Without a word, Sarah hung up and fell into her seat on the couch.

12

Nola Langston tugged at the bottom of her dress and swept her hands over the front of it, smoothing it back into place. Then she reapplied her flaming red lipstick and checked her hair as a sweaty, panting Mr. Johanssen leaned against his desk.

In the twenty minutes they'd spent behind the locked doors of his office, she'd given him what he'd wanted, transforming herself from polished executive to street whore in an instant.

In exchange, he'd made the call that allowed the million dollars to be brought up from the vault.

Now, as she waited for the cash to be delivered to Johanssen's office, the bank executive stood up straight, adjusted his clothing, and watched her. He knew that she had given him more than he could handle. Still, he wished his body would allow him to take her again.

"Ms. Langston," he said, straightening his tie. "It was a pleasure helping you to expedite your transaction."

Nola smiled and sat down in the chair in front of his desk. "The pleasure was all mine," she said.

They both knew this was a lie.

As Johanssen walked slowly around his desk and sat down, there was a knock on the door. His secretary entered, along with a security guard. She was carrying a metal briefcase. She looked at Nola and then at Johanssen. Her eyes said that she knew what had transpired.

She handed the briefcase to Johanssen, who handed it to Nola. She opened it and examined its contents. Satisfied that everything was in order, Nola took a pen from him and signed for the transaction.

As the secretary left the office with the guard, she glanced at Nola, rolled her eyes, and walked out with her lips pursed in a look of disgust.

"I'll take care of closing the account for you, Ms. Langston," he said.

"Thank you," she said, nodding her good-bye as she stood up and began to walk toward the door.

"Ms. Langston?" Johanssen called out to her.

"Yes?" she said, turning around.

"If there's anything else I can ever do for you . . ."

Nola smiled and looked down at the briefcase. "Anything I need done from here on out," she said, "I'm sure I can do for myself."

She turned around and walked out of his office, crossed the bank's lobby, and was about to walk out into the warm embrace of the summer air when she saw them out of the corner of her eye.

Frank was walking quickly across the lobby, pushing Marquita while holding something at the small of her back.

Marquita's eyes pleaded with Nola, silently begging her to do something.

For an instant, Nola was frozen. She looked at Marquita and saw her eyes stretched wide by fear. She looked at Frank, and knew that he would harm Marquita if he had to. She looked at the two of them, and imagined them together in her bed.

Forced to choose between her own flesh and blood and money, Nola chose the latter.

She bolted out the bank's doors with the briefcase in hand, and dashed into Center Square's lobby. Frank pushed Marquita out of the way and ran after Nola.

Pushing past the people lined up on the escalator, Nola weaved her way to the bottom, with Frank in hot pursuit.

She pushed through a set of revolving doors and past a donut shop beneath the giant clothespin, and ran right, through the transit system tunnels that had helped her to escape from the detective.

"Nola!"

Frank was behind her, closing fast, as she ran between the curving, tiled walls that separated Philadelphia's subway system from the New Jersey Transit lines.

"Nola, wait!"

As he rounded the curve, Frank spotted Nola and fired. The bullet whizzed past her and ricocheted off the tiled walls as she ducked left and ran back toward City Hall.

Dashing past the fountains, Nola ran up the steps to Dilworth Plaza as Frank stumbled behind her.

When he reached the top, he stopped and watched her run toward Fifteenth Street. With Nola out in the open, he could take her down. Holding the weapon out in front of him, he prepared to take his final shot.

"Drop the gun, Frank!" a voice said from across the court-yard.

Nichols looked over at Detective Hubert, who had him in his sights. Then he looked around and saw uniformed police running at him from every direction.

Two of them had grabbed Nola and were bringing her back with the briefcase.

Knowing that it was all but over, Nichols knelt down and placed his weapon on the ground beside him.

As the police took him into custody, he wasn't thinking of the money, or of Nola, or his business. When they stood him up and walked him across the courtyard to a waiting vehicle, his only concern was Jamal.

Keisha and Jamal had already decided that they would make the couple drive them as far as the last stop on the Market Frankford elevated train line, and that they would find their way to Jamal's friend from there. Neither of them had thought any further than that. And in reality, they didn't want to.

Jamal knew, just as Keisha did, that the longer they stayed on the run, the slimmer the chance for them to end it all peacefully. There was only one certainty at this point: Jamal would be blamed for the commissioner's murder. And if he was caught, he would die, one way or the other. Their only chance of being together was starting their lives anew, because life as they knew it had already ended.

Keisha glanced over at Jamal as the car's driver stopped at a red light. And as the thirtysomething, brown-skinned couple with the wedding rings and fearful expressions sat stiffly in the front seat, Keisha imagined herself and Jamal as a real couple. She imagined spending her life looking at him.

When she'd glimpsed his body as the two of them changed clothes, both in the factory and at her aunt's house, she'd marveled at his black skin and his muscles, taut and strong, stretched over his sturdy frame. She'd forced herself to look away, only to have her eyes drawn back to him by an attraction that went well beyond what she saw.

She was attracted to the dark side—to a lifestyle she'd seen, but never been a part of. It was an attraction that she couldn't shake, because the sight of him was the opposite of everything she'd ever known.

It was a different reality. One that was hard and powerful, like the gun she now held in her hand.

"Can you tell us where we're going?" the driver asked, snatching her back to the moment.

"Just keep movin'," Jamal said as the smell of the chicken the couple had purchased at KFC permeated the car.

Keisha could feel her stomach beginning to turn. She hadn't eaten since the night before, and apparently Jamal hadn't, either.

Reaching over the front seat, he snatched the bag of chicken and opened it.

"Why don't we just stop now?" the driver said, glancing over at his wife, whose face was now red with fear and humiliation. "You take the car, and we walk away."

"You heard what he said," Keisha warned. "Keep moving."

Jamal ripped open the striped box and tore into its contents with ferocity born of hunger.

"You want some o' this?" he said, turning to Keisha with hot grease and chicken crumbs smeared against his face.

Still holding the gun at the back of the driver's head, she turned and looked at Jamal, whose jaws were filled to capacity.

He looked like one of the squirrels she'd often seen on her strolls along Temple University's campus, the ones that picked the heels of cheesesteaks out of the trash and gnawed them with reckless abandon.

She started to smile.

"What you laughin' at?" he said, chomping into a breast and ripping the meat from the bone.

The woman looked at her husband, her eyes pleading for him to do something. He looked into the rearview mirror and saw Jamal eating and Keisha laughing, and he knew that this was his chance.

He slammed on the brakes and the car skidded forward. The gun flew out of Keisha's hand and landed on the dashboard as the car came to a halt in the middle of Frankford Avenue.

The driver threw the car into park and reached for the gun as Jamal, his eyes stretched wide, leaped over the seat and grabbed him by the neck.

The man's wife reached over and started hitting Jamal, and Keisha climbed over and started punching the back of her head.

The gun fell onto the floor, near the accelerator. The driver tried to bend down to get it, but Jamal dived headfirst onto the floor. The driver tried to stomp him while his wife tried to grab Jamal's legs. Keisha reached around and locked her forearm around the woman's neck, choking her as Jamal fought his way off the floor and held the gun aloft.

With the driver staring down the barrel of the nine-millimeter and his wife immobilized by a forearm at her throat, the struggle was over.

"Get out," Jamal said, his chest heaving up and down. "Get out 'fore I kill both o' y'all."

The man reached behind him and pulled the door handle, getting out of the car on one side. Keisha released the wife, who got out on the other side.

Jamal took the wheel and drove off with a skid. But by then a police car was behind them.

Jamal's breath caught in his throat as he told himself not to panic. He took one hand off the steering wheel and placed it on the butt of the gun.

The cop began to blast his horn. At that moment, Jamal knew that his only choice was to run.

He slowed down slightly and angled toward the curb as if he were pulling over. The cop followed. Then Jamal whipped the steering wheel around, stomped on the accelerator, and darted back into traffic.

He swerved along Frankford Avenue, the car's engine humming as he shot between the huge steel columns that held up the Market Frankford elevated line.

The cop followed, his siren echoing off the steel girders as he tried to keep up with Jamal. The heavy traffic and the relatively narrow street made the chase hazardous. But both the hunter and the prey knew that what happened in the next few moments could change their lives.

Jamal slammed on the brakes, whipped the car to the left, and moved into the opposing traffic. The cop tried to do the same, but swerved back into his own lane to dodge an oncoming SUV.

Jamal looked in the rearview mirror and saw the cop coming up fast. In seconds they would be parallel to each other. Jamal reached down and grabbed the gun, then looked up and saw a bus coming straight at him.

He stood on the brakes while snatching the steering wheel to the right. His tires screamed against the asphalt and he stopped on an angle, right in front of the speeding police car. He put his head down and braced for the collision.

The police officer swerved at the last second, barely avoiding Jamal's car. He tried to stop but couldn't, and the car smacked into one of the steel girders holding up the train tracks. Time seemed to slow to a crawl as his siren died and his spinning lights flashed against the walls of the bars and stores lining the avenue.

When Jamal and Keisha looked up, the officer was unconscious in his car. There was the sound of fast-approaching sirens in the distance, and the smell of gasoline in the air.

They both got out of the car and walked quickly away from the crash, melting into the crowd of commuters who stopped to look at the wreck. By the time the police began to arrive, Keisha and Jamal had climbed the steps leading to the train tracks.

Keisha reached into the purse her aunt had given her and found a few wrinkled dollars in the bottom.

She thrust them at the cashier, and the two of them went through the turnstile, squeezed between the train's closing doors, and boarded the Market Frankford elevated line toward Center City.

John Anderson's mind was racing as he pulled into a rare metered parking space on Ninth Street between Market and Chestnut in downtown Philadelphia.

As he looked across the street at patrons walking in and out of the post office, his thoughts were a hodgepodge of love, hatred, confusion, and fear. He wanted to kill Jamal. He wanted to embrace his daughter. He wanted to love his wife.

But as he turned off the car and put it in park, his recent past came flooding back in fuchsia-colored snapshots, and he remembered why he couldn't do any of those things.

He saw his tongue against the skin of the woman who'd seduced him, his lips on a vodka-filled bottle, his laughter in the shadows of her bedroom, and his tears in the middle of the night.

He saw each of them, separately and together, as he unbuckled his seat belt and tried, unsuccessfully, to focus on the matter at hand.

John looked at the passenger seat, and the gym bag containing the sawed-off shotgun. Then he opened the glove compartment and searched for the Bible that he'd pushed to the rear.

He found it and laid it on the seat next to the gun. Then he looked at them both, and tried to decide which one was of more value. Which one would bring his daughter back to him? Which one would earn his wife's respect? Which one would change his life from the miserable mess it had become?

With those questions lingering in his mind, John reached up and turned the rearview mirror toward him. He examined his red eyes, the gray stubble of his beard, and the haggard expression on his face. He was tired, in more ways than he cared to think about. But he would have to cast the weariness aside in order to do what he must.

He pushed the mirror back into place. As he did so, he noticed a car about thirty feet to his rear with its hazard lights on. It was sitting in one of the two lanes of traffic.

This was a fairly common sight in Center City, where couriers often made deliveries to office buildings. But the driver of the blue Chrysler wasn't moving. He was sitting in his car, waiting, though it wasn't clear for what.

John took his hand off the mirror, but he continued to watch the driver in the blue car. He was young and dressed like an older man, in a conservative blue suit, and glasses that didn't quite fit his face.

John couldn't be sure, because weariness played tricks with his vision. But even from a distance, it looked like the man was watching him.

John opened the door as if he were exiting the car. Then he looked back and saw the man in the Chrysler do the same.

174

He closed the door and saw the other driver hesitate before closing his own. John was sure that the man was following him.

Reaching across the seat for the gym bag containing the sawed-off shotgun, John clenched his jaw and opened the door. He was about to get out of the car and make the first stop on his quest to find Keisha. But then he thought about it, and knew that he'd forgotten something. He reached across the seat and grabbed his Bible as well.

He put two quarters in the meter and looked back for the man in the blue car. He was gone. John looked down the street to see if he had driven away, but there was no sign of the man or the car.

John shook his head and hoped that fatigue hadn't caused him to imagine it. Then he turned and walked down Ninth Street, toward the Gallery Mall and the Strawbridge's where Keisha worked.

He descended the steps into the mall and turned left before climbing the steps that led to Keisha's job. He hadn't been there in a while, and was momentarily confused.

He found a directory near the bank of ornately designed elevators in the middle of the store, took one of the elevators to the upper floors, and walked quickly to the management offices, glancing behind him all the while.

A secretary greeted him as he walked through a set of glass doors.

"Can I help you, sir?" she asked with a smile.

"I'm looking for a manager," John said while nervously clutching his bag.

"Do you need to talk to a manager from a certain department?"

"I'm not sure. See, my daughter's been working here for the summer. And now, she's missing."

John paused to allow the truth of those words to sink in. He didn't know that speaking them would cause him such pain.

"I'm so sorry," the secretary said, her face creasing in sympathy. "Please have a seat."

"No, I'm fine standing. If I sit down I might go to sleep. I've been up all night."

"That's understandable."

"Anyway, I'm wondering if I might be able to talk to her supervisor, or someone who could tell me some of the places she liked to go, the people she hung around with, that sort of thing."

"What's your daughter's name?"

"Keisha Anderson."

"Oh, that's your daughter. I've been seeing that on the news all morning. I'm sorry."

"If you could just get me her supervisor," John said impatiently. He was already growing tired of the sympathy.

"Of course," the secretary said, getting on the intercom and calling for a manager.

It took a few minutes for the woman to come up on the elevator. But when she arrived, with her hair curled perfectly and her slim brown frame ensconced in a flowing summer print, it was clear that she was a woman of style. The type of woman that Keisha had always wanted to be.

"Mr. Anderson," she said, extending her hand. "I'm Sheila Jackson. I work with your daughter in Women's Wear."

"My pleasure," he said, taking her hand.

"Would you like to rest your bag?"

"No," he said, a bit too quickly, and held the bag tightly to his side. "I really don't plan to be here that long."

"I see," she said, looking at him strangely. "Well, I heard about what happened on the news, and I have to say, I'm a bit confused. I thought they knew who your daughter was with. So I'm wondering exactly how I can help you."

"I just think there's more to this than what the cops are saying," he said. "I think there might even be more people involved."

"Well, in any case, Keisha's a lovely girl. Whatever I can do to help, I'd be happy to."

"Actually, I was hoping you could answer a few questions for me."

"Sure."

"Do you know if Keisha had any friends who stopped by when she was at work? Male friends?"

"Not that I know of," the manager said. "She generally stayed by herself. I mean, there were boys, and, frankly, men, who were interested in her. But Keisha never gave them the time of day."

"Did she make a lot of phone calls or receive a lot of phone calls here at work?"

"No," the manager said. "She was a little bit of a loner. She usually ate in the food court by herself. The only person I ever saw her have lunch with was your wife."

"My wife?" John was surprised. He'd never heard his wife talk about meeting Keisha for lunch.

"Her name is Sarah, right?"

"Yes, that's right."

"I met her once," the manager said. "She seemed very nice. Pretty, too. You're a very lucky man."

"Thank you," he said, taking a business card from his back pocket. "If you remember anything else, can you give me a call?"

She looked at his card as he turned to walk away.

"Actually, Reverend, there was one other thing."

"What's that?" he said, stopping in his tracks.

"I always thought Keisha might make a great buyer. So I sent her down to our sister store, Lord & Taylor, to meet with our regional buyer for women's wear—Nola Langston."

The color drained from John Anderson's face.

"Maybe Nola might remember something that could help you. Would you like her number?"

"No, thanks," John said, walking out of the office. "I think I know how to reach her."

Ishmael parked the Chrysler in the public parking garage on Tenth Street and walked half a block to a phone booth on Market. If things happened the way he wanted them to, he would walk back to the garage and drive away before anyone could catch him. But first he had to kill John Anderson.

He stood at the phone booth, holding the phone while pretending to make a call. He didn't want to chance John spotting him the way he had a few minutes before. So he stood with his back to the mall entrance that John had used, waiting for the reverend to come out.

Reaching into his jacket, he wrapped his hand around the butt of his nine-millimeter and imagined how it would feel to pull the trigger. The thought of it made him anxious to do it. But he told himself that he would have to wait. Disposing of John Anderson on a Center City street, where Ishmael was most likely to be caught, would only defeat the purpose.

He couldn't spend the rest of his life with his lover if he was jailed for murder. But he knew in the back of his mind, where secrets and rage dwelled together in an uneasy union, that his lover's embrace would not be his only reward for killing the preacher.

Ishmael's greater prize would be the look in John Anderson's eyes when he told John what he knew. It was a look that he'd imagined for weeks. Ishmael would have the satisfaction of that look because he would deliver the killing blow while standing face to face with him.

With that thought fresh in his mind, Ishmael turned around and watched as John walked up the steps that led out of the Gallery Mall. When he saw that John was walking toward him, Ishmael hung up the phone and walked to the corner of Tenth Street.

He ducked inside a bank and stood at a counter by its large window, which overlooked Market Street. Picking up a pen, he pretended to fill out a deposit slip while waiting for John to pass by.

A few seconds later, John did. His gait was a step slower than it had been a few minutes before. His eyes were unfocused, as if he were walking in a dream. His face was ashen gray, and his mouth hung open in apparent shock.

Ishmael could have walked up from behind and put a bullet in his brain. John would have never known what hit him.

But this wasn't the time or the place. So Ishmael waited a few more seconds before putting down the pen and walking out of the bank to follow John Anderson.

It wasn't until he saw John walk to Thirteenth Street and into Lord & Taylor that he stopped. He knew that the pastor would have to come back to his car sooner or later. So he walked back to Ninth Street to prepare for the confrontation as his mind filled with thoughts of the woman who would give him his ultimate reward.

Kevin Lynch and Detective Hubert had spent the last half-hour going through the wealth of material they'd gotten from Nola and Frank upon their capture, and splitting the information into separate files.

Lynch believed that it was best to talk to Nola first. With all Frank Nichols had done to her, she should be more than willing to talk. And the more information she gave, the easier it would be to pursue a case against Nichols for the commissioner's death.

Although Lynch was angry that he had missed Keisha and Jamal back at the projects, the evidence laid out before him was encouraging.

If Lynch's hunch was right, Nola was the missing link in the Nichols organization. And if he was able to break her, finding Jamal and Keisha would be easy.

He grabbed the file, a plastic bag filled with Nola's personal effects, and the briefcase filled with the money. Then he walked out of his office and down the hall to the interrogation room.

"How are you, Ms. Langston?" he asked as he walked inside.

Nola was sitting at the head of the table with a detective on either side of her.

"Annoyed," she said, sounding like a petulant child.

"You guys can take a break," Lynch said, dismissing the detectives as he sat down at the other end of the table.

As they walked out of the room, taking great pains to steal final glances at Nola, Lynch opened the file, taking his time so she could watch him remove all the personal papers and cards they'd taken from her purse. Next he removed her makeup and cell phone from the plastic bag.

Finally he put down the cash-filled briefcase, hoping that the sight of it would make her nervous. But as he looked across the table and saw the arrogant smirk that played on her lips, he could see that it did no such thing.

"Why'd you try to elude the detective I had trailing you this morning?" Lynch asked.

"I didn't *try* to elude him. I did," she said with a chuckle. "I don't like people following me around."

"Frank followed you," Lynch retorted.

"And I got away from him, too."

"Yeah, you did," Lynch said while flipping through the file. "Was that before or after he screwed your daughter and tried to kill you?"

Nola stopped smiling, and Lynch knew he had her.

"Tell me something," he said. "You and Frank Nichols, I assumed the two of you were just lovers, but you're business partners, too?"

"You know what they say about assuming," Nola said coolly.

Lynch smiled. "Alon Enterprises. That's Nola spelled backward. Clever name. Was it your idea?"

"Actually, it was Frank's. He thought it would be nice to name the business after me, since I was the one who came up with the concept."

"And what concept was that, Ms. Langston?"

"I told him that he should open some coffee shops on a few college campuses. Maybe do some vending as well."

"Did you tell him to filter the drug money through the business, too?"

Nola smiled. "I don't know what you're talking about."

"Okay," Lynch said, sliding her withdrawal slip across the table. "Tell me how Alon Enterprises sells a million dollars' worth of coffee to college kids in a year."

Nola looked up at Lynch with a seductive grin. "It was *really* good coffee, Lieutenant. Some people have even called it addictive."

"Cut the shit, Ms. Langston," Lynch said impatiently. "I don't have time for it. And frankly, neither do you. Your name is on a business that launders drug money under the direction of Frank

Nichols, and you made an illegal transaction in an attempt to clean out the assets of that business."

"I made an emotional decision that any woman might make if she found out her man was sleeping with her daughter," Nola said with a knowing smile.

"An emotional decision to steal a million dollars in drug money?"

"I don't know anything about drug money, Lieutenant. As far as I know, that money is all legitimate. I'm the second signer on the business account, I created the business, I grew the business, and given the fact that Frank is wanted in connection with the commissioner's murder and tried to kill me this afternoon, I think a jury would agree that I had every right to try to protect my interests."

"Frank didn't seem to think so."

"He's a hothead," she said, crossing her legs so her short linen dress rose up to the top of her thighs.

Lynch walked back around to his end of the table and picked up her cell phone from the pile of personal effects.

Nola's self-assuredness seemed to waver as she watched him walk toward her with the phone in his hand.

"Cell phones are interesting little pieces of technology," he said as he toyed with the buttons. "Yours, for instance, is billed to Jamal Nichols—Frank's son, and his right-hand man in his drug business."

"That doesn't mean I know anything about any drugs," Nola said.

"Maybe not. But it doesn't mean you don't, either."

"Look, Frank gave me that as a business phone, and that's what I use it for," Nola said, her voice a little more jittery. "How am I supposed to know who the phone's billed to?"

"I understand," Lynch said. "I think cell phones are one of the best business tools you can have. You can make calls from virtually anywhere. You're always accessible, and you always have the ability to get in touch with the people you need to."

Lynch began to press her buttons—all of them.

"I keep my schedule on my cell phone," he said with a grin. "I send e-mails with it, too. I even use the calculator and that little picture phone thing. But you know, sometimes it's the simple things that make technology so great. Things like the phone book function."

Nola looked up at Lynch, who was once again standing over her.

"It lets you put all your important numbers in one place," he said as he scrolled through her list. "For example, you've got Frank Nichols, your daughter, Marquita, your job. You've even got Jamal Nichols here."

He bent down in front of her and put the phone on the table so she could see what he was doing.

"And when you go back and scroll through the recent calls on your phone, you've got a call to Frank this morning, which explains one of the calls we saw on his phone from Jamal. But then there's three others that are a little more difficult to explain. Calls to you from Jamal Nichols. One at seven-forty, another at seven-forty-one, and another at seven-forty-two."

He stood up and looked down into Nola's face. "That's after he snatched Keisha Anderson. But, of course, you already know that, because you're the one who told him what to do with her."

"So what am I, a crime boss now?" Nola said with a nervous giggle. "That's ridiculous."

"Is it?" Lynch said over his shoulder as he walked to the other end of the table and sat down. "Then what's this?"

Lynch reached into the pile and extracted a small slip of paper. He unfolded it, slowly, and read the message that it contained.

"Keep the package for an hour. If you don't hear anything, get rid of it."

Lynch put the paper down and stared across the table at Nola. "You wanna tell me what that means?"

"Could be a note from work," she said, looking away from him. "I don't really remember, to be honest with you."

Lynch stared at her for along moment. "Okay," he said. "That's fine. The notes and the calls could all be a coincidence.

"The business stuff, that's a little different. Because frankly, Ms. Langston, a first-year accounting student could look at the books of Alon Enterprises and see that there's drug money there.

"Now, maybe you can get away with it," Lynch said as he began to gather her things. "Maybe you lick your lips just so, and bat those beautiful eyes, and a jury believes that a Wharton graduate like yourself was a partner in a business and knew nothing about its primary source of revenue."

Lynch stood up.

"But why chance it? You've still got a lot of years ahead of you, Ms. Langston. Would you rather spend those years in prison for laundering drug money, or would you rather just tell us what we need to know about Frank and Jamal's involvement in the commissioner's murder, and come out with a slap on the wrist?"

Nola wanted to respond, but she couldn't speak. She was too afraid.

Lynch knew that, so he walked toward the door to give her fear a chance to set in.

"Whatever you decide," he said as he reached for the doorknob, "you need to make it quick, because Jamal Nichols is still on the loose with Keisha Anderson. And you don't want him to do anything else that might be traced back to you."

Lynch was about to leave the room when Nola finally relented.

"Lieutenant?"

"Yes, Ms. Langston?"

"I'm ready to call my attorney."

13

"*Gimme the* gun," Jamal whispered to Keisha.

They were sitting between seats that obscured their hands from the view of the other passengers on the nearly empty elevated train.

Just one day before, Keisha would've been afraid to remove the gun from her purse, regardless of the fact that no one could see her. But now she didn't care.

She took the gun out of the purse and handed it to Jamal, knowing that it was better for him to have it, in case they needed to use it.

She wouldn't have trusted him enough to hand over the weapon just a few hours before. But each of them had demonstrated what the other meant to them, not only through their words, but through their actions.

Her life was literally in his hands, she thought as she looked down into the streets below the fast-moving train. And his life was in her hands as well.

As the el train slowed down and pulled into the Allegheny Avenue station, Keisha thought of the struggle in the car, and the look she'd glimpsed in the woman's eyes as she'd choked her. Keisha imagined that it was a look much like the one she had worn the night before, when the men attacked her in the playground.

It was odd, she thought as she looked at Jamal, that loving him had made her stronger. Perhaps it was because she had something worth fighting for now. Or maybe it was because she had someone who was willing to fight for her.

Whatever it was—the energy of the streets, the struggle to survive, or the power of their love—it was enough to transform her from a victim to a conqueror, from a little girl to a woman. It was enough to make her into someone she had always wanted to be.

As the doors closed and the train pulled away from the station, she was concerned with only one thing—their next move.

"Where do you think we should go?" she asked, laying her head on Jamal's shoulder.

"I don't know," he said. "But wherever it is, I want it to be away from all this."

"Away from all what?" she said, looking up at him.

"My father, your father, the drugs, the guns, the lies, everything."

He looked at her and imagined that she was still the little girl he'd met five years before.

"I want to go someplace where we can be those two little kids again. Where it don't matter what family we from. I wanna go where we ain't gotta be lookin' over our shoulders to see who comin' at us, tryin' to take what's ours."

Keisha furled her brow. "We don't have anything that anyone would want to take."

"You wrong," Jamal said. "We got what everybody else tryin' to get. All them people chasin' paper, chasin' men, chasin' women, chasin' ghosts, they tryin' to get what we got. They tryin' to get somebody to care about them."

Jamal shook his head and sat back in the seat. "You got people out here doin' whatever—workin' theyself to death, slingin' dope, sellin' ass, takin' loot—doin' whatever they gotta do just to get somebody to notice them. And you know what? None o' that shit they doin' don't mean nothin'."

Keisha looked out the window as the train passed by spray-painted names scrawled upon walls, and wondered if the people who'd written them were looking for someone to notice them.

"Are you trying to get noticed, too?" she asked absently.

He took her chin in his hand. "Only if you the one lookin'."

Keisha touched his face. "I am," she said.

Jamal looked into her eyes and pressed his lips against hers. She pressed back, and their bodies told them that it was time. They each felt their hearts beating faster than they'd ever beaten before. And as their blood rushed to the nether regions of their bodies, stiffening Jamal and softening Keisha, they knew that they would explode if they couldn't touch one another.

"Keisha," he said, suddenly disengaging from their kiss, "we here."

He hastily peered out the window and looked at the placard identifying the station name. It said Somerset.

"Follow me," he said, jumping from his seat and running toward the door with Keisha in tow.

The train squealed to a stop, and he took her by the hand and led her across the platform and down the steps to Kensington Avenue. They crossed against the busy street's traffic, walked into a dilapidated bar, and in the next instant they were face to face with Frank Nichols's only friend.

Kevin Lynch sat in his office with an assistant district attorney whom he'd called in to draw up a plea agreement for Nola Langston. True to his reputation, Robert Harris handled it immediately.

One of the few black assistants on staff at the DA's office, Harris was there for only one reason: he was good. He had the highest conviction rate of any assistant DA. But there was more to his winning ways than his ability to manipulate the law.

With boyish good looks that often yielded comparisons to Denzel Washington and an enduring sense of style that never seemed to fail him, Robert Harris cut a dashing figure in the courtroom. But he had higher aspirations. And winning a conviction in the murder of the police commissioner would help him to achieve them.

"Thanks for handling this so quickly, Robert," Lynch said, sitting down behind his desk as he looked over the plea agreement that Harris had drawn up in exchange for Nola's cooperation.

"Not a problem," he said while flicking a speck of dust from his tailored, single-breasted pinstriped suit. "Darrell Freeman was a good man. If this Langston woman can connect Frank Nichols to his murder, I think it's well worth the deal."

"Good," Lynch said, flipping to the last page of the agreement. "Now if her lawyer can just convince her to take it, we can get the ball rolling."

"I took a good look at Ms. Langston, Kevin. You're not going to have a problem getting her to take it. She's not jail material."

Harris smiled a mischievous grin. "Nothing that fine should go to waste behind bars."

Lynch shot a sidelong glance in the attorney's direction. He was well past the point of being mesmerized by Nola, and was about to tell Harris as much when a detective knocked on his office door.

"Lieutenant Lynch," the detective said, "Mrs. Anderson is here about her daughter. Do you want to talk to her now, or would you rather wait until you're finished with Ms. Langston?"

"Is Reverend Anderson with her?" Lynch asked.

"No. She says she doesn't know where he is."

"Okay," Lynch said. "Send her in."

The detective nodded and went outside to get Sarah.

"Robert, could you give me a few minutes with Mrs. Anderson? I need to talk to her about her daughter."

"No problem," the assistant DA said. "I'll be right outside when you're ready.

"Thanks."

The prosecutor opened the door just as Sarah walked in. He nodded a greeting and left the room while she sat down with Kevin Lynch.

"I got here as soon as I could," Sarah said, rushing to the seat in front of his desk. "Is Keisha okay?"

"As far as we know," Lynch said uncomfortably.

"Why does everyone keep saying that?" Sarah said, exasperated. "Just tell me what's wrong!"

"Okay," Lynch said, getting up from his seat and sitting down on the side of his desk. "We think your daughter is helping Jamal Nichols."

"What do you mean, 'helping'? He kidnapped her—took her right off the street this morning, and we haven't seen her since. She would've come home if she could have. She wouldn't be—"

"Mrs. Anderson," Lynch said, cutting her off. "Jamal and one of his father's men traded shots with a police officer in an alley about an hour ago and shot that officer to death. Keisha was apparently with them when it happened, and she chose to run away from the scene with Jamal."

Sarah was momentarily shocked into silence.

"That's impossible," she finally said. "Keisha would never do anything like that on her own. He must have forced her to go with him."

Lynch didn't want to make her feel worse, but he didn't want to spare her the reality, either. So he told her the truth.

"Mrs. Anderson, your daughter helped Jamal Nichols escape from the scene of that shooting. They stole clothing from two prostitutes and carjacked a man at gunpoint. After that, she helped him hide in her great-aunt's house up in the Northeast, and the two of them disappeared."

"What are you talking about?" Sarah asked, sounding confused. "Carjacking? Guns? Keisha's never used a gun in her life."

"That remains to be seen," he said carefully. "But Keisha *did* hide Jamal in a woman's house off Frankford and Academy. The woman identified herself as your husband's aunt. Her name is Margaret Jackson."

Sarah was about to argue, but then she remembered. Margaret was her dead father-in-law's oldest sister. She'd come to visit the church occasionally over the years, but had stopped coming as she'd gotten older.

"Okay, I remember Margaret," Sarah said. "But why would Keisha hide Jamal there, and why would Margaret let her do that? I don't understand."

"Neither do we," Lynch said, folding his arms. "That's why I asked you to come down here."

Sarah tried to digest what Lynch was saying to her, but it was impossible for her to focus. She couldn't imagine her daughter going along with such a thing. It wasn't like her.

"Maybe Keisha knows Jamal from the neighborhood or from church, or something," Lynch suggested.

"She doesn't know him," Sarah said firmly. "And even if she did, she would know to stay away from him. Not just because of what he does, but because of who he is. We don't associate with the Nichols family."

"Could the two of them have had some kind of friendship that you and your husband didn't know about?"

"I really can't believe what you're asking me," Sarah said. "You act like I don't know my own daughter."

Lynch tried to be gentle. He could tell that Sarah was truly shocked by the news.

"Mrs. Anderson," he said, "I know all this must be very hard to believe, and maybe there's a reasonable explanation for it. We think Margaret Jackson could give us at least part of it, but so far she's refused to talk to us. I was actually hoping that your husband could talk to her—maybe get her to give us an idea of where they went."

"I haven't seen John in hours," Sarah said, wringing her hands. "He left the house saying he was going to find Keisha, and he hasn't been back since."

"Do you know where he went?" Lynch asked.

"God only knows," she said with a sigh.

Sarah leaned forward and looked into Lynch's eyes. "Lieutenant, I want you to let me talk to Margaret," she said earnestly.

Lynch saw that she was determined. She was not going to be denied the opportunity to find out for herself what was going on with her daughter.

That was good, Lynch thought, because the old woman was at least as headstrong as Sarah.

"Okay," Lynch said, getting up from the desk, opening the door, and leading her past the waiting assistant DA.

"I'll be right back, Robert," Lynch said quickly.

The prosecutor nodded and watched them walk down the hall to an office where the old woman was waiting.

When he opened the door and led Sarah inside, Lynch saw Margaret Jackson begin to look around as if she could see who had walked into the room.

"Mrs. Jackson, I've brought someone to see you," Lynch said.

"I hope it's somebody who can tell me when y'all gon' fix the doors you busted down out at my house."

"Actually, Aunt Margaret, it's me, Sarah," she said, sitting down in front of the old woman and grasping her hand. "It's good to see you again."

"I wish I could say the same," Aunt Margaret said. "But I'm not seein' too well these days."

"I'm sorry to hear that," Sarah said, shifting in her seat as she tried to think of a way to broach the subject.

The old woman spared her the trouble.

"You here to ask me about Keisha," she said, settling back into her seat.

"Yes, Aunt Margaret, I am. Do you know where she went?"

The old woman looked up toward the ceiling. She closed her eyes tightly, like she was concentrating on retrieving some distant memory.

"Do you remember how your family acted when you were about to marry my nephew?" she said.

Sarah thought back twenty years, and saw herself sitting at her mother's kitchen table, listening to her go on about how Sarah had just gotten her life together, and how she was taking an incredible risk in joining a family like the Andersons. She remembered that talk like it was yesterday. It was that talk that convinced her that she should marry John. Years after that fateful talk, she'd shared her mother's sentiments with her husband, and he'd apparently shared them with Aunt Margaret.

"Yes, I do remember that," Sarah said. "It was a turning point for me."

"I guess it was," the old woman said. "I imagine if somebody tried to tell me about my future husband's family being drug dealers and murderers, I wouldn't want to listen, either. 'Cause when you love somebody, can't nobody tell you nothin' about 'em. And if they do, that just make you love 'em even more."

Sarah looked up at Lynch, who was standing there listening to the old woman confirm what he'd tried not to believe.

"Keisha just like you, Sarah. She come from a preacher's family, and she done spent her whole life tryin' to do right. She told me she knew Jamal from when they was little. He was the first boy she ever kissed. And she loved him ever since then."

"Why didn't she tell me anything about that?" Sarah asked, confused.

"Same reason you ain't tell your parents everything you did," Aunt Margaret said with a sad smile.

"This isn't about me, Aunt Margaret," Sarah snapped.

The old woman reared back, surprised at Sarah's attitude.

"I know it ain't about you," she said. "It ain't about me, either, Sarah. It's about Keisha's choice. I tried to tell her that boy wasn't no good for her, even told her 'bout what his father did to my brother. But she ain't wanna hear that."

"She wasn't afraid?" Sarah asked.

Aunt Margaret tried to figure out a way to make her understand, just as Keisha had made her understand.

"Sarah," she said, speaking in hushed, motherly tones, "I think Keisha just tired. She wanna live without worryin' 'bout what anybody think about her."

"But she's out there with a murderer," Sarah said.

"She don't think so," the old woman said. "She said the boy ain't do it, and that's why they runnin'. She don't wanna see him go to jail for somethin' he ain't do."

"If that's what she believes, she could come back and tell the police that," Sarah said frantically. "She doesn't have to stay out there with him."

"She love the boy, Sarah. And he said he loved her, too. And when they said it, I could feel it down in my soul."

"So you let Keisha go back out on the streets with him because you thought you felt something?" Sarah said in disbelief.

"Sarah, I couldn't have stopped her if I wanted to," Aunt Margaret said gently. "I'm ninety years old, and I'm blind. I'm gettin' weaker all the time. But they gettin' stronger, 'cause they love each other."

"I just want her to come home," Sarah said, sounding anguished. "I just want to know she's all right."

Lynch watched the old woman and saw in her face that there was a conviction to her actions. She believed she'd done the right thing in helping them. And when she spoke again, he understood why.

"I done learned a few things in my life, Sarah," she said, her soft voice growing louder with each word. "And one o' the things I learned is that you might only get one chance in life to really love somebody. The only one who should be able to take that chance away is God."

The old woman smiled and squeezed Sarah's hand. "I ain't God, Sarah. And neither is you. Let the child be."

Sarah looked around at Kevin Lynch, then back at her husband's aunt. "I'm not trying to take away her chance to love somebody, Aunt Margaret. I just want to know where she is."

"I can't help you there," Aunt Margaret said. "But I do know this. Keisha growin' up and tryin' to find her own way. You was a preacher's daughter, just like she is, and you tried to find your way, too."

"But I came back," Sarah said.

"And she will, too," Aunt Margaret shot back.

Then her face softened, and she reminded Sarah of the reason why her daughter would eventually return to her roots.

"Bring up a child in the way he should go, and when he is old he won't depart from it," she whispered.

At that, Sarah dropped her eyes and began to weep. Aunt Margaret put her hand against her face and wiped her tears.

"You got to believe God, Sarah. You got to believe he can take care o' Keisha better than you and John ever could."

Sarah wiped her eyes, patted Aunt Margaret's hand, and stood up.

And as she and Lynch left the room and walked back down the hallway toward his office, Lynch received a phone call.

Keisha and Jamal had carjacked another vehicle, and an officer had been injured in a pursuit.

Homicide detectives were already on the scene along with district officers, and Acting Commissioner Dilsheimer was en route.

Though their victims had provided fresh descriptions that were already being broadcast on police radio, the two of them had escaped once again.

14

Jamal and Keisha sat in the back room of the bar on Kensington Avenue as the owner looked Jamal in the eye and told him everything that Keisha had made him forget.

Joe Vega, an old white man with a pockmarked face and a nose that had been flattened by too many bar fights, wore his white hair slicked back in the style of days gone by and walked with a slight limp. But his knowledge of the streets was as fresh as that of an eighteen-year-old. And today, it was much better than Jamal's.

Keisha listened along with Jamal as Joe voiced the very things that Frank Nichols would have, if he were there. Jamal took it all in because, if he'd learned anything from his father, it was that Joe Vega was like family, and he was to be trusted above anyone else whom Frank dealt with.

Frank's relationship with the old man had begun ten years before, when they were cellmates in Graterford State Prison.

Frank did a year with Joe before he was acquitted at trial for a murder in which the witnesses disappeared. Joe wasn't as fortunate. He was found guilty of armed robbery, and ended up doing the minimum of a five- to ten-year sentence.

But the two stayed in touch. And during those years that Joe remained there, Frank regularly sent money, and accepted the occasional collect call. When Joe got out, he looked Frank up, and Frank helped him to open a bar. The place was nothing fancy, but it was enough to pay the bills and keep Joe out of jail.

Over the years, whenever things got too hot in North Philly, Frank went to Joe's bar to conduct the transactions necessary to keep his drug business flourishing. Million-dollar deals had taken place in the back of Joe's seedy little establishment. And whenever they did, Frank was always sure to pay Joe a little something off the top.

Joe never forgot that. And so, when he heard about Jamal's supposed involvement in the police commissioner's murder, he expected Jamal to come to him, because he knew that the police would have all of Frank's places staked out.

Now, as Jamal sat before him with Keisha by his side, Joe paced in front of the two of them, asking the one question that had plagued him since he'd heard the news.

"Why?" he asked, his face twisted in anguish. "Why would you shoot the police commissioner? Are you outta your mind, Jamal? Or don't you even have one?"

"I didn't do it," Jamal answered calmly.

"Bullshit! They've got your picture all over the television. Everybody in Philadelphia knows what you look like. You *and* your little girlfriend here. She's gonna get you jammed, you know. You do know that, don't you?"

"I'm willin' to take my chances."

"Are you? Well, let me tell you this, Jamal. They said on the news that they've been holdin' your father for questioning for the last hour. Nola, too."

For the first time, Jamal began to look worried. But then he thought about the way he'd disobeyed his father's orders. And he began to think that he was better off with his father in jail than he was with his father on the outside.

He knew what his father would tell him to do. He would tell him to keep running. And Jamal intended to do just that.

"Jamal, it's hot out here right now," Joe said. "You can still go someplace nice and forget about all this. But you gotta lose the girl."

"I can't do that," Jamal said matter-of-factly.

"Why?"

" 'Cause I love her."

Keisha looked at Jamal, grateful that he could embrace their love so easily. The two of them clasped hands, their fingers interlocked with one another.

Joe watched their display of affection and rolled his eyes in disgust.

"You're jokin' about this, right?" he asked hopefully. "I'm sure she's a nice girl and all, but she don't know nothin' about the streets. She's a preacher's daughter, for God sakes!"

"She saved my life, Joe. She had my back when anybody else woulda jetted. That gotta mean something, right?"

Joe put both hands on Jamal's shoulders and looked him in the eye.

"She's gonna get you caught, Jamal," he said in measured tones.

"Caught for what?" Jamal said. "I ain't do nothin' to get caught for."

"Then stop runnin' right now and turn yourself in. Tell 'em you ain't shoot the commissioner, and it's all a big misunderstanding. Tell 'em you can explain."

"You know I can't do that, Joe."

"Yeah, I know you can't, 'cause they don't wanna hear that shit."

Joe stood back and ran his fingers through his hair as he tried to think of the best course of action for Jamal to take. He didn't want to see Frank's son make a mistake that could cost him his life. But it looked to him like the boy was going down that path.

"Jamal, let's forget about whether you did what they said you did," Joe said while holding his hands out in a placating gesture. "I'm not even worried about that right now. I'm worried about you.

"I'm worried that you screwed up somehow, didn't do what your father told you, and now what shoulda been a little problem is bigger than anything I seen in all my sixty years. But it ain't too late to make it right, Jamal. Ditch the girl. I can keep her here for an hour or two, you can go wherever you're gonna go, and she can just reappear—presto. You're gone, she's back home. Problem solved."

Jamal looked at Joe, and he knew that what he was telling him was the right advice, if the streets and their codes were the only thing worthy of consideration. But then he looked at Keisha. He thought of her fierce loyalty and her willingness to leave everything for him. He knew that there was no way he could leave her. Not now, not ever.

"You right, Joe," he said, turning his gaze on the grizzled barkeep. "I messed up. I ain't do what my father wanted me to do. I did what *I* wanted to do. But Joe, if you love my father—and I know you do—you'll help me out this one time, and you won't ever have to worry about seein' me again."

Joe looked from Keisha to Jamal, and knew that he would never get through to him. The kid was making a mistake, Joe thought. But his father had prepared for this day, just like he'd prepared for everything else over the years. So all Joe had to do was pass on what his father had left.

"What do you need?" Joe asked with a frustrated sigh.

"We need money, some clothes, and a ride," Jamal said. "Anything we need after that, I can get it myself."

Joe stared at them for a moment. Then he shook his head and walked to the back of the room. Unlocking a cabinet, he reached in and removed a sealed manila envelope with Jamal's name on it, and walked back over to Jamal and Keisha.

"Your father must have known this day was coming," Joe said, handing the envelope to Jamal. "He left this for you."

Jamal unsealed the envelope and began counting hundred-dollar bills. He knew before he'd finished counting that there was more than enough for the both of them.

He counted out five thousand dollars. "This is for you," he said, offering the money to Joe.

"Your father already took care o' me," Joe said. "I got an envelope stuffed away somewhere, too. You keep that for yourself. You're gonna need it."

Joe went to the back of the room and opened a door. There was a stairway on the other side.

"There's men's and women's clothes upstairs in the closet. I'm sure my girlfriend won't mind if you borrow a pair o' jeans and a blouse or somethin'. You might want to shower and get somethin' to eat, too."

Joe looked at his watch. "It's one o' clock now," he said. "Lay low here for a couple hours, let 'em look for you up in Frankford 'til the trail goes cold. At five o' clock, I'll close up the bar and take you wherever you want to go. That's rush hour. Lot of traffic, but you're a lot less likely to be stopped for somethin' stupid. Until then, Jamal, my home is your home. My apartment is through that door and up those stairs."

Jamal got down off the stool, and Keisha followed.

Joe looked at Keisha and spoke to her for the first time. "I wasn't tryin' to be hard on you," he said. "But his father's like a brother to me. He's really the only family I got."

Keisha smiled. "I understand," she said. "Just know that you can never care for Jamal more than I do. As long as we understand that, I think we'll all be fine."

Joe was surprised. He hadn't expected her to respond that way. But it was the right response. Maybe Jamal wasn't so stupid after all.

"Thanks for everything, Joe," Jamal said with all the sincerity he could muster.

"Thank me when this is over," Joe said with a wave of his hand. "We're not out of the woods yet."

Swirling red and blue lights painted the dark street under the el tracks as a crowd of onlookers watched a disheveled police tow truck driver load the mangled police car onto his flatbed.

The officer who'd chased Keisha and Jamal had already been transported to the hospital with a head injury, and officers from the department's Northeast division had fanned out to search for Keisha and Jamal.

The streets around the accident site had been blocked off quickly. The el was no longer running into or out of the Bridge-Pratt station. Transit police had boarded every one of the twenty or so buses that were idling in the transportation hub when the accident took place.

In an ambitious effort to ramp up the search, Transit police were also going door-to-door in the vicinity of every el stop from Bridge-Pratt to Center City. And housing police were assisting with the search of a housing project that was within walking distance of the Bridge-Pratt station.

Still, no one was operating under the illusion that it would be easy to find Keisha and Jamal in the streets of Frankford, a working-class, integrated neighborhood that was suffering, like communities all over the city, under the weight of an out-of-control drug epidemic. There were people on every block who looked just like Keisha and Jamal.

But their saving grace was the couple whose car they had tried to use to escape. The husband and wife were still traumatized from their short ordeal with the gun-wielding teens. But their anger at being victimized outstripped their fear.

Unlike those who remained silent in the wake of crimes committed against them, these two were willing to talk. They'd already given Keisha and Jamal's descriptions to the police. And now, as they stood before the first camera to arrive at the scene, they were about to repeat the descriptions for the world.

A white-haired reporter stood before the wreckage of the police car, with the couple's green Ford, cordoned off by crime scene tape, visible in the background.

As his cameraman turned on his light, the reporter checked his notepad and, after a silent countdown from the station, spoke with a mixture of grave sincerity and shocked disbelief.

"This is Frank Wilson, reporting live from the latest scene of an incredible crime spree that has thus far claimed the lives of seventy-year-old Emma Jean Johnson, Police Commissioner Darrell Freeman, and Officer Jim Hickey. Just about fifteen minutes ago, an unidentified police officer was seriously wounded while chasing a car belonging to this couple—the second vehicle to be carjacked in connection with these crimes."

The reporter held out his arm to allow the couple to step into the frame.

"Mr. and Mrs. Jack Williams have agreed to speak exclusively to Channel Ten about their ordeal," he said before turning to the couple. "Mr. Williams, how did this happen?"

"My wife and I were in the drive-through at KFC when an elderly couple approached us. When I rolled down the window to see what they wanted, the woman put a gun to my head and they forced their way into our car."

"And these two elderly-looking people, what did they look like?"

"From the pictures I've seen, it looked like Jamal Nichols, the man who shot the police commissioner this morning, and Keisha Anderson, the girl he supposedly kidnapped.

"But Nichols didn't have the dreadlocks anymore, and he was wearing an old-looking fedora and an oversized gray suit. He was wearing glasses and using a walker. Keisha Anderson had on a long flower-print dress with a wide-brimmed straw hat and a purse.

"The odd thing about it is, she was the one with the gun," Mrs. Williams said. "She didn't look like someone who'd been kidnapped to me."

"So it appeared that she was working with Jamal Nichols?" the reporter asked.

"I'm not sure if working is the right word for it," Mr. Williams said. "She looked like she was enjoying it. At one point she even laughed. That's when I slammed on the brakes and tried to take the gun, but I couldn't get it, and they forced us out of the car.

"Right after that, the police officer in that car came and chased them," he said, turning his head to look at the wrecked police car. "And you see what happened after that."

"Were you able to see where they went?"

Mrs. Williams looked up at her husband, then at the reporter, and shook her head regretfully.

"I wish we did," she said. "But everything happened so fast after that, with the police car crashing and everybody running, that it was really hard to see anything.

The husband wrapped his arm around his wife. "Right now, we're just glad to be alive."

A police officer approached the couple and pulled them away from the camera just as four more news vans arrived on the scene. He put them into a nearby police car before the other reporters could stick microphones in their faces.

As the police car drove away with the witnesses, the reporter turned toward the camera and read from his notepad.

"Again, if you're just joining us," he said, "there are witnesses who now allege that Keisha Anderson, who was originally believed to have been kidnapped, is actually Jamal Nichols's accomplice in what is turning into one of the biggest crime sprees this city has ever seen.

"Stay with Channel Ten as we follow all the developments in this rapidly changing story. I'm Frank Wilson, reporting live from Frankford for Channel Ten News."

As the reporter spoke those last few words, a black Mercury arrived at the scene, and Acting Commissioner Dick Dilsheimer got out of the car to survey the damage. He was quickly mobbed by reporters.

As a jumbled mass of voices shouted questions he could barely understand, the acting commissioner raised his hands to quiet the reporters, and spoke with authority as his comments were broadcast live throughout the region.

"The officer who was injured in this pursuit is fine. As you know, we can't say the same for Commissioner Freeman and Officer Hickey, two public servants who were slain in the line of duty while trying to protect the citizens of this city. I can assure you that this department is doing everything possible to find those people responsible for these crimes."

He began to walk away amid more shouted inquiries, but one question stood out above the others.

"What are your comments regarding the newest allegation, that Keisha Anderson is working with Jamal Nichols?" shouted the reporter from Channel 10, speaking so loudly and clearly that Dilsheimer was forced to turn around and respond.

"Anyone involved in these crimes against the citizens of Philadelphia will be brought to justice," he said firmly. "We will investigate vigorously to find out who they are and what role they played. We will arrest them, charge them, and allow our criminal justice system to run its course."

The commissioner turned and walked away, speaking with his commanders as the reporters rushed to file their reports.

But even as the latest chapter in Keisha and Jamal's odyssey was broadcast across the Delaware Valley, the people closest to the investigation were still trying to figure out how it began.

Kevin Lynch reached up and turned off the television in his office, having just watched the commissioner address the media about the latest turn of events.

"Well, I guess the old lady was right," he said, turning to the assistant DA as the two of them prepared to go in to question Nola Langston. "Keisha's in love with Jamal Nichols."

"I don't think that changes what we need from Nola," Robert Harris said, adjusting his tie.

Lynch sat down in his chair. "You're right. It just narrows things down a bit."

Lynch's eyes took on a faraway look. He looked like he was someplace else.

"What is it?" Harris said, studying his face.

"I don't know how her mother didn't see it," Lynch said. "She had no idea."

"Maybe it was an on-again-off-again type of thing," the prosecutor said.

"Or maybe they just kept it so well hidden that by the time everyone figured it out, it was too late," Lynch said while rubbing his chin.

"Well, I wouldn't worry about it," the prosecutor said. "Because the key question now isn't even the extent of their relationship. It's how much of a role the girl played in everything Jamal's done to this point."

"I think it's pretty clear that she's helped him," Lynch said. "She flagged down the cars, she helped him hide out, she held the gun. I mean, all that stuff makes her an accomplice, but I still can't see her doing much more than that."

"Why not?" the prosecutor asked.

"You didn't see her this morning at the protest," Lynch said. "She had this innocence about her—this sweetness that you don't see much in kids these days."

"She knows how to play innocent, Kevin. She's a PK."

"A what?"

"A PK—preacher's kid. When I was coming up, we all knew to stay away from the preacher's kid, because they would be the ones doing all the crazy stuff, and getting you in trouble for it.

"Preacher's kids are the Eddie Haskells of the world, Kevin.

They can be real polite and sweet when they need to be, but behind the scenes, when nobody's looking, they're the main ones raising hell."

"I really wasn't trying to think of it that way," Lynch said. "Thanks for bursting my bubble."

Robert Harris smiled. "You're a homicide detective, Kevin," he said. "You're supposed to look for the worst in people. But instead, you're always trying to find the best."

Kevin leaned back in his chair. "That's what makes me good at what I do. I see people for who they can be, not necessarily for who they are."

"So, do you think Keisha Anderson can be worse than what you thought she was?"

"I think the key to that question is that shooting up in the Twenty-fifth District. When we get the results back from Ballistics, we'll know a little bit more about how far Keisha Anderson went. Until then, we'll just have to get all we can from the witnesses we have."

There was a knock at the door.

"Come in," Lynch said.

A detective stuck his head in the door. "Ms. Langston's attorney has gone over the plea agreement," he said. "He says his client is ready to talk."

"Good," Lynch said, taking his jacket from the back of the chair.

"It'll be interesting to see how her story matches up with what we know," the prosecutor said.

"Or if it matches up at all," Lynch said.

The two of them walked down the hall to the interrogation room, and walked inside to hear Nola's side of the story.

It was hot in Joe's apartment. The single oscillating fan that circulated the summer air throughout the living room made it seem even hotter.

But as Keisha and Jamal looked around at their spartan accommodations, they were thankful for the simplicity. It allowed them, for the first time in years, to focus all their senses on one another.

It was almost like the playground on a Friday night at dusk. There was no television, no stereo, no CD player. The only electronic items in the apartment were a dust-covered radio and an ancient-looking laptop computer that looked as if it hadn't been used in ages.

The only visible source of entertainment was a pile of books in one corner of the room that stretched from the floor to the ceiling.

A small mirror hung on a nail above an end table. And a couch and chair were pushed against opposite walls in the room. The hum of the old refrigerator was the only sound, other than their breathing. But their breathing was all they wanted to hear.

"Keisha, I need you to know somethin'," Jamal said, placing his hand against her face.

"What is it?" she said, moving close to him and looking in his eyes.

"Remember in the car, when I said you can't always have everything you want?"

"Yes," she said, walking up to him until she was inches from his face.

He looked down at the floor.

"I lied."

Keisha touched his face, and swept her hands through his freshly cropped hair.

He looked into her eyes and saw a mixture of fear and desire.

She knew that it was time to test the fantasies they'd spun, to see if they could possibly come true.

Jamal reached down and gingerly guided her lips to his own. He kissed her tenderly, his eyes watching hers to see what she was feeling. He didn't want to miss a second of the moment he'd waited for all his life. He'd known sex before. But neither of them had ever known love.

Keisha reached up and took off the jacket he was wearing. Then she unbuttoned his shirt, grabbed him by the shoulders, and pulled him against her.

He pulled away and looked into her eyes, and slowly began to unbutton the cotton dress she was wearing. When he undid the last button, they both watched it fall to the floor.

They peeled the remaining clothing from their sweat-soaked bodies as they explored each other's mouths with probing tongues. Then, as they stood naked before one another, with every fiber of their beings longing to be touched, they realized that they weren't standing alone.

Every dream they'd had about each other, every thought they'd had about this moment, every forbidden pleasure they'd secretly entertained, was there, standing between them, daring them to take them for themselves.

Jamal ran his hands through her hair and along her cheek, over her breasts, and down to her secret places. He took her in his arms and carried her to the bathroom. Then he placed her in the shower, turned on the water, and watched it cascade over her body's every curve.

Stepping over the rim of the tub, he stood behind her and took the soap between his fingers, and with his bare hands, he washed every inch of her body. He rinsed her with the water, and then he rinsed her with his mouth.

Keisha felt his fingers everywhere, probing her, caressing her, loving her. She felt her body growing softer, more yielding, as he pressed himself against her. His lips were on her neck, and on her back, and down her spine, causing every part of her body to tingle at his touch.

She reached back and pulled him closer, closed her eyes and lost herself in the rhythm of his movements, opened her mouth and allowed herself to give voice to what she felt.

She placed her hands against the slick, tiled wall and pushed herself against him until her body pulled him in, and they were one.

They moved to the beat of their hearts, slowly at first, and then faster, until they lost control. She squealed with delight at the sensation of his love, and his voice joined hers in a shouted harmony of passion.

They clawed and gripped one another, holding on for dear life, until their love burst forth from their bodies in streams of ecstasy. They were both left breathless at the end, trembling as the water poured over them and hoping that their love would never end.

15

Lynch sat at the far end of the table with the assistant DA on his right. Nola and her lawyer were at the other end. Both of them looked anxious. That was good, Lynch thought. It meant that Nola's lawyer believed that it was best for her to cooperate.

"This is Assistant District Attorney Robert Harris," Lynch said by way of introduction. "Mr. Harris, this is Nola Langston and her attorney, Ryan Gold."

"Charmed," Harris said, staring at Nola. "I'm sure."

He took out his copy of the plea agreement. "Mr. Gold," Harris said, "the state is willing to abstain from filing any serious charges against your client—that is, felony charges—in exchange for full cooperation, with the stipulation that her testimony leads to a conviction in the murder of Commissioner Darrell Freeman. Of course, we have no say concerning any federal charges, but we're willing to recommend leniency with respect to any federal charges that may be filed."

Gold looked at Nola. "I'm not sure we can take that agreement," he said.

"I'm offering your client the moon and stars," Harris said, grinning seductively at Nola. "She can't possibly want any more than that."

Gold looked at Nola, then back at the flirting assistant DA, and shook his head.

"My client maintains that she doesn't know anything about the circumstances of Commissioner Freeman's murder, simply because she was not in Philadelphia at the time. What she can give in exchange for that agreement—the moon and stars, as you call it—is testimony about the events leading up to the shootings that have taken place over the past few days."

"Will it give us Nichols?" Lynch asked.

"It'll give you the truth," Nola said, speaking up for the first time.

Lynch looked at Nola and saw that the flirtatious grin was gone, and her legs were no longer crossed. Her flawless hair was beginning to contract in the humidity of the closed-in room, and she had a haggard look in her eyes. She was tired, from what Lynch could see. And she just wanted to get it over with.

"Okay," Lynch said. "Tell us the truth."

"In exchange for what?" her lawyer interjected.

Harris leaned over and whispered something to Lynch.

"We can give her the same deal if her testimony leads to a conviction in at least one of the three murders connected with this thing, and a racketeering conviction against Nichols," Lynch said.

Nola looked at her lawyer. He nodded.

She leaned back in her chair and took a deep breath.

"First of all, you're on the wrong track," she said. "If you think this thing is about Frank and Jamal Nichols, you're wrong."

"Well, who is it about, then?" Lynch asked.

"It's about Reverend Anderson. It's about money. And it's about me."

Nola smiled at the assistant district attorney, who was once again enthralled with her, because he could see in her eyes that she was ruthless.

"I used to date mobsters," she said, returning the prosecutor's hungry gaze. "Something about bad boys and their big guns has always turned me on."

She paused as the men in the room shifted uncomfortably in their seats, no doubt picturing the double entendre.

"They can afford to feed my expensive tastes. But they always seem to die. A few years ago, I decided that if I kept dating those kinds of men, it was only a matter of time before I got caught in the crossfire. So I figured I needed a different type of man—a *good* man.

"A friend suggested I try church, and told me about this growing congregation down in North Philly. So I decided to give it a whirl.

"I got there and I was pleasantly surprised. There was a lot to choose from—businessmen and lawyers, even a doctor or two. But they all seemed to have these problems."

She sat back in her chair and crossed her legs again as she thought back on the power that her body had given her, even in the church.

"After a few Sundays," she said, fixing her eyes on each man at the table, "I decided that the only man I wanted there was the pastor. He seemed so big and strong standing up there in that pulpit.

"So I went to him after the service one Sunday and asked if he could come and pray with me. I told him I needed a special kind of healing. Then I stuck my business card in his Bible, and right before my eyes, he went from man of God to just man. And that's when I knew I had him."

"That's all very interesting, Ms. Langston," Lynch said impatiently. "But we need to know how all this plays into the commissioner's murder. And if it doesn't have anything to do with it, we need to know what does."

Nola smiled. "The commissioner was murdered because I slept with Reverend Anderson. I slept with him, and he did what men do because he was weak, just like every man I've ever known."

She spoke directly to Lynch, daring him to refute what she was saying.

"You see, Lieutenant, men want what they want, and they do whatever they have to do to get it," she said with a wicked grin. "But they never think of consequences, only pleasure. They think that just because a woman sleeps with them, she's their friend. And so they talk. They tell us all of their problems—the things their wives don't want to hear.

"And then they expect us to spread our legs and solve each and every one of them."

She paused to revel in the shocked expressions on their faces.

"Reverend Anderson was no different," she continued. "He was a nice man, a spiritual man, but a man nonetheless. So after we'd been seeing each other for a while, sneaking away to places where his congregation and his wife couldn't see, he started to open up to me.

"He told me about this man, Frank Nichols, who'd killed his father and stolen everything he had. He told me how Nichols had become one of the biggest drug dealers in the city. He told me that he was going to bring Nichols down one day.

"The good reverend also told me about his own past in the drug business," Nola said, speaking with some degree of satisfaction, as if the pastor's sins justified her own.

"He talked about hurting people, even killing people, back in the sixties."

"People like who?" Harris interjected.

"He didn't say," Nola answered. "He just said that he'd made some mistakes as a young man, and that the only thing that could make him kill again was his daughter, Keisha. He said that if anyone ever laid a hand on her, he would kill them, just as sure as he was sitting there talking to me."

"So it seems you had your bad boy and your good boy, all rolled up into one," Lynch said. "Why'd you leave him? Because he was married?"

"Don't be silly," Nola said with a smile. "I really didn't want to leave him, because sleeping with him was . . . spiritual. But he couldn't support my lifestyle on what he made. I need money, Lieutenant. I can get sex from anybody."

"So you found Frank Nichols," Lynch said matter-of-factly.

"Yes, I did. And oh, what a find he was. See, there's something about small-time gangsters like Frank. They're always looking for a woman with class—someone to lend them social standing. So that was the first thing I offered.

"I walked into his bar one day with a business proposition. I told him that I'd heard a lot about him, and that I wanted him to invest in a company I was starting. Of course, the only thing he could see was how I looked. So he flirted, and I let him. And for six months, I strung him along while I learned everything I could about his business.

"By the time we finally laid down, I had my finger on the pulse of everything he was doing. The drugs, the prostitution, everything.

"Soon after that, he started giving me little assignments, telling me to make phone calls and deliver messages."

"What kind of messages?" Lynch asked.

Nola shrugged. "The same kind of message you saw. Words on a strip of paper that could have been about anything. He'd just leave them in my purse and tell me to make a phone call at a certain time, and that was it. I never knew what it was about. And to be honest with you, I didn't care. The only thing I cared about was what was in it for me. I brought up my business proposition to him again, and he acted like he didn't want to hear it. So I did what I had to do to make him listen. I played with his manhood."

Harris and Lynch exchanged glances as Nola's lawyer turned his head, embarrassed and at the same time intrigued by her choice of words.

"I bought him a tailor-made Armani tuxedo," she said with a self-satisfied grin. "And I took him to see the Philadelphia Orchestra at the Kimmel Center. He'd never been there before, but I could tell, by the way he was sitting there, looking around at the people with *real* money—people with fortunes he could never dream of having—that he felt inferior, just like I wanted him to.

"Then I took him home that night and made him feel like a man again. I told him he needed some legitimate money to fall back on. Something that could take him to the next level, and make him like the people we'd seen that night. I started Alon Enterprises for him, made myself the second signer on his account, and watched him filter the drug money through the business. Then something crazy happened."

"What do you mean?" Lynch asked.

"Reverend Anderson got wind of my relationship with Frank, and he started calling me five times a day," she said. "Sometimes he'd hang up. Sometimes he'd leave these long, pitiful messages, asking why I'd betrayed him with Frank. I never returned the calls, and eventually I changed my number. When he couldn't take his anger out on me anymore, he did what any man would do. He turned his anger on Frank.

"John was determined to get him for stealing me. That's why he started trying to drive crack out of the neighborhood. It had nothing to do with healing people and saving lives, like he claimed it did. It had everything to do with hurting Frank Nichols.

"Frank knew that, and it pissed him off. When I saw how it was affecting him, I saw it as an opportunity."

"What kind of opportunity?" Lynch asked.

"It was a chance to take control of the situation," she said. "I got in Frank's ear, and told him that the only way to get back at John was through Keisha. I convinced him to get Jamal to follow her, and he did it. They started talking about kidnapping her and holding her for ransom, but I didn't think they were really gonna do it, and I didn't feel like sitting around waiting.

"So I hired two guys to scare the girl last night," she said. "I didn't tell them to hit her, but I knew she would go back to her father and tell him what happened. I figured he would blame Frank."

"So what did you expect to happen?" Lynch said.

"I expected that John would go after them, and Frank would do something stupid and get himself in trouble. I figured, no matter what, that I would end up with the money."

Lynch shot a troubled look in the prosecutor's direction. Then both men looked at Nola's lawyer. They were all thinking the same thing: Nola was diabolical, and dangerous. But she still needed to give them more, if she was going to walk for her part in it.

Lynch stood up, reached back, and massaged his neck. It had been a long day.

"Ms. Langston," Lynch said with a frustrated sigh. "There's really only one thing I need to know. Did Frank Nichols ever give the order for Jamal to kill John Anderson?"

"Frank gave a few orders in the last few days," Nola said, looking around the table and connecting with each face. "Orders he told me he was going to give, to put the whole feud with John to rest."

"Did you hear him give these orders?" Lynch asked.

"No, but right before I left for New York, he told me that he was planning to have Jamal murder John Anderson."

"So Jamal takes a shot at John last night, misses, and hits the old woman on Diamond Street?" Lynch said.

"That's right," Nola said. "But that wasn't good enough. Frank wanted Jamal to finish the job. That's why he had him take another shot this morning. Of course, we all know how that turned out."

"So where does the whole kidnapping thing come in?" Lynch asked, shooting a look in Robert Harris's direction.

"I'm really not sure," Nola said. "I mean, I know that was something they'd discussed before, but like I told you, I never believed it would happen."

"So if you never believed it would happen, how'd you know what to tell Jamal when he called you this morning after he'd snatched the girl?" Lynch asked.

"The same way I always knew," Nola said, growing nervous.

"Frank had given me a message to relay to him, and that's what I did. I relayed the message."

"If you were in New York and he was with your daughter, when did he have a chance to tell you what to say?" Lynch asked.

"He gave it to me before I left to go to New York," Nola said. "He said, 'If Jamal calls you, I want you to tell him this.' Then he stuffed the paper into my bag, and I left."

Lynch sat back in his chair and looked at the assistant district attorney sitting next to him. Harris was no longer impressed with Nola's looks. From the look on his face, Lynch could tell that he was more concerned with the gaping holes in her story.

Nola's lawyer watched the two of them and felt the need to interject, because he saw that things were going badly for his client.

"She's given you what you asked for," Ryan Gold said, sitting up in his chair. "She's willing to testify that Frank Nichols gave the order to kill John Anderson, and that Jamal Nichols attempted to carry it out, killing Commissioner Darrell Freeman and Emma Jean Johnson."

"That would be fine if your client's testimony were true," the prosecutor said, getting up from his seat. "But we all know there's something missing here. It's up to Ms. Langston to tell us what it is."

"I can't give you what I don't have, Mr. Harris," Nola said anxiously. "All I can give you is what I know. The rest is up to you."

"No, the rest is up to you, Ms. Langston," Lynch said, getting up from his seat. "If you want the deal, you have to give us something we can use.

"And when you revise your story, I want you to consider this. Keisha Anderson isn't with Jamal Nichols because she was forced to be. She's with him because she wants to be."

The young lovers had spent the last hour devouring one another with their hands and with their mouths. Now, as they sat in the quiet of the simple room, listening to the echoes of the voices emanating from the bar downstairs, they were feeding their hungry eyes with the only sight they wanted to see—each other.

They lay on the small bed together, Keisha feeling the whisper of Jamal's breath against her neck. She tried to think only of the moment, only of their love, only of herself. But she couldn't, because something inside her kept bringing her back to the tragedy that had created this perfect moment.

It was difficult for her to reconcile her own pleasure with the death and destruction that had taken place all around them. She knew that she should be mourning with those who mourned, and praying for the families of those who'd lost people whom they loved as much as she loved Jamal.

But Keisha swept those thoughts aside, and instead immersed herself in thoughts of Jamal. She wanted to know who he was. She wanted to know who he wanted to be. But more than anything, she wanted to know what had brought him to her.

"Where'd you come from?" she whispered.

"From the playground," he said with a playful smile. "Remember?"

She tapped his arm. "Stop playing, Jamal. I really want to know. I mean, Frank Nichols is your father, and I've always seen him. But I only saw you that one summer, and this past month. How come?"

Jamal's smile faded as he considered a question that he'd never posed to himself. Where did he come from? In many ways, he didn't know. But what he did know, he was willing to share with Keisha, just as he was willing to share everything else.

"My mom and pop met in the early 'eighties, somewhere between heroin and crack. That's how my pop tells time. Whatever his hustle was, that's what time it was. The 'seventies was heroin. The 'eighties was cocaine. Then, around 'eighty-five or so, it was crack.

"Of course, he had other things that helped tell time, too. Women and whatnot. But they was just somethin' to do while he waited for his money to roll in off them corners.

"Some o' his women knew that, some of 'em didn't."

"Did your mother know?" Keisha asked.

"Like I told you before, my mom was a college girl," Jamal said, flipping onto his back and putting his hands behind his head as he stared at the ceiling. "She wasn't like them hoes he was used to. She was strong, smart, too good for his sorry ass."

Keisha could see that the memory had stirred something bitter inside him.

"Jamal, if you don't want to talk about it anymore, it's okay," she said, reaching over to caress his chest.

"It ain't like I don't wanna talk about it," he said. "I guess I just never had a reason to get too deep with it."

"Don't let me be the reason for you talking about something that hurts you," she said, running her fingers along his face.

"You the best reason I got," he said, touching her hand with his own.

He took a deep breath before he continued.

"My mom was goin' to Temple law school when she met my pop," Jamal said. "She wanted to practice international law, travel around the world, see things she ain't never see before.

"She ain't care who Frank Nichols was, or what he could do for her. My mom was the type who could always do for herself. Frank liked that, at least he did at first."

Jamal smiled as he imagined his parents in their younger days.

"My mom told me that when they met, Frank was talkin' all this revolutionary shit about how black folks should work inside the system, get what they needed from it, then go back and use what they learned to do they own thing."

Jamal laughed. "He ain't tell her 'bout the system he came through. And he ain't tell her what business he was in, either. All she knew was, he gave her a ride home in a nice Benz, and asked if he could take her out the next day.

"My mom was a year away from finishin' law school when she had me, and she dropped out. She remind me o' that every time she get a chance, like it's my fault she ain't finish when she wanted to."

"But you know it's not your fault, right, Jamal?" Keisha asked earnestly. "You know you couldn't have done anything to change what happened before you were born, don't you?"

"Yeah, I know," he said, with a grim look on his face. "I know 'cause my mom spent years tellin' me it was Frank's fault. And for years, I believed her. Still do."

Jamal was silent for a moment, trying not to remember the things that had shaped the violence that raged in his heart. But he couldn't deny the memories, even though he'd tried to suppress them. They were there. And he had to tell Keisha about them, because he didn't want to be like his father.

"My mom went back to Temple when I was little, and finished her last year o' law school. My pop kept comin' around and tryin' to make it work with her. But she ain't want no drug dealer, and after a while he hated her for bein' too good for him.

"The first time I saw him hit my mother, I was five. She was talkin' 'bout takin' me away somewhere like California—

someplace where Frank could never see me. He smacked her in the mouth and told her she better not ever say nothin' like that again. She got a restrainin' order to keep him away for a year."

Jamal sighed and tried to keep the memories from consuming him.

Keisha kissed him on his cheek. "It's okay, Jamal," she said in the hope that it would take his pain away. "It's okay."

He turned and looked into her eyes, and knew that what she'd said to him was right. It was okay. At least, it was going to be. As long as the two of them could be together, it was all going to be okay.

"Is that why I never saw you?" Keisha asked. "Because your parents couldn't get along?"

Jamal nodded. "My mom thought she was protectin' me from him," he said. "And maybe she was. But the only thing I saw was, I ain't have no father. And I was mad about it."

He reached down and held her hand as he recalled the only piece of his childhood that really mattered. The piece that Keisha had given to him all those years before.

"For years, she wouldn't let me see him," Jamal said. "She wouldn't even let me talk to him on the phone. When I turned thirteen, I had to beg her to let me go down there, just that one time.

"When I finally did come down to North Philly to spend the day with him, he ain't have time for me. He was too busy makin' money. When I asked him if he was gon' take me out, he handed me fifty dollars, said, 'Happy Birthday,' and sent me on my way.

"I walked around the corner to the playground on Fifteenth Street," Jamal said. "Then I met this little girl who looked like she needed somebody."

Jamal touched Keisha's face as she smiled and looked into his eyes.

"That little girl made me forget about what was wrong," he said. "And she made think about what was right. I told her I would come back and see her every Friday after that. And even though I had to sneak out the house to do it, I did."

"Is that why your mother sent you down South?" Keisha asked, searching his eyes.

"Yeah, but it ain't make no difference. I started gettin' in trouble in school, and then I stopped goin', 'cause they wasn't teachin' me nothin' anyway. I started doin' what I wanted to do, 'cause, what difference did it make? I ain't have no father."

Keisha looked at the pain in his face and knew that it was the source of his anger. And as he continued to tell her where he'd been, she couldn't help wondering where he would go from here.

"My mom brought me back up here two years ago," he said, breaking into her thoughts. "But by then it was too late. By the time I was sixteen, I had got locked up twice for hustlin'. It wasn't even like I had to do it, 'cause my mom had enough money to get me whatever I wanted.

"But I ain't wanna get it like that. I wanted to get it myself. She finally gave up. She told me if I wanted to be like my pop, I could go down North Philly and see what it was like to be him."

Jamal turned away from Keisha and looked back up toward the ceiling.

"That's when she put me out," he said gravely. "And my pop, he put me to work."

John Anderson had spent the past half-hour wandering through Lord & Taylor, trying to summon the courage to go to Nola's office and ask her about Keisha.

It was odd, he thought, that he could draw from the Bible to counsel others. But in recent years, he had seemingly lost the ability to apply it to his own life.

In his mind, there was only one word that could explain his spiritual malaise: Nola.

He hadn't talked to her in months, and he wasn't keen on doing so now. And so he walked to the sportswear section, pretending to browse through tank tops and shorts, sneakers and socks.

Of course, John wasn't really sorting through clothing. He was sorting through his memories of Nola.

Their affair had been a whirlwind—one that had snatched him into its vortex and spun his life completely out of control.

She'd shown him things he'd never seen before, and seduced him with more than just her stunning beauty. There were lunches at five-star restaurants on Rittenhouse Square, and afternoons filled with the shouts and whispers of their frantic lovemaking.

They often rented suites in Center City's finest hotels. But they made love in other places as well. Places that excited him in ways he'd never imagined. The Crystal Tea Room, located on the upper floors of the Wanamaker Building, was a vast, exquisitely appointed dining room that had hosted presidents and royalty alike. But on the days when Nola wanted him, it played host to their sin. So did her office, and her living room, and the executive washroom at Lord & Taylor.

He tried not to think about the way she felt in his arms, or the scent of her perfume in his nostrils, or the sensation of her lips against his. He tried to block out the incredible sense of guilt he felt every time he'd taken her. He attempted to forget the heartbreak she'd imposed on him by sleeping with his enemy.

Instead, he willed himself to the escalators for the one-floor climb to her office. He dragged his feet as he stepped off the moving stairs and rounded the corner.

He wondered if the sick feeling he had about Nola's meeting Keisha was correct. Nola had, after all, betrayed him with Frank Nichols. Perhaps she had betrayed him with his daughter as well.

What if she had told Keisha of their affair? What if she had taken her to the places where they had gone? What if she had shared the things that he had told her about his past?

John didn't really want the answers to those questions. He was about to go back to the escalator and leave the building when one of Nola's coworkers—a manager in the evening wear section of the store—spotted him and called out his name.

"Reverend Anderson," she said, walking over to him, with her hand extended. "It's been such a long time since we've seen you. How have you been?"

"Fine," he said, hiding behind a fake smile.

He wondered if Nola's colleagues still believed that he was just her pastor, or if they knew that he'd stepped over that line long ago.

"I guess you're looking for Nola," said the blonde manager.

"Yes, I am," John said.

"Well, she was here this morning," she said. "But she only stayed for a minute."

"Do you know if she went home?"

"I'm not sure. But I do know that she won't be back here today. Is there anything I can help you with?"

"I actually just came to ask Nola a few questions about my daughter, Keisha. I understand the two of them worked together a few times this summer."

The woman's smile brightened. "Oh, yes, Keisha's a wonderful young lady. She and Nola hit it off very well. How's she doing, by the way?"

"She's missing," John said solemnly.

The woman's smile disappeared. "I'm so sorry to hear that."

"Yeah," John said. "Me, too."

He clutched the bag he was holding and half-turned to walk away. "If you hear anything from Nola, can you ask her to give me a call?"

"That's not a problem. I'm sure we'll hear from her tomorrow."

"Thanks," John said with a weak grin.

As he descended the escalator and walked toward the door, he asked himself the questions he hadn't dared to think about until then.

What if the secrets he'd told Nola had led to his daughter's kidnapping? Would he be able to forgive himself if they had?

16

When Sarah Anderson returned home from police headquarters, she closed her front door and leaned back against it.

Her head was still reeling from the things they'd told her about her daughter's involvement with Jamal. And while she refused to believe most of it, she knew that there was only one way to see if any of it was true.

Slowly, she walked to the steps, climbed them to the second floor, and stood outside her daughter's closed bedroom door. It felt strange standing there, knowing that Keisha was gone. But Sarah had to know if Aunt Margaret was right about Keisha and Jamal, so she twisted the doorknob and walked in.

Looking around the room, she saw that Keisha's things were still in place, just as they had always been. Her Bible was on her nightstand, next to her bed. Her magazines—everything from *Essence* to *Vogue*—were on the opposite side.

Sarah walked over to the bed, turned on one of Keisha's bed-side lamps, and looked down at her Bible. It was opened to the fifth chapter of Ephesians. Sarah's face creased in a wry smile. She wondered if Keisha had learned more about family through Paul's ancient letter to the church at Ephesus than she had from watching her parents.

Did she know that husbands were to love their wives, that wives were to respect their husbands, and that children were to honor their parents, as the Bible commanded? Or did she believe what she saw—that husbands were to honor themselves, and wives were to despise their husbands for doing so? Was what she saw in her home the reason she'd chosen the opposite of every-thing she'd been taught?

Sitting down on Keisha's bed, Sarah picked up the *Essence* magazine. It was a bible of a different sort—the tome that black women used to measure the pulse of their own unique culture.

Sarah could see that Keisha had gone through its pages with a fine-tooth comb, circling the images that depicted the style and grace of black women. They were images that reflected Keisha's own aspirations and potential—images of the woman that she wanted to be.

Sarah went through every drawer in Keisha's nightstand, des-perately searching for a clue that would give her some indication of Keisha's state of mind. She found receipts from clothing Keisha had purchased, and notes she'd written to herself about everything from scripture lessons to homework assignments.

She found a few fashion sketches her daughter had drawn, using herself as a model. The drawings were impressive, Sarah thought as she looked through them. She'd never seen them be-fore. But then, there were many things she'd never seen about Keisha.

Sarah went to her daughter's closet and began rifling through her things. She checked inside pockets and shoes, in pocketbooks and book bags. She went through her makeup and toiletries, sniffing and prodding and poking and searching for something that would tell her what she needed to know.

And after she'd ransacked Keisha's room, searching every inch of every one of Keisha's possessions, she found everything her daughter should have had, and nothing that she shouldn't. There were no indications anywhere that Keisha had ever wanted a boyfriend, let alone had one. There were no phone numbers, no names, no love notes, no diaries. There was nothing.

Sarah lay back on Keisha's bed, allowed her head to sink down into the pillow, and inhaled the fruity scent of the body spray her daughter loved to wear. She thought that by lying there, she would somehow be closer to Keisha. She thought that she could put herself inside her daughter's head.

But Sarah was too tired to think. She'd spent too much time thinking over the past day and a half and was utterly exhausted, both mentally and emotionally. Now she just wanted to rest. And as she drifted off to sleep, the voice in the back of her mind grew louder with each passing second.

Sarah felt her eyelids flutter as the voice continued to call out to her. And then, out of the clouds of her subconscious, she saw the voice take shape. It took on flesh and bone, and a face that was all too familiar.

Keisha was on the other side of the room, standing in the mirror in an evening dress, putting the final touches on her makeup. She didn't look like the girl Sarah had seen the night before. Now she looked like a woman.

"Keisha, there's something I need to know," Sarah began, trying to find the best way to pose the question.

"You want to know why I'm with Jamal?" Keisha asked, saving her the trouble. "I'm with him because he noticed me."

"Lots of people notice you, baby."

"You don't," Keisha snapped, staring daggers into her mother's eyes. "You never have. You're too busy feeling sorry for yourself to notice anybody."

Sarah was almost too stunned to respond. "That's not true, Keisha."

"If you noticed me, you would've seen something different about me the day I met Jamal when I was little," she said with a mocking laugh. "You would have seen how much I'd changed in the weeks since I've been seeing him again. But you didn't. You couldn't."

"Keisha, I was just under a lot of strain, honey. Your father—"

"Don't blame my father," Keisha said. "At least I knew he cared about me."

"But he never cared about me!" Sarah shouted. "You think you know something about being a woman? Well, you don't. You don't know what it's like when the man you love stops looking at you the way he used to. You don't know what it's like to have him treat you like an employee instead of his woman. You don't know what it's like to beg for his attention, just to watch him give it to everybody else."

"Oh, but I do know what it feels like to be a woman," Keisha said with a Cheshire cat grin. "Jamal showed me exactly what it feels like."

She got up and sashayed across the room with her hand on her hip.

"It feels good," she said, looking in the mirror and checking her hair. "*Real* good."

Sarah was dismayed as she looked at her daughter and saw herself. She knew the kind of girl she'd been at Keisha's age, and so she accused her of doing what she would have done.

"You've been sleeping with him all along, haven't you?" Sarah asked rhetorically. "You probably were with him last night when you made up that story about being raped."

Keisha wheeled around to face her mother.

"That's how I know you don't know me," she said angrily. "Because if you did, you wouldn't say anything like that."

Sarah regretted making the accusation. But she was about to regret it even more.

"I'm not the way you were when you were my age," Keisha said, walking to the bed and standing over her. "I don't lie and sneak and plot and connive the way you did."

Sarah wanted to move, and struggled to run away from the truths she knew were coming. But her body wouldn't budge from that spot, no matter how hard she tried.

"You thought you were too pretty and too smart to waste away in church," Keisha said mockingly. "And you thought you were too mature for boys your own age."

Keisha bent down until her face was only inches from Sarah's.

"You wanted men," Keisha spat. "But you see what men did for you, don't you?"

Sarah wanted to scream, to lash out, to do anything but listen to her daughter speak such things.

"I'm with Jamal because I love him," Keisha said, standing up and walking toward the door. "Not because of what he can do for me, or what he can give to me."

She looked down at her mother as if she were trash.

"That's a lot more than I can say for you."

Keisha opened the door, and a ringing sound filtered in from the hallway. Sarah watched her daughter as the ringing grew louder.

She wanted to ask her to come back. She wanted to ask her for another chance. But somehow, Sarah knew that it was too late for that. And as the sound of the ringing grew louder, Keisha walked through the door and closed it, forever shutting herself off from her mother.

The ringing became unbearable. Sarah couldn't listen to it any longer. And when her eyes snapped open and she awakened from her dream, she realized that the ringing was coming from the phone.

Sarah ran out into the hallway and picked it up.

"Hello?" she said tensely.

"Mrs. Anderson, we're sending a car to pick you up," a detective said over the phone.

Sarah waited with baited breath for the other half of the message.

"It's about your daughter."

Kevin Lynch was walking down the hall with the assistant DA. The two were on their way back to the interrogation room for another round of questions with Nola Langston when one of Lynch's detectives stopped them.

"Lieutenant Lynch," said the curly-haired Detective Hubert. "There's something I think you ought to see."

Lynch knew that the detective who'd captured Frank and Nola wouldn't have stopped him for anything frivolous. That's why Lynch was nervous about talking to him.

"Can it wait?" Lynch said. "I'm about to interview Nola Langston again. We really need to hear what she's got to say."

Hubert looked from the prosecutor to Lynch with a look of grave concern.

"When you see this," the detective said, "what Ms. Langston says might not matter a whole lot anymore."

Assistant DA Robert Harris was accustomed to being interrupted by now.

"Go ahead and take a look," Harris said. "I can wait out here if you want."

"No," Hubert said. "You probably need to see this, too."

"It'll be quick, right?" Lynch said as the two men followed the detective to one of the offices at the far end of the hall.

"That depends on what you mean by quick," Hubert said.

The three of them walked into the darkened room, and Hubert walked over to a laptop hooked up to a monitor on the table.

"Have a seat, gentlemen," Hubert said.

Lynch and Harris sat down in folding chairs as Hubert reached for the mouse and clicked it so that the film could begin.

"We got a tape in about an hour ago from one of the news stations and downloaded it into the computer," Hubert said. "The footage is from their chopper. We were able to enhance it a little bit, but not much."

Hubert paused the film and directed the mouse across the screen until it was poised over the man on the rooftop.

"This is the shooter right here," he said, moving the prompter to another part of the screen. "Over here is the commissioner, working his way through the crowd to get to Anderson. Right in front of Anderson is his daughter, Keisha."

Hubert clicked the mouse, allowing the film to play in slow motion.

"You'll see the commissioner grab Anderson from the vehicle and start pulling him through the crowd," Hubert said, moving the prompter until it was next to Lynch's image.

"You're here, Lieutenant," he said, narrating the action.

"Right about here, you run into the alley, and a minute later, we see you running toward the shooter on the roof. There are gunshots, the commissioner is hit, and he falls."

Hubert clicked the mouse again, causing the film to play frame by frame.

"Keisha Anderson has fallen down at this point," he said, moving the prompter to the middle of the screen. "Here she is, right here.

"Now, you'll see Jamal Nichols running into the picture, picking her up and carrying her through the crowd."

Hubert stopped the film and walked up to the television screen, pointing his finger at the focal point of the picture.

"But if you look on the roof, here," the detective said, "the shooter is still up there, struggling with you, Lieutenant, right as Jamal Nichols takes Keisha Anderson out of the picture."

Lynch got up to take a closer look at the screen. It was hard to make out the men's faces because the film was shot from overhead. But there was no doubt that they shared similar features, hair, and body types.

"Run it again," Lynch said quietly.

Hubert went back to the laptop and ran the film again, this time without interruption. The result was the same. Clearly, the man on the roof and the man who'd taken Keisha Anderson were two different people. That could only mean one thing.

"Looks like Jamal Nichols didn't shoot the commissioner," Lynch said, almost to himself.

"But we've still got every cop in the city thinking he did," Hubert said. "The question is, do we do anything differently, or do we just focus on catching him, and sort it all out later?"

For the first time in the investigation, Lynch wasn't sure what to do. Jamal Nichols could have been involved, even if someone else did the shooting. But if he wasn't involved and he was cornered by police who believed that he was, the results could be deadly.

"Has Ballistics gotten anything back yet from that shooting in the Twenty-fifth?" Lynch asked.

"No," the detective said. "But that's the other thing I wanted to talk with you about. We got prints on the gun they found near the body of the alleged shooter, Joseph Barnes."

"Is that Nichols's guy they found dead in the alley?"

"Yeah."

"Good," Lynch said. "If Ballistics matches the bullets with the gun and the Crime Lab guys find powder burns on his hands, we got him."

"Maybe that's where Nola's testimony comes into play. Because if we can make a case that Frank Nichols gave an order that led to the girl's kidnapping, and Jamal Nichols was an accomplice to that officer's murder while carrying out that order, maybe we can get a jury to connect the dots."

"That's a long stretch," Lynch said to Harris.

"You haven't seen me work a jury."

"It might be a moot question," Hubert said.

"Why?" Lynch asked.

"They found someone else's prints on the gun, too."

"Were they Jamal's prints?" Lynch asked, although he already knew the answer.

"No," the detective said gravely. "Whoever these prints belong to doesn't have a record, so we don't have a match in the system."

"I see," Lynch said. "So the shooting takes place in an alley where prostitutes hang out, and the only other people there are Jamal Nichols, Joseph Barnes, and Keisha Anderson."

"Let me guess which one doesn't have a record," the assistant DA said.

Lynch sighed and sat back down in the folding chair. "Our little girl just grew up," he said.

"Yeah," Hubert said. "I guess she did."

"Well," Lynch said with a sigh, "we'll just have to see what happens when the stuff comes back on the bullets."

"That could take weeks," Hubert said.

"I know," Lynch said. "In the meantime, we keep looking for them. Jamal's still wanted for investigation in connection with that shooting in the Twenty-fifth, and we want to ask him some questions about the shootings of Emma Jean Johnson and Commissioner Freeman."

"What about the girl?" the detective said.

"She's wanted for questioning, too. But we have to make it clear to the guys on the street that it's just that—questioning."

"Okay," Hubert said. "I'll pass that on to the district commanders."

"No, I'll pass it on to the commissioner and let him give the order," Lynch said. "They'll take it a lot more seriously if it comes from the top."

"Okay," Hubert said. "But there's still one thing we haven't addressed."

He reached down for the mouse and moved the prompter across the screen.

"Who's he?" Hubert said, pointing the prompter at the man on the rooftop.

No one in the room had an answer.

17

Breaking into the car was easy. It was the waiting that was difficult.

Ishmael had been hunkered down in the back seat of John's car for the better part of twenty minutes. He'd spent the time repeatedly imagining what it would be like to kill him.

He wanted to put John's head on a plate for his queen, just like the Bible stories he'd heard as a child. But this would provide more than just the queen's satisfaction.

Ishmael looked up to see if the preacher was within sight. When he didn't see him, he pulled out his cell phone and dialed his lover once again. Her voice mail came on, and he refused to leave another message.

He would tell her about it in person, when he met her that evening at the safe house. He would take her in his arms and describe the look on John's face, the words from his mouth, the sound of his heart beating against his chest and fading, slowly, to nothing.

Ishmael looked up again from the back seat and saw John round the corner with the bag swinging from his shoulder. Reaching into his jacket pocket, Ishmael extracted the gun, chambered a round, and tightened his fingers on the butt.

He heard footsteps approaching the driver's side of the car and stopping. Keys jangled and pushed into the lock, and then the door opened and the car listed to the side as John got into the driver's seat.

Ishmael waited for John to start the car, and before he could put it in gear, Ishmael sprang up and pressed the gun against the back of the preacher's neck.

"Don't move," he said, reaching around him to adjust the rearview mirror so that they could see each other's faces.

John looked at the reflection and recognized Ishmael as the man he'd spotted earlier, in the blue car. His face was filled with a rage unlike anything he'd ever seen before. Reasoning with him would be difficult. But he knew he had to try.

"Do I know you?" John asked while slowly moving his hand toward the gym bag.

Ishmael laughed. "Nah, you don't know me, man. But you ought to."

"Why is that?" John asked, his hand edging ever closer to the bag.

"I'm the one in your dreams, askin' how you can preach when you worse than the people you preachin' to."

"I don't know what you're talking about," John said, reaching into the bag and trying to close his fingers around the sawed-off shotgun.

"But God knows," Ishmael said, smiling. "And so do I."

"What do you mean?" John asked, though he feared the answer more than he feared the gun the man was holding.

"Nineteen sixty-five," Ishmael said. "Fifteenth and Diamond, 'round midnight, you drove around the corner in a Cadillac. You rolled the windows down and pointed a sawed-off out the window."

The color drained from John's face, and his grip loosened on the gun. Tears stung his eyes. And yet his tormentor continued to speak, giving voice to his darkest secret, and weight to his greatest guilt.

"You ain't care about nothin' but doin' what your father told you to do, did you, John? You wanted to please him, 'cause you thought he loved Frank more than he loved you, didn't you?"

"Who are you?" John asked, feeling as if he were falling from a great height, and spinning ever faster toward the ground.

"You was always scared Frank was gon' steal your father from you, wasn't you?" Ishmael asked, happily observing the tortured look on John's face.

John let go of the gun as Ishmael spoke, and the tears of thirty-five years began to flow.

"Who are you?" he asked through grief-stricken sobs.

"You ain't care who I was when you pulled that trigger, did you? All you cared about was Frank Nichols bein' more like a son to your father than you ever coulda been.

"You was weak," he spat. "You was nothin'. Just like you is now."

John wanted him to pull the trigger. He wanted his misery to end, but it wouldn't. It couldn't, because Ishmael wouldn't allow it to.

"You did everything your father told you to do, and it still wasn't enough, was it? 'Cause Frank Nichols stole him from you anyway. But he ain't steal him the way you thought he would. He took him away with bullets."

John leaned forward and put his head on the steering wheel. His soul was wracked with pain as the tears continued to fall.

He sobbed as the grief he'd covered with anger came pouring out of his eyes. He sobbed as the sense of loss overcame his desire for vengeance. He sobbed and waited for God to have mercy, and end his life with the gun that was leveled at his neck.

"How did you know?" John cried as the tears soaked his face. "How did you know?"

Ishmael leaned over the back seat and whispered in John's ear.

"I knew because somebody took my father the same way they took yours—with bullets. They took him on a summer night on Diamond Street, with a sawed-off stickin' out a Cadillac's window. They took him and they ain't think twice about the little boy he left behind. They took him and my life was over, 'cause nobody wanted me but him.

"I waited thirty-five years to find out who killed my father," Ishmael said with quiet triumph. "Who woulda thought I would hear it from somebody you thought loved you?"

John looked up from the steering wheel, his eyes red with fatigue and grief, and stared into the mirror at the man who planned to murder him.

"Nola told me about what you did to my father," Ishmael said. "Then she told me about what you did to her. She told me how you beat her and raped her."

"That's not true," John mumbled as he tried to understand what he was hearing.

"She told me how you tied her up for days."

"No, I didn't," said a bewildered John.

"She told me you would kill her if she told anybody."

"That's a lie," John said, his voice growing stronger.

"I told her I would kill you first."

Ishmael pressed the gun against the back of John's head and squeezed the trigger.

There was the tap of metal against metal. And in that moment, they both realized that the gun had jammed.

John grabbed the gym bag and swung it, hitting Ishmael in the head with the heavy metal of the sawed-off shotgun. Ishmael fell back against the seat, and John pushed open the driver's-side door and fell out into the street.

An approaching car braked hard, and John jumped up to avoid being hit. Ishmael emerged from the back seat and grabbed him from behind, choking off his air with a forearm at the neck.

John flipped the younger man over his shoulder, dropping the bag in the process. When it hit the ground, the sawed-off discharged, the blast echoing along Ninth Street. Cars came screeching to halt while their drivers watched the two men fight violently in the middle of downtown traffic.

Ishmael got up and swung wildly at John, who ducked the blow and delivered a vicious hook to Ishmael's midsection, knocking the breath from his body. Ishmael doubled over, wrapped his arms around John's knees, and pulled, flipping him onto his back.

Ishmael jumped on top of him and began flailing wildly, hitting him hard across the jaw, then flush on the nose, before John grabbed his suit jacket and flung him off with a mighty heave.

Ishmael looked over at the gym bag and spotted the sawed-off sticking halfway out. It was five feet away from both of them, in the middle of the street. John followed his eyes to the gun, and the two of them raced to get it.

The younger, quicker Ishmael grabbed it first, and pulled the gun from the bag. John froze in his tracks as Ishmael aimed the gun in his direction.

"Drop it!" said a voice from the post office across the street.

Ishmael looked over and saw two postal policemen leveling their weapons. Sirens wailed as police cars approached from four blocks away, at police headquarters. Motorists on Ninth Street stared wide-eyed at the spectacle.

John took it all in—from the anxious looks on the faces of the policemen to the disbelieving stares of cowering passersby. But it wasn't until he looked into Ishmael's face that he knew how the standoff would end.

"Drop the gun now!" the police officer repeated.

Ishmael's finger tightened on the trigger as John dived between his car and the one parked in front of it.

There was a loud blast as Ishmael fired the shotgun. There were dozens of popping sounds as the officers emptied their weapons.

When the shooting finally stopped and John raised his head, Ishmael lay dying in the street. The officers ran over to him and John ran to his side as well.

As blood streamed from the wounds in his face and chest, Ishmael uttered one final word.

"Nola," he said.

And then he closed his eyes.

Keisha got up from the bed, walked over to the window, and peered out between the edge of the shade and the windowsill.

She could see that the activity on the street below was beginning to increase, especially on the other side of the street, near the Market Frankford el, where a group of transit police were gathering on the platform.

Keisha's heart beat faster as she watched them confer with one another. She was sure they were looking for her and Jamal. But then the police disappeared down a stairway, and she calmed down.

As she closed the shade, Jamal came up behind her and wrapped her in his arms. The warmth of his touch was comforting, as was the sound of his voice in her ear.

"I don't think you wanna be all up in the window," he said. "Ain't nothin' out there but trouble."

"There's trouble in here, too," she said, backing away from the window while wearing a devilish smile.

"How you figure that?"

"I'm trouble," she said, turning to face him.

"No you not," he said. "You innocent."

"Not as innocent as I used to be," she said, taking his fingers between hers and placing them in her mouth.

He kissed her on her forehead and wrapped his arms around her. Melting into his embrace, she allowed herself to rest in his strong arms as she lay her head against his chest. She wished that she could stay there for the rest of her life, but she knew that they would eventually have to face the world outside.

It was a world trying desperately to destroy their love, a world Keisha believed that she could do without. Jamal was in no hurry to think of the world, either. He only wanted to think of her.

"So, you asked me where I came from," he whispered in her ear. "The least you could do is tell me where you came from, too."

"We come from two different worlds," she said, looking up at him.

"Yeah, we do," he said in a melancholy voice. "In mine, you gotta decide what you gon' do, when you gon' do it, and who you gon' do it to. If you take too long to think about it, you might never have to worry about thinkin' again. 'Cause somebody gon' make the choice for you.

"Your world a little different than that," he said. "But I'm only guessin', 'cause I don't really know a whole lot about it."

He sat there, looking at her, and waiting for her to fill in the blanks. Keisha was uncomfortable doing so, because she knew that she should tell him about more than just herself.

"What do you want to know about my world?" Keisha asked.

"Whatever you want to tell me."

"I always wanted to be a designer," Keisha said. "I used to make little drawings of my little fashion ideas and hide them in my drawer.

"I like long walks in the park, horseback riding, and intimate dinners for two," she said with a giggle.

"Oh, so you a personal ad now?"

"No," she said. "I'm just someone who hopes she can have a real life again someday, after all this is over."

Jamal knew what she meant, but he didn't want to deal with such harsh reality at the moment. He just wanted to learn about her.

"After this is over, I'm takin' you on my yacht, and we gon' sail around the world," he said, putting his arm around her.

"Yeah, okay," she said, grinning at him.

Jamal looked at her and saw something wonderful in her smile: something sexy, and sensual, and vulnerable, and sweet; something that needed to be loved. He wondered how much love she'd gotten to this point. And he wondered how much more he would have to give.

"Tell me 'bout your father," he said.

"Why?"

"'Cause I asked you."

"You gotta do better than that," she said playfully.

"All right. How I'ma know how to treat you if I don't know how he treats you?"

"Good answer," she said, leaning back against the headboard.

"My father was always around," Keisha said. "I always knew he loved me, and he showed me that whenever he had the chance. But even though he was always there physically, he wasn't there emotionally, and that's the one thing I always hated. I wished that he had more time for us."

Keisha looked down at her hands and began twisting them around each other. It made her nervous to talk about her background. She smiled at how much she'd changed.

"What's funny?" Jamal asked.

"I'm just thinking about how easy it was to tell you everything when we were kids, and how hard it is now."

"You was tellin' me about the movies you liked to see and the games you liked to play. That's easy. Now you tellin' me about your life. That's hard."

"Yeah," she said with a faraway look in her eyes. "It is."

"What's your mom like?" Jamal asked.

Keisha laughed. "That's a good question," she said. "Sometimes it's hard to tell, because she keeps a lot inside."

"My mom like that, too," Jamal said. "But I think she do that 'cause she ain't tryin' to let nobody see when she hurtin'."

"Maybe my mom is, too," Keisha said. "She's always talking about how hard it is to be married to a preacher, because you have to share your husband with everybody else."

Keisha looked at Jamal.

"I guess it's hard to be a preacher's daughter, too," she said. "Not just because you have to be this perfect child. That's just part of it. The other part is, you need to have your father to yourself sometimes, and people just don't want to let him go."

"So why would he wanna be a preacher, then?" Jamal asked. "He coulda went and got a regular job in a factory or somethin'.

He coulda went to school and been a lawyer, or a doctor, or a teacher. Why preach?"

Keisha sat back and thought about the question. She'd never heard anyone ask it before, yet everyone around her acted as if they knew the answer. Keisha, for one, wasn't sure. She only knew what she'd been told.

"My father told me once that he was called," Keisha said. "He said it's like something inside you, this voice pulling at you, telling you what you're supposed to be."

"So where the voice come from?" Jamal asked.

Keisha thought he was being facetious. But when she looked at him, she saw that he really wanted to know.

"God speaks to us in a lot of different ways," she said, speaking as if in a trance. "He speaks through the scriptures, he speaks through believers, he speaks though a voice inside of us—the voice of the Holy Spirit."

Jamal looked at her and thought about the voice inside her. He wondered if he had such a voice as well. And if he did, what was it telling him now?

"You want some water or somethin'?" he said, changing the subject.

"No, I'm fine."

"You sure is," he said, reaching over and kissing her on the cheek.

She smiled weakly.

"I wish I coulda seen some o' those drawings you did," Jamal said. "I know you got a lot o' talent."

"That's the same thing Nola used to say," Keisha said.

There was a moment of uncomfortable silence.

"You know somebody named Nola?" Jamal said as a sick feeling rose in his throat.

"Yeah," Keisha said. "Nola Langston. She's a buyer for

Strawbridge's and Lord & Taylor. I worked with her a few times this summer."

Jamal's jaw dropped. He thought about Nola's hold over his father, and how she'd used it to get him to start a business that Jamal thought gave Nola too much control. He thought about Nola pushing for them to use Keisha to get to Reverend Anderson.

Keisha could see the change in his face, and she was concerned.

"What's wrong?" she asked.

"Nola Langston works with my father," he said, speaking quickly while getting up and searching through his pants pocket for his cell phone.

"Is that the Nola Joe said was in jail?" Keisha said, shocked.

"Yeah." Jamal feverishly scrolled though his phone book until he found the number he was looking for.

He pressed the speed dial, listened for a moment, then punched in a code when he was prompted to do so. He listened again, and his face went from hopeful to dismayed.

"What is it, Jamal?" she asked.

He sat down on the bed beside her and put his face in his hands.

"Nola Langston is the one who told my father to snatch you," Jamal said slowly. "She tried to get you killed."

Keisha gasped. "Oh my God."

"She cleaned out my father's business account, too."

"How much money was in the account?" Keisha asked.

"A million dollars."

Keisha's eyes widened as she tried to imagine that much money. She couldn't.

"Keisha," Jamal said, grabbing a pair of sweatpants from Joe's closet. "Nola set this whole thing up."

He started rifling through Joe's shirts as Keisha looked at him, confused.

"Come on and get dressed, baby," he said over his shoulder. "We gotta go."

"I thought we were waiting until five o'clock."

Jamal stopped and walked over to Keisha.

"They made it look like me and my pop had somethin' to do with the police commissioner gettin' shot," Jamal said. "Then they stole a million dollars o' my pop's money.

"Why do you keep saying 'they'?" Keisha asked.

"'Cause you don't set up shit like that by yourself," Jamal said. "Somebody helped her. And until we find out who it was, we gotta go. Now, come on."

Just as Keisha got up from the bed to put on her clothes, they heard the sound of many voices downstairs in the bar. They could only make out part of what they were saying. But the part they could hear was enough.

They were saying, "Police."

Joe Vega saw the officers gather at the el stop, watched them descend the stairs and spread out along the block, and observed them showing everyone the pictures they were carrying in their hands.

The officers had spent the better part of the last fifteen minutes canvassing the block, going door-to-door, looking for Keisha and Jamal.

No one else on the block had seen them. That was good. That meant that no one was paying attention.

And Joe knew that the chances of his drunken patrons recalling two people they'd seen for all of fifteen seconds were slim to none.

He watched the transit cops walk in, and knew that he would be able to get rid of them even before they opened their mouths. He only hoped that Keisha and Jamal would know to remain still and quiet, no matter what they heard downstairs. Because if they began to move around, or worse, began to panic, Joe wouldn't be able to control what happened next.

Joe pulled out a rag and began wiping down the bar as the officers fanned out, and began looking around without even announcing their presence.

"Can I help you?" Joe said, making sure the annoyance came through in his voice.

"Police officers," said a sergeant who was leading the other officers through the bar.

The sergeant didn't bother to say anything else, and now Joe was really annoyed.

"I said, can I *help* you?" he said, putting down the rag and staring daggers through the sergeant.

"We're just looking around," the sergeant said.

"Looking around for what?" Joe said. "Something that's written on a warrant, I hope."

"No," the sergeant said, walking over to Joe. "We were actually looking for these two."

He held up pictures of Jamal and Keisha, side by side on a single page. The pictures weren't recent. Jamal still had his dreadlocks, and Keisha looked like a little girl.

"Nobody who looks like that comes in here," Joe said, picking up his rag and wiping the bar even harder.

"What do you mean by that?" the sergeant said.

"I mean, look around," Joe said. "You're the only black person in here. There aren't any black people drinkin' in my bar. Not that they can't come in. They can come in all they want to.

But they don't feel comfortable in my bar, understand? They just don't feel comfortable here."

The sergeant, who was about six-three and 240 pounds, looked like he wanted to finish flattening Joe's out-of-joint nose. Instead, he just shook his head and called out to his officers, who were still snooping around, checking bathrooms and looking under tables.

"Come on, guys," he said, waving his hand. "Let's go."

He turned back and looked at Joe as he left.

"Thanks for the hospitality," said the sergeant.

"Yeah, whatever," Joe said, without looking up.

When the officers were a safe distance away, one of Joe's patrons looked down the bar at him.

"Why'd you tell him black people don't feel comfortable here, Joe? Your *girlfriend's* black, for God's sakes."

"I was just breakin' his balls," he said with a laugh. "You know I hate cops."

"Yeah, but—"

"Just go with the flow, man. Don't worry about it. Have a beer on the house. Everybody have a beer on the house!"

A cheer went up from the six inebriated men stationed at various areas of the bar.

Joe poured the beers and looked toward the ceiling, thankful that Jamal and Keisha were quiet while the cops did their little inspection of the place.

He still thought that they should wait until five o'clock to leave the bar. But Jamal had other ideas.

18.

Fire Rescue transported Ishmael to Jefferson Hospital with five bullets lodged in various parts of his body. One of the bullets had collapsed a lung, ricocheted off one of his ribs, and landed dangerously close to his spine.

Still, he managed to breathe, albeit barely, while doctors worked to stabilize him. It didn't look like he would be able to hold on that much longer, given the damage the other bullets had done to his organs.

But while there was still breath in his body, there was testimony to be had. And so Lynch—along with Detective Hubert and Assistant DA Harris—made his way to the hospital as soon as he heard the news.

When Lynch and the others arrived, John Anderson was already there.

"Are you okay, Reverend Anderson?" Lynch asked.

"A little shaken up, but I'll be fine."

"Your wife was concerned about you. Nobody knew where you were."

"I was looking for my daughter," John said with a slight edge to his voice.

"Okay," Lynch said, noting the tension in the preacher's demeanor. "We'll talk a little later."

Lynch ran down the hall, with Harris and Detective Hubert close behind.

"Where are you going?" a young resident asked Lynch as he ran through the emergency room with his cohorts.

"I'm looking for the shooting victim who was brought in from Ninth and Market ten minutes ago," Lynch said.

"He's in cubicle five, but I don't know if you can—"

Lynch was gone before he finished the sentence, snatching open the cubicle's curtains to reveal the bloody mess that was Ishmael.

People were at work all around him, prodding and clamping, slicing and removing. Ultimately, he wasn't going to make it. And Lynch, for the first time in his career, was unconcerned with that cruel reality.

"Let me in here," he said, tossing aside two nurses and a doctor as he made his way to the head of the bed. "I need to talk to this man now."

"Somebody get Security in here," said one of the doctors.

"I *am* Security," Lynch said, holding up his badge while bending down over the patient.

"Mr. Carter, can you hear me?"

Ishmael nodded.

"Take that damn oxygen mask off his face so he can talk!" Lynch shouted to a nearby doctor.

"Officer, I really don't think—"

Lynch snatched off the oxygen mask.

"What are you doing?" the shocked doctor asked.

"He's gonna die, isn't he?" Lynch screamed in the doctor's face. "Isn't he!"

The doctor nodded nervously.

"Well, get the hell outta my way and let me do my job before he dies!"

The doctors backed away from the bloody bed as Lynch waved over the assistant DA and Detective Hubert, who were standing a few feet away.

Hubert turned on a handheld video recorder as Lynch bent over Ishmael's face and began asking questions.

"What's your name son?"

He labored to breathe before pushing out two tortured words. "Ishmael Carter."

"I don't know what you believe, Mr. Carter," Lynch said, staring intensely into his eyes. "But you're going to die soon, and when you do, you're going to have to answer to someone. When they ask if you stood up like a man and admitted what you did, I think you'll want to say yes."

A tear formed at the corner of Ishmael's eye as he winced in pain and nodded, almost imperceptibly.

"Okay then, Mr. Carter, I want you to listen very carefully, and answer all my questions."

Lynch looked back at Hubert to make sure the video camera was on. Then he turned back to Ishmael.

"Did you attempt to kill John Anderson?" he asked.

Ishmael nodded.

"How many times?"

He lifted a weakened arm and held up three fingers.

"Last night on Diamond Street, around ten o'clock, you drove by in a car and shot at him?"

Ishmael nodded.

"A woman named Emma Jean Johnson was killed in that shooting. Do you admit to her murder?"

A rapidly weakening Ishmael nodded again.

"This morning from the rooftop, you shot at John Anderson and you struggled with me, as well, right?"

Ishmael nodded.

"And that's when you shot the police commissioner?"

Ishmael tried to catch his breath to speak, but couldn't. He nodded again.

"Did you try to kill John Anderson again this afternoon?"

Ishmael nodded while grimacing in pain.

"Why did you want to kill John Anderson so badly?" Lynch asked, searching his eyes. "Did someone put you up to it?"

Ishmael labored to get the word out of his mouth.

"No," he said.

"So you did this all on your own?" Lynch said.

"La," Ishmael said.

"Lieutenant, I think that's all one word," Hubert said. I think he's trying to say—"

"No-la," Ishmael said, with tears in his eyes.

As the blood from his lung began to bubble up through his mouth, he said it once more.

"No-la Lang-ston," he whispered. And with that, he died.

Lynch backed away from the gurney.

"Hubert, I need you to get Mr. Carter's clothing and personal effects," Lynch said. "Go through them and see if there's anything there we can use."

"Okay, Lieutenant," Hubert said before turning and hustling down the hall.

Lynch slowly moved out into the walkway that ran the length

of the emergency room. The staff he'd ordered out of the cubicle looked at him as if he were a murderer.

Walking up to one of the doctors standing shell-shocked by the desk, Lynch leaned in close and whispered, "I think you can sew him up now, Doctor. The operation was a success."

And with that, Lynch and Harris walked out of the operating room, armed with the testimony of a dead man.

Now, Lynch thought as he approached the preacher at the center of it all, the commissioner would finally be able to rest in peace. And so would Ishmael.

Shortly after she received the call, a detective showed up and transported Sarah Anderson to police headquarters.

There she heard the news that was spreading through the department like wildfire. Ishmael Carter, the man who'd shot and killed the police commissioner while trying to kill her husband, John, had died in the emergency room at Jefferson Hospital. But not before making full confessions in the murders of the commissioner and Emma Jean Johnson.

John was all right. He was waiting for her at the hospital, along with Lynch and some other law enforcement officials. Sarah didn't care about that. All she wanted to hear about was Keisha.

She was still haunted by the dream, and still wondering if Keisha hated her in reality.

Sarah walked down Eighth Street toward the hospital, taking in the summer breeze as she passed the spectacular mural on the wall adjacent to police headquarters. It depicted adults and children of many races, all striving for some unseen goal, breaking through impossible barriers, reaching ever higher for their dreams.

Sarah could remember when she was one of those people, striving for something beyond what she could readily comprehend. Now she was just a mother and a wife—roles that didn't seem quite as important as they'd been made out to be.

Crossing Arch Street, she walked under the bridge toward Market and passed by Strawbridge's, where she sometimes met Keisha for lunch, back when her daughter still loved and respected her. Back when the two of them were still friends.

Sarah wanted that back, she thought as she crossed Market Street and headed toward the hospital. She wanted that back more than anything in the world. If only they would find her daughter, everything would be okay again.

They would be able to go before the people of God and share a testimony that would go well beyond what God did for them in days gone by. They would be able to share how God had blessed them, even in the face of impending death. They would be able to say that they'd been delivered from their enemies.

Yes, she thought as she arrived at the hospital, that would be quite a testimony. It might even be enough to heal the wounds in their family.

"Can I help you?" said the woman at the information desk.

"I'm Sarah Anderson. I'm here to meet my husband, John, and Detective Lynch."

"Oh, certainly, Mrs. Anderson," the woman said, getting up and pointing down the hall. "They're right back there in the waiting area outside the emergency room."

"Thank you," Sarah said, walking slowly down the hall while she watched her husband and Detective Lynch huddled together in a corner.

The closer she got to them, the more it looked like John was upset about something. And the detective's questions—if that's what they were—seemed to make him even more upset.

258

Lynch saw her just as she got within earshot. John put his hand on his head and turned away, as if he didn't want to look her in the eye.

Lynch greeted her warmly. "How are you, Mrs. Anderson?" he said, taking her hand in both of his. "Thanks for coming down."

"I got a call that there was some news about Keisha," she said, craning her neck to get a look at her husband.

"There is," Lynch said gravely. "But it's not good."

"Well, what is it?"

"Like I was explaining to your husband, she's still alive," Lynch said. "And from what we can tell, she's still with Jamal. But we've got two more witnesses who say Keisha held them at gunpoint, and that she and Jamal carjacked them, shortly after leaving Margaret Jackson's house."

"So, where are they now?" Sarah asked anxiously.

"They were last seen at Bridge and Pratt," Lynch said. "We've had officers searching for them, but we haven't turned up anything so far."

"John, you said you went looking for her," Sarah said. "Did you find anything?"

"No," he said, turning around to reveal the swelling on the left side of his face.

"What happened to you?" she said, reaching out to touch his face.

"I was attacked by a man with a gun," he said. "Turns out it was the same man who killed the police commissioner."

"I heard something about him being shot by the police," Sarah said. "But I had no idea that he was fighting with you."

"Seems I've been his target all along," John said, holding his jaw as he spoke.

"But why would he want to kill *you?*" said a bewildered Sarah.

Lynch looked at Reverend Anderson, who sat down on the couch in the waiting area and stared into space.

"John?" Sarah said, walking over to her husband and repeating the question. "Why was he was trying to kill you?"

"Sit down, honey," he said softly. "We need to talk."

As Sarah sat down next to her husband, Lynch and Assistant DA Harris exchanged knowing glances and walked to the far end of the hall.

"Sarah," John said, reaching out to take her hands in his, "there's something I have to tell you."

His grave expression made her nervous. "What is it, John?"

"I love you, Sarah," he said, avoiding her eyes. "I always have. I want you to know that."

"I love you, too," she said, more out of reflex than anything else.

She watched him with narrow eyes, silently urging him to go on. But for the first time in a long time, John Anderson didn't know what to say.

"What is it, John?" she asked, growing impatient.

"I don't know how to tell you this," he said nervously.

"Just say it."

He took a deep breath before he continued. "Before he died, the man who tried to kill me said someone I knew had put him up to doing it."

"Who?" Sarah asked eagerly.

John looked at his wife with an apology in his eyes, and her heart began to break even before he spoke her name.

"Nola Langston."

Sarah's eyes began to fill up with tears. She thought of all the lonely nights she'd spent without him, of all the sacrifices she'd made over the years, of all the times she'd longed for his touch.

She was hurt, and defiled, and angry. But she needed him to say it aloud. She needed to hear it from his lips.

"Who's Nola Langston?" she said, her voice cracking with emotion.

John squeezed his wife's hands as if it would ease the pain. "We had an affair."

With tears streaming down her face, Sarah pulled her hands away from her husband's and stood up. Then she slapped him as hard as she could and stormed down the hallway.

John's shoulders slumped and his head bowed down as he watched his marriage crumble before his eyes.

Lynch and Harris watched it, too. They felt sorry for John. But more than that, they felt empathy for his wife.

"Let's take Reverend Anderson back to Homicide," Lynch said, walking toward the door. "And then let's bring Nola and Frank together in one room."

"What about Keisha and Jamal?" Harris said.

"We still need to find them," Lynch said. "And sooner rather than later."

Keisha and Jamal stood at the door, waiting nervously for Joe to come up the stairs and tell them what they already knew.

They didn't have to wait for long.

Joe opened the door and walked inside, and saw in their faces that they didn't want to stay there any longer.

"We gotta go now, Joe," Jamal said, speaking quickly. "We can't wait 'til five."

Jamal was tying a belt around the baggy sweats he'd found in Joe's closet. The sweats were the only clothing belonging to the short, pudgy man that would fit on Jamal's six-foot frame.

Keisha was already dressed. She was wearing a pair of jeans and a modest top belonging to Joe's girlfriend, whose dimensions were roughly the same as hers, albeit a little less curvaceous.

"Before we go, Jamal, I think you better turn on the television," Joe said.

"For what?"

Joe walked over to his table, picked up the remote control, and turned on the television. As he flipped through the channels, they saw pictures of Ishmael Carter on every station. And every picture was accompanied by words spoken in the same grave-sounding tone.

Joe settled on Channel 3, and put down the remote so they could watch.

"And again, for those just tuning in, thirty-five-year-old Ishmael Carter, in an apparent deathbed confession, has admitted to the murders of seventy-one-year-old Emma Jean Johnson and forty-nine-year-old Police Commissioner Darrell Freeman. Sources familiar with the investigation say that Carter implicated former model Nola Langston, pictured here, as his accomplice in a murder plot against Reverend John Anderson of North Philadelphia. Our sources aren't yet sure of the motive behind the alleged plot.

"And in a related story, Jamal Nichols, initially wanted in connection with Commissioner Freeman's murder, is still at large. Keisha Anderson, pictured here, was at first believed to have been kidnapped by Nichols in a feud between the two families.

"But CBS Three has learned that Anderson is suspected as a possible accomplice in several crimes committed in the aftermath of the commissioner's murder, including the murder of Officer Jim Hickey of the Twenty-fifth Police District.

"Stay with CBS Three for continued coverage of this stunning crime spree, and the two families at the center of it."

Joe turned off the television, put the remote control down on the table, and looked at both Keisha and Jamal.

"Are you sure you still wanna do this?" he asked.

Jamal and Keisha looked at one another, and they were sure of only one thing. They wanted to be together, no matter what the cost.

Lynch watched two detectives lead a handcuffed Frank Nichols into the interrogation room. Frank's lawyer and Assistant DA Harris were close behind.

Nola and her lawyer, on the opposite side of the room, watched with open mouths as a wincing Frank Nichols sat down.

Frank saw them looking, and tried to contort his face into the haughty expression Nola was accustomed to. But when she looked at him, all she could see was defeat.

His expression was haggard, and his grimy clothing made him look more like a homeless man than a drug lord.

After the initial shock of seeing him that way, Nola found herself smiling. Whatever happened to her from that point would be okay, she thought. She could rest in the fact that Frank was already ruined.

Nichols saw her smile, and though his expression remained impassive, he inwardly wondered what Nola had told the detectives. More importantly, he wondered what it would mean to him.

"Mr. Nichols, aren't you going to say hello to Ms. Langston?" Lynch asked with a slight smile.

Frank glanced at Lynch and said nothing. He didn't want to tell or show them anything they didn't already know about his relationship with Nola.

"I'm sorry," Lynch said. "What was I thinking? You probably wanted to apologize to her first, for sleeping with her daughter last night, and taking a shot at her today."

Nichols raised his middle finger.

Lynch smiled at the vulgar gesture.

"You'll have men wanting to do that to you soon enough," Lynch said. "Right now, I think we ought to focus on the business at hand."

The assistant DA handed Lynch a folder, which he opened and began skimming through.

"Mr. Nichols, this is the testimony that Ms. Langston's offered to us so far," he said.

Nichols shot a murderous glance in Nola's direction. She responded with a single raised eyebrow that infuriated Nichols all the more.

"She says that you gave orders for Jamal to kill John Anderson, and to kidnap Keisha," Lynch continued. "Of course, Ms. Langston has every reason to lie to us."

"What do you mean, lie?" Nola said heatedly as her lawyer tried to calm her down. "Everything I told you was true, right down to—"

"Right down to cleaning out the Alon Enterprises bank account this afternoon," Lynch said.

Frank's angry expression turned to outright rage as he lunged across the table and tried to grab Nola. The two detectives in the room grabbed him by the shoulders and sat him down in his seat.

"Counselor, I suggest you keep your client under control," the assistant DA said, speaking for the first time. "This type of violence won't help him when this thing goes to trial."

"You mean *if* this thing goes to trial," Nichols's lawyer said. "From what I can see, all you've got is Ms. Langston's word, which, in light of her attempted theft of a million dollars, isn't worth a whole hell of a lot."

"Actually, counselor, we've got a little more than that," Lynch said. "We've got phone records, notes, and most of all, we've got something that neither one of these fine people counted on."

He flipped a page in the file and stared at it thoughtfully.

"We've got videotaped testimony from the man who shot the police commissioner this morning," Lynch said.

He looked around the room, knowing the lie he was about to tell was a tremendous gamble, but one that he was willing to take.

"In that testimony," he said gravely, "he implicates Ms. Langston and your client."

He turned to Nichols and his lawyer.

"Now, you can take a chance and let us go forward with that testimony," Lynch said. "Or you can tell us the truth about your client's role in this whole thing."

"And what about me?" Nola said. "We had a deal."

"The deal was, your testimony leads us to a conviction, and you get a slap on the wrist," Assistant DA Harris said. "But your testimony, while entertaining, won't lead us to a conviction by itself.

"Now, if you can fill in the holes," Harris said, "maybe we can honor the agreement. But as it stands, considering that we're talking about a conspiracy that led to the murders of three people, including the police commissioner and a Twenty-fifth District officer, I'm sure your lawyers will agree that you're both looking at the maximum."

"Which is?" Nola asked.

Harris looked her directly in the eye.

"Death."

There was a moment of deadly silence as everyone in the room reflected on that reality. Nichols's lawyer turned to him and whispered something about a conference. But Frank didn't need to talk to his lawyer.

Even the prospect of the death penalty was too much for him to risk. Especially to protect Nola Langston.

"You was supposed to be so damn smart," he said to Nola while shaking his head.

"Shut up, Frank," she snapped. "They don't know anything. They're bluffing."

"You told me all I had to do to get to John was get to Keisha," he said.

He turned to Lynch and told him the truth.

"All I wanted John to do was stop fuckin' with my business," he said. "I didn't want him hurt, I didn't want him killed. I just wanted him to stop."

"So why were there people taking shots at him?" Lynch asked.

"I don't know," Nichols said. "All I know is that I told Jamal to have a talk with John's daughter, scare her a little bit."

"That's a damn lie, Frank, and you know it," Nola shouted. "You ordered the kidnapping, and you wanted her killed if John didn't agree to stop the antidrug stuff."

"Okay!" Frank shouted. "I told him to snatch the girl! But I never told him to kill nobody!"

"What about when the girl was attacked and John came down to your bar?" Lynch asked. "I mean, he disrespected you in front of your men. Weren't you angry about that?"

"I never told anyone to kill John Anderson," Frank said. "No matter what you say, I'll never admit that, because it never happened."

"And I guess you never told anyone to kill his father, either, right?" Lynch said.

Once again, the room went silent as everyone looked at one another and waited for the other shoe to drop.

"I loved his father," Nichols said solemnly. "Things happened the way they happened, and I'm sorry. But I loved John's father, and I hated to see him die that way."

"Yeah, right," Nola said. "You could care less, Frank. You ordered his murder the same way you ordered Jamal to kill John. That's why Jamal gave them the confession, because he knew you'd be all too willing to talk."

Lynch and Harris looked at each other. Then they looked at Nola.

"I never said Jamal was the one who gave the confession," Lynch said.

"But Jamal was the one who was shooting at John," Nola said, looking confused. "It had to be Jamal!"

"Actually," Lynch said, "it was a man named Ishmael Carter."

Frank looked confused. "I don't know no Ishmael Carter," he said, looking at his lawyer.

"Neither do I," Nola said, her eyes darting about the room.

"Sure you do, Ms. Langston," Lynch said. "He looks just like Jamal."

"I don't know what you're talking about," Nola said.

"Ms. Langston, don't say anything else," her lawyer said. "Let me handle this."

"There's nothing to handle!" she shouted. "I don't know any Ishmael Carter."

"You slept with him to get him to murder John Anderson," Lynch said. "It was the perfect setup to make it look like Jamal and Frank Nichols were behind it."

"That's a lie," Nola said.

"You did it so you could walk away with that drug money."

Nola tried to calm down. When she spoke, she enunciated every syllable.

"I don't know any Ishmael Carter, Lieutenant."

"Yes, you do."

"How do you know that?"

"Because Ishmael said you told him to murder John Anderson," Lynch said calmly. "It was the last thing he said before he died."

Sarah Anderson stood in the middle of the bedroom she'd shared with her husband for the past twenty years and cried uncontrollably as she thought of John's affair.

Thinking back to her mother's long-ago warnings about John and his family, Sarah shook her head and wondered how she could have been so stubborn. But then, as she thought back on her disdain for her mother, Sarah knew the answer to that question.

Sarah's mother was the woman who'd decided to stay with Sarah's father even after Sarah told her that she'd caught him with another woman in his office.

Sarah hated her for that decision, even though it was made in a time when powerful men were allowed such indiscretions, and women were obliged to ignore them.

Perhaps it was that hatred that caused Sarah to disregard her mother's warnings and instead make a promise to herself. Sarah would never allow a man to treat her as her father had treated her mother—like an accessory to be cast aside at his convenience.

She hadn't kept that promise to herself. She'd become her mother—an insignificant person dwelling in her husband's shadow. And for years, she'd been paying the price.

Sarah looked around their bedroom at the memories it contained—their bed was their first piece of furniture. John had broken the doorknob on the closet. And as she thought back on the hope she'd had for her marriage, she cried a little harder at the disappointment.

Sarah had known for a long time that her marriage was all but over. But she'd hoped that it would end differently.

There was only one thing left for her to do now. But knowing that didn't make it any easier.

She walked over to the closet in the corner of the room, opened it, and removed her suitcase. She hadn't used her old satchel in years, she thought, as she opened it and threw it onto their bed.

The last time she'd packed it was fifteen years ago, when they'd gone to Florida for the first and only time as a family. She remembered Keisha splashing at the edge of the pool. She recalled John lifting Keisha, and then Sarah, onto his shoulders, and carrying them into the water.

She remembered laughter during those days, and passion during those nights. And she remembered how things began to change after that.

Their lives became consumed with the minutiae of maintaining their home and their church. And in the process, their happiness dwindled away to nothing.

Sarah looked at the suitcase, which appeared to be almost new, and wished that she'd used it more during their marriage. Perhaps if they had gone to other places and seen other things, there would still be passion between them instead of discord. Perhaps if they had taken more time for themselves, they would still see possibilities instead of endings.

Sarah thought of all of these things, and her tears fell against the hardwood floor like raindrops.

Opening the chest of drawers, she retrieved the remainder of her clothing, except for a skirt, a blouse, and a pair of heels, and threw it into the suitcase. She scrounged the makeup she rarely used from the top drawer, and took it with her into the bathroom.

She opened the cabinet beneath the sink, took out her electric curlers, and plugged them into the wall. Then she dropped her dowdy clothes to the floor and turned on the shower's hot water.

Sarah opened the curtain, and a cloud of steam filled the room. She stepped into the water and allowed the heat to penetrate every fiber of her being. She was going to wash away twenty years of unhappiness. And then, she thought with a smile, she was going to go on with her life.

Even with the confession in Commissioner Freeman's murder, Keisha and Jamal couldn't chance being caught.

If they were ever to go to trial, the carjackings and gun charges would yield significant time. But when the dust settled and the truth about Officer Jim Hickey's murder was revealed, they wouldn't be facing years anymore. They'd be facing death.

The decision was an easy one. They were going to run.

When they told Joe what they'd decided to do, he nodded solemnly, because he knew the criminal justice system better than most.

A confession could be overturned, even if it was genuine, because prosecutors were often more concerned with appearances than truth. Better to have a live defendant who could be sentenced to death by the Commonwealth of Pennsylvania than a dead one who couldn't.

And even if Keisha and Jamal managed to avoid a death sentence, they would get life without parole. Their ability to love— the very thing that had brought them together—would be systematically stripped away.

No, Joe thought as he waited for them to decide their next move. They couldn't turn themselves in. They definitely had to run.

"We gotta get as far away as we can right now," Jamal said, walking over to Joe.

"And go where?" Keisha asked.

"We could drive to Canada," he said.

"My car won't make it that far," Joe said. "And I wouldn't trust nothin' else to get you there safe."

They were all silent as they tried to think of the best route of escape.

Jamal looked at Joe. "Can you get us on a plane?"

"I could get you tickets on the Internet. Question is, where would you go?"

"What about the islands?" Keisha said.

"You need passports to get there?" Jamal asked.

Joe walked over to his laptop as Keisha and Jamal followed. "My girl used to fly there a lot," he said. "She told me all you need is a birth certificate."

"We ain't got birth certificates, and we ain't got time to get 'em," Jamal said.

Joe booted up the computer and logged on to a Web site that provided discount airfare.

"I got a friend a couple blocks away who makes birth certificates and driver's licenses. He can have 'em made up for you in ten minutes."

"I don't know if we can wait that long," Jamal said.

"What other choice you got?" Joe said.

Keisha and Jamal looked at each other, knowing that Joe was right. They could use fake identities, or they could take their chances and be caught and tried for murder.

Jamal grabbed Keisha's hand and held it tightly as Keisha looked into his eyes.

"Make the call," Jamal said.

19

John Anderson was siting alone in a dim cinderblock room just down the hall from where Nola Langston and Frank Nichols were trying to decide just how much of the truth they wanted to tell.

It was odd, he thought, that he should find himself here, on this side of the fence, when he'd begun his journey on the other side. But here he was. Strange as it seemed, he was willing to accept it.

"How are you, Reverend Anderson?" Lynch asked as he breezed into the room.

"I'm tired," he said.

"Physically or mentally?"

"Both."

Lynch sat back and looked into the preacher's eyes. He saw the fatigue of which John spoke. But he saw something else there as well. John looked like a man at the end of a long struggle, a man who was tired of fighting.

There was at least one more battle for the preacher to fight, Lynch thought as he looked at him. And Lynch was about to draw first blood.

"Why didn't you tell me that you'd had an affair with Nichols's girlfriend?" Lynch said.

"I guess I didn't think it was important."

"You didn't think it was important to tell me about someone with intimate knowledge of both you and the man behind your daughter's disappearance?"

John shrugged. "I thought I could find Nola's connection to all this on my own."

"Is that why you had that sawed-off in your bag?"

John didn't answer.

"We had detectives talk to a few people on the scene. They saw you get in the car with the bag."

"I wasn't going to—"

"Look," Lynch said. "All I wanna know is, did you know that Nola was the cause of your daughter being kidnapped, and did you plan to kill her with that gun?"

John didn't know what to say. So he didn't say anything.

"Reverend, I like you," Lynch said. "But here's the truth, whether you like it or not. Your daughter's missing, and she's probably with Frank Nichols's son because she wants to be. Your marriage is in trouble because you slept with another woman right under your wife's nose. You've got Nola Langston telling people that you're a murderer. And if you think folks are going to be flocking to your church once they find all that out, you've got another think coming."

Lynch leaned in close to John. "You don't have a whole lot left to lose by telling me the truth," he said.

John Anderson sat back in his chair, knowing that the battle that raged inside him was all but over. The man he'd been was just about dead now. And the voice inside him—the one that had called him to the ministry—was loudly telling him to surrender.

John smiled as he heeded the voice and decided that it was time to let go. It was time to allow the secrets that had held on to him for so long to turn to dust. It was time to throw that dust on the grave of the man he used to be.

The preacher looked into the detective's eyes. And then he looked past them and stared, red-eyed, into the past he'd avoided for so long.

"There was a small-time dealer named Ben Carter," John said softly. "He tried to sell heroin near one of my father's spots. My father didn't like competition, so he told me to handle it for him. In the summer of 'sixty-five, I did. I shot him down on Diamond Street on a clear August night."

He shook his head sadly at the memory. "It seems like nothing's been clear for me since then."

John rubbed his tired eyes with his fingers.

"I guess I never thought Ben would have a son who loved him as much as I loved my father," he said. "A son who would have the guts to do what I never did—avenge his father's death."

"Are you saying Ishmael Carter is the son of the man you killed?"

"Yes," John said. "That's what he told me right before he tried to kill me."

"Did he tell you anything else?"

"He said that I'd abused Nola—tied her up and burned her and threatened to kill her. He said Nola told him that I was the one who'd killed his father. And he talked about the shooting as if it was yesterday—like he'd been carrying this rage his entire life."

"The things he accused you of doing," Lynch said. "Was any of it true?"

274

"Not the part about me abusing Nola," he said. "I never did anything like that. But the part about Ben Carter, well, yes, like I said before, I killed him."

A tear fell from the pastor's eye, and he quickly wiped it away. "I murdered a man, Lieutenant Lynch. And after all these years, I guess it's finally time for me to face that."

Lynch's face fell as he took in John's admission, because he knew that the pastor's punishment was just beginning. Though John had managed to avoid Ishmael's street justice, he would soon face the wrath of the criminal justice system. And the system wouldn't be so kind.

John could see the sadness in the detective's eyes. But he knew that there was more to his plight than what appeared on the surface.

"Lieutenant," he said, leaning forward in his chair, "there's a story in the Bible about Paul and Barnabus being jailed. They sang and praised God all night, until their shackles fell off and the bars of the jail swung open.

"Their Roman jailer was about to kill himself for allowing them to escape. But they stayed, and they ministered to that man, and they saved him and his family."

Lynch looked up into the preacher's face.

"My ministry isn't in that church on York Street, anymore," John Anderson said with a smile. "That's why it doesn't matter what the world thinks about the things I've done."

John pointed his finger to a point somewhere in the distance. "My ministry is out there, in whatever prison they decide to send me to. That's God's purpose in all this, Lieutenant. And I think, after all these years, I finally understand that."

Lynch sat back in his seat and thought about what John had said.

"Who knows, Reverend Anderson?" he said after a long pause. "He might have a bigger purpose for you than prison."

John nodded as Lynch regained his bearings and returned to the questions at hand.

"There is one thing that still doesn't make sense about what Nola told us," Lynch said.

"What's that?"

"She said you never told her who the victim was," Lynch said. "Is that true?"

John remembered mentioning his past involvement with his father's drug business to Nola. But he didn't remember giving her names.

"Yes," John said. "I guess it is."

"Then how would she know who you'd killed?" Lynch asked. "And how would she track down the man's son, and put him up to killing you? Better yet, why would she even bother?"

"I don't know," John said. "Maybe Frank told her to."

"Did Frank know that you killed Ben Carter?"

"No," John said. "No one knew, as far as I could tell. My father gave the order directly to me. He didn't tell anyone else, and neither did I. I didn't even know that anyone else knew, until today."

"That's the other thing that's bothering me," Lynch said. "This guy, Ishmael Carter, pops up and tries to kill you, and he swears on his deathbed that it was Nola who put him up to it. But when I confronted her about it, Nola acted like she'd never heard of Ishmael Carter. I even described him, which wasn't hard, because he looks like an older version of Jamal Nichols. She still acted like she didn't know him, and from what I could see, she was telling the truth."

Anderson smiled. "Nola can be very . . . convincing, even when she's telling a lie."

Lynch grunted in response.

"Are you sure there wasn't anyone else who knew about you shooting Ben Carter?" he said absently.

Reverend Anderson spent the next few minutes in deep thought. And then realization swept across his face, along with something else. Something infinitely deeper.

"There is one person," he said, looking up at the detective. "But before I take you there, there's something I want you to do for me."

A detective opened the door to the interrogation room where Frank Nichols was waiting with his lawyer.

"Counselor, we're getting ready to transport your client to a holding cell downstairs," the detective said.

"Is he being charged?"

"Not yet. But we can't hold him here any longer. We need this room."

"Okay," the lawyer said, gathering his papers and walking toward the door. "Frank, you call if you need me."

Nichols nodded. He wasn't in the mood to talk anymore. Especially not with the looming threat of being charged with the commissioner's murder.

But that wasn't his most pressing problem. His worst problem was on its way into the room.

The door eased open, and Frank looked up from his seat as a detective escorted John Anderson inside. The detective unlocked the pastor's handcuffs and shot a look at Frank Nichols. Then he closed the door behind him and locked it.

"John," Nichols said with a stiff smile. "What a surprise."

The pastor didn't waste any time. He walked slowly around

the table, the sound of his heavy footsteps filling the room, and stopped in front of Frank Nichols. Towering over him, he asked the question that had haunted him for thirty-five years.

"Why did you kill my father?" he said, staring down into the smaller man's face.

Frank looked down at his hands and tried to come up with an answer. He couldn't.

"He took care of you like you were his own son," John said with quiet anger. "I even thought he loved you more than me. And then you killed him."

Nichols sighed as he felt the familiar rush of guilt over the only crime he'd ever regretted.

"It wasn't that simple, John," he said quietly. "Other people was in it, too. People who thought your father was outta control. When they came to me—"

John Anderson reached down with gigantic hands and snatched him out of his seat.

"I don't care who came to you!" he said, shaking with rage. "You were like a son to him! You were supposed to protect him, the same way he protected you!"

Frank reached up and pushed John's hands away from him. Then he looked up into the taller man's face.

"That was always the problem with you, John," he said, as his eyes bugged out with rage. "You was always worried about the next man."

"He was my father!" John shouted.

"Yeah, he was," Frank said, nodding in agreement. "He taught me everything I know. But your father knew the game he was in. He knew somebody was gon' take him out sooner or later. He probably was glad I had enough heart to do it."

Enraged, John yelled and swung wildly at Nichols's jaw.

Frank ducked the right hand and threw a hard left hook and right cross to John's midsection.

The bigger man doubled over, and Nichols kneed him in his chin. John fell backward and Nichols pounced, landing one punch to John's jaw before brute strength overcame quickness.

With one hand, John grabbed him by the collar and flung him into the side of the steel table. Then John flipped over and straddled Frank's chest so that he couldn't move.

He smashed his fist into the middle of his face. There was the sound of cracking bone and a spurt of blood as Frank's nose gave way.

"I told you I would see you if anything happened to my daughter, didn't I?"

John pounded his fist into his temple as Frank tried in vain to fend off the blow.

"Where your guns at now, huh?" John pummeled him, causing his head to bang against the concrete floor. "Who you gonna kill now, Frank?"

He slapped him with the front of his hand. Then he slapped him again with the back.

John raised his fist to punch him again. But there was no use. No matter how many times he hit him, the emptiness was still there. His father was still dead. His daughter was still missing. His life was still in a shambles.

Panting and glaring down at his defeated enemy, John wiped his bloody knuckles on Frank's shirt and got up off the floor.

"Where's my daughter?" John said, turning his back on the bloody mess that was Frank Nichols.

Frank pulled himself up from the floor and sat in one of the chairs. "I ain't seen your daughter."

John wheeled around. "But you know where she is," he said earnestly. "Your son's got her."

"I ain't heard nothin' from my son," Nichols said, wiping his bloody face with his shirt. "But if your daughter is with him, you might not wanna blame me for that. She just might wanna be there."

John recognized the truth in Frank's words, and his anger began to dissipate. The hatred that he'd harbored for years began to ease. And at last, he started to feel a sense of peace.

"If only we'd been like our kids," John said as he sat down on the other side of the table. "Maybe we could've looked past the hate. Maybe all those people wouldn't be dead."

John looked across the table at his enemy. "I forgive you for what you did to my family, Frank," he said with a sigh. "It's the only way I can ever be free."

When they emerged from the bar's back entrance, Jamal was holding Keisha tightly, refusing to let her go for even one moment. Keisha held onto him for dear life, knowing that she had finally found the boy she'd lost so long ago, the boy who'd grown into the man she loved.

Jamal opened the back door, and they both slid into the back seat.

Joe Vega's old Chevy Malibu was a virtual jalopy, more suited to the occasional trip to the market than it was for the two-hour drive to Newark Liberty International Airport. But they had little choice but to go there. Philadelphia's airport would be crawling with police, and leaving from there was a risk they weren't willing to take.

Even now, after leaving Philadelphia and driving for an hour and a half on the New Jersey Turnpike, Keisha and Jamal lay together in the back seat, covered with a thin sheet.

They lay that way as much for expediency as for comfort, because they knew that New Jersey's state troopers would be less likely to stop a lone white driver like Joe than they would a car with black passengers.

As the car labored along in the slow lane at fifty miles per hour, Keisha lay on the tattered back seat with her arms around Jamal, watching him as he slept against her bosom.

She marveled at the peace that covered his face, and wondered what was going through his mind. She hoped that his thoughts were of her and the love that they shared. She hoped that his peace came from the knowledge that she would always be his. She hoped, in that space in the back of her mind where doubt continued to linger, that he would always be hers as well.

If there was fear in Keisha's heart, it came only from the thought of losing Jamal. She was no longer afraid of what the next moment would bring. Nor was she intimidated by the magnitude of their dilemma. She was now just a woman in love, enraptured by her very first lover and giddy with hope for the future.

If they lived modestly in Jamaica, they had enough money to last them for a lifetime. And if they didn't, they would learn how to make more. But it wasn't about the money, as far as Keisha was concerned. It was about Jamal.

She ran her fingers along his face, tracing the shape of his lips, his eyes, and his nose.

He awakened slowly and looked into her eyes, and his whole being brightened in a smile.

"What you lookin' at?" he whispered.

"Us," Keisha said with a grin.

"I thought you was just lookin' at me," Jamal said.

"When I look at you, I see us," she said seductively. "Swimming in clear ocean water in Jamaica."

"Can you swim?" Jamal asked.

"No."

"Neither can I."

"All right," Keisha said with a grin. "How 'bout we just stick our feet in the ocean instead?"

They smiled and looked into each other's eyes, trying to see their futures as they were, rather than seeing them as they wished them to be.

Neither of them wanted to face the reality of their plight. They were on the run for a growing list of crimes, and though they seemed to hold their destiny in their hands, both of them were increasingly aware of the net that was closing around them.

"Jamal, we're almost there," Joe said, speaking over his shoulder. "I'm gonna take you to the terminal for Air Jamaica. You've got e-tickets. Just go to the desk and give 'em the confirmation number. You should be all right from there."

"Thanks for everything, Joe," Jamal said. "I'll never forget it."

"You two just take care of each other," Joe said as he took the airport exit from the turnpike. "You do that, and everything else will take care of itself."

Keisha smiled, knowing that Joe was right. But Jamal knew that things could go wrong. So he told her what he wanted her to do if things didn't go as planned.

"Keisha," he said, stroking her hair. "I want to you to promise me somethin'."

"What?"

"If anything happens to me—"

"Stop right there," she said, putting a finger against his lips. "Nothing's going to happen to you, Jamal. I won't let it."

He gently removed her hand from his lips.

"I know you won't, baby," he said with a reassuring smile. "But just in case it does, I want you to promise me somethin'."

"What?"

"I want you to promise that you'll take this money and disappear—start a life on your own someplace where nobody knows you."

Keisha took a deep breath. She didn't want to think about anything happening to Jamal, because it would be just like having something happen to herself.

"If you love me, Keisha, you'll promise me that," Jamal said, staring into her eyes.

She kissed him gently on the lips.

"Nothing is going to happen to you, Jamal," she said firmly. "But if it makes you feel better, I promise I'll do what you said."

"Good," Jamal said, leaping out from beneath the sheet as the car pulled to a stop at Terminal B. "Let's go."

The two of them stepped out of the car and watched as Joe pulled away. Then they entered the airport and walked cautiously to the check-in desk while fighting the urge to look around them to see if anyone was watching.

Because it was midafternoon, well after the morning rush, things were moving slowly. There was no line at the desk, so they were able to get their boarding passes without having to wait. Their flight would begin boarding in fifteen minutes, which gave them plenty of time to catch the Airtrain to Gate B40.

The security checks were easy as well. They went through without incident, largely because they had virtually nothing. They'd left the gun in Joe's car, knowing that they'd be checked for weapons. And neither of them had keys, carry-on bags, or even wallets.

Keisha had the cash-filled envelope stuffed down the front of her pants. If anyone asked, she was prepared to say that the money was a wedding present and that she was keeping it there for fear of being robbed.

But no one asked, so she didn't have to offer any explanations. It was all so easy that even Jamal was beginning to relax a bit.

He spotted a gift shop in the terminal and smiled.

"Keisha, I want to go over here and get somethin'," he said. "I'll meet you at the gate."

"You're not meeting me anywhere," Keisha said with an attitude. "I'm coming with you."

Jamal sighed. "I can't even buy you a little gift without you bein' right there next to me? Suppose I wanna surprise you?"

"I don't like surprises," Keisha said seriously.

"Well, you'll like this one," he said. "Go to the bathroom or somethin'. I'll meet you right there in front o' the gift shop."

Keisha crossed the concourse and went into the bathroom, thinking all the while of what kind of surprise Jamal would find for her.

He was enough of a surprise, she thought as she washed her hands and splashed water against her face. She'd always expected that love would somehow appear and wrap its arms around her. She'd never expected that it would be someone from another world—someone with whom the only thing she had in common was love.

As she checked her hair in the mirror, she noticed a woman in a security guard's uniform out of the corner of her eye. She was standing near the entrance to the bathroom and looking out into the terminal while whispering something into her hand held radio.

A few seconds later, the area of the terminal she'd just come from with Jamal erupted in bedlam.

Keisha ran out of the bathroom to see security guards and police running toward the area directly outside the gift shop. She could hear them screaming something about a security breach as she watched them converge on someone in the hallway. She saw sticks flailing and fists flying as five police officers and security personnel tried to subdue a single person.

As she watched other officers join the mêlée, she realized with mounting horror that Jamal was nowhere in sight. That could only mean one thing. He was the man they were trying to subdue.

"Final boarding call for Air Jamaica Flight eleven thirty-six, at gate B-forty," a voice said over the public address system.

Keisha watched helplessly as dozens more officers ran past her to join those already locked in battle near the gift shop.

Tears streamed down her face as she listened to the voice over the PA system as it once again announced the final boarding call for her flight.

She looked around once more, hoping that Jamal would somehow emerge and join her at the gate. But she knew in her heart that he wouldn't, just as she knew in her heart that she would have to keep her promise to him.

She turned and ran to the gate just as the flight attendant was about to close the door, and showed her boarding pass and identification.

Keisha ran through the portable tunnel to the plane, her tears nearly blinding her as she made her way to her seat.

She sat in her seat with her face in a pillow, and cried for the love she'd lost. She cried for the memories she'd left behind. And as the plane took off fifteen minutes later, she cried for the family she'd been so anxious to forget.

Kevin Lynch was physically and emotionally drained when he walked out of the interrogation room and into his office. He'd seen too much destruction take place in a single day. Now he just wanted it to be over.

Although he believed that finding Jamal and Keisha would now be all but impossible, he was somewhat comforted by the facts laid out in the preliminary Internal Affairs report he found on his desk regarding the Twenty-fifth District police shooting.

According to the report, Officers MacAleer and Hickey had raped a prostitute in their wagon just prior to Hickey's shooting death, which occurred while MacAleer was still in the wagon with the prostitute.

The rape was consistent with the officers' behavior over the past two years, the report said. They had previously been under investigation for stealing drugs from addicts, sexually assaulting prostitutes, and robbing drug dealers. No charges had been brought to that point, though charges against MacAleer were still being considered.

The fact that they were dirty didn't make it right, Lynch thought as he closed the report. But it certainly made the whole thing easier to swallow.

There was a knock as Lynch unlocked his drawer and grabbed his gun.

"Come in," he said.

Detective Hubert walked in. "I went through Ishmael Carter's personal effects," the detective said.

"And?"

"Ishmael dialed one number on his cell phone all day long," he said gravely. "And it wasn't Nola Langston's."

"So whose was it?"

"I called the phone company, and it looks like the number belongs to Jamal Nichols," Hubert said. "Of course, that makes no sense at all, since Carter apparently had no contact with the Nichols organization."

"What's the number?" Lynch said.

"It's 215-555-8708."

Lynch opened his drawer and retrieved his file on the case. He was halfway down the list of numbers called and received by Nola and Frank when he found a match.

"Looks like that's one of the numbers that called Frank Nichols's phone this morning," Lynch said.

"So, do you think Jamal had two cell phones on him?"

"Apparently all the cell phones they used were in Jamal's name," Lynch said. "But as far as I can tell, he only had one of them."

"So who had the other?" Hubert said.

"That's what I was going to find out," Lynch said. "Come on."

Lynch put on his jacket and the two of them walked out into the hallway just as two detectives led Reverend Anderson out of the interrogation room.

"I'll take him," Lynch said as he and Hubert met them in the hallway. "You two follow us."

"Okay, Lieutenant," one of the detectives said.

As Lynch took John's arm, the preacher whispered, "Thank you for letting me handle that."

"It's okay, Reverend," Lynch said quietly. "Are you ready to handle this, too?"

John nodded as he walked to the elevators with the four detectives. They rode down to the first floor, moved into the parking lot, and got into the unmarked police cars for the last ride Reverend Anderson would know as a free man.

As he bent to get into the back of the car, he thought of the day that he got saved, the way that he'd crawled out of the pew after the sermon, preached from John 3:16, had touched him like nothing ever had. He thought of the tears he'd shed on that day—

the first time he'd ever cried in public—and the freedom that those tears represented.

He was free from the things he'd done, free from the prison of his guilt, free from the shame of his past, free from the legacy of his father. But he didn't know how to handle his freedom.

Perhaps now, with his guilt out in the open, he could finally be truly free. There was just one more thing that he had to do, he thought as Detective Hubert slowed down and Lynch dialed the number.

Reverend Anderson watched helplessly, hoping that the call would go unanswered. When it didn't, he was heartbroken, because he knew that what he'd suspected was true.

Lynch turned to him and nodded.

Reverend Anderson got out of the car, trotting across the street to the stretch of sidewalk in front of his church.

The woman dropped the cell phone she was carrying and turned just as he approached her from the rear. Her beautifully made-up face was practically glowing with hatred.

Her hair fell just past her shoulders in long, sweeping curls. Her tight knit dress dipped low at her breasts and rode high against her thighs. Her curvaceous body was on display for all to see, and all John could do was stand there, aghast, and stare at this woman he didn't know.

"Surprised, John?" his wife said.

"Sarah, I—"

"You what?" she snapped as the detectives jumped from their car and leveled their weapons.

"Where'd you get the phone, Sarah?" John asked.

"From Keisha. She left it lying around one day and I just picked it up. I used it to track down Ben Carter's son. I even used it to call Frank Nichols."

Sarah saw that the detectives were aiming at her, and she pulled a gun from her purse. John moved toward her, and she pointed it at his head.

She saw him looking at her in disbelief, and she laughed.

"This is what you wanted, right?" she asked him with a madness playing in her eyes. "You wanted a woman who looked like this. A woman who would do all the things you wanted her to do, whenever you wanted her to do them."

"Mrs. Anderson, drop the gun," Lynch said as he approached her slowly from the street.

"No, you drop the gun!" she said maniacally.

The neighbors began to gather along the street, watching with open mouths as the preacher's wife held a gun at his head.

"John, I knew," she said, shaking her head. "Every time you went downtown to meet her, I knew."

"But it's over, Sarah," John said earnestly.

"It's not over 'til I say it's over!" she screamed.

Lynch walked onto the sidewalk to try to get a clear shot while Hubert circled around the other way. Sarah saw them and moved around her husband until his body shielded hers.

"Even Keisha taught me things about Nola," Sarah said with a chuckle. "Keisha and I would have our little lunches, and she'd just chat all about this lady at work named Ms. Nola. Ms. Nola thought she was talented, and Ms. Nola was so pretty. That's the only thing she ever talked to me about was Nola.

"I told Ishmael my name was Nola. I told him how you killed his father, and it hurt him so bad that I slept with him to make the pain go away. Then I told him I would be all his if he would just make you stop abusing me."

Sarah laughed derisively. "I figured I could get Ishmael to kill you and say Nola made him do it. But it didn't work out that way."

Sarah raised the gun.

"Drop it, Sarah," Lynch said in a warning tone.

"I guess I have to do it myself," she said, ignoring the detectives.

She cocked the hammer on the pistol and started to squeeze the trigger.

A single shot rang out, and Sarah fell to the ground in front of the church.

Seconds later, Mother Wallace and the others who'd talked with Sarah earlier came stumbling out the church on unsteady legs. With their hands over their mouths and their eyes stretched wide, they watched her blood soak into the sidewalk.

As Sarah's eyes stared vacantly toward heaven, John knelt over her and brushed her hair away from her face. He kissed her lips and whispered in her ear.

"I'm sorry, Sarah," he said, looking into her dead eyes through tears. "I'm so sorry for what I did to you."

The neighbors walked silently to the spot where Sarah had fallen. The church folks did the same. And in that moment, the two worlds came together to encircle John as he looked up to heaven and yelled out the only prayer he had left.

"Forgive me!" he shouted over and over as tears streaked down his cheeks. "Forgive me!"

20

The hours seemed longer in the humid island air of Negril, Jamaica. The effect of this for most was an abiding sense of bliss.

But for Keisha, staring out the glass doors of the bungalow they'd reserved and into the lush greenery of the garden, the stillness was torture.

She couldn't stop thinking of Jamal, the only man she'd ever loved. She was to have shared the rest of her life with him here, in the island paradise she'd always dreamed about.

But now she didn't know if he was alive or dead. She didn't know if she was, either. All she knew was that she was filled with regret.

After reading the news on the Internet of her mother's death and her father's impending imprisonment, she regretted that she'd never said good-bye to them because she thought that she'd have another chance.

She regretted taking the money and leaving Jamal in the hands of the police. She regretted that she'd never had the chance to tell him how much he'd changed her with his kiss. She regretted that when it counted the most, she'd refused to stay and fight, in spite of her promise to do otherwise.

Keisha sat down on the king-sized bed and inhaled the scent of the room. It was damp, and salty, and sweet, like the mist of the ocean, or the taste of her tears.

She'd cried enough of them to make an ocean of her own, and still the pain was there, like a wound that wouldn't stop bleeding.

She took a bath, and as she tried and failed to soak the hurt away, she thought of all she'd been through with Jamal: the summer nights as children, the feud between their fathers, the plan to leave the country, the gunshots, and the running.

She'd survived all of that, she thought, only to die of a broken heart.

Keisha got out of the tub and dried herself, then dressed quickly and walked outside to walk barefoot along the white sands of the beach.

She stopped when she was directly in front of the setting sun, and watched its red and orange burn blue against the clouds.

"Why, Jamal?" she asked as she watched the beautiful Jamaican sunset pour over her like so much warm water. "Why did you make me think you would always be with me?" She sobbed softly as the sun dropped into the sea.

"Because I will," a voice said, seemingly from somewhere deep inside her.

She turned around, and out of the gathering shadows, she picked out the shape of his eyes, eyes she would never forget, staring at her from a few feet away.

Keisha ran to him and threw her arms around his neck. She

kissed his face and held his hands and touched him everywhere, just to make sure that he was real.

"Jamal," Keisha said, kissing his fingers one by one. "It can't be you."

He kissed her back, tasting her salty tears.

"What happened?" she asked, searching his eyes. "How did you get away from them?"

"That wasn't me they grabbed, Keisha. That was some dude who snuck a gun into the terminal. When I saw 'em grab him, I just went the other way. Then I got the next flight down."

She kissed him before he could say another word. And when she'd had her fill of his lips, she stood back and looked into his eyes.

"So now what?" she asked seductively.

"You tell me."

Keisha turned to go back to their bungalow, and her smile shone through the rapidly falling darkness.

"You rollin' with me or not?" she said, holding out her hand.

He looked into the sunset. Then he turned his gaze on Keisha. He gave his hand to her. And in that moment, he gave her his heart, as well.

"Ride or die," Jamal whispered.

They were the same two words she'd whispered to him before—words he'd never fully understood until that moment. As he stood there on the beach, looking into Keisha's eyes, he pledged his loyalty and his life to her. He was going to ride with her until the end of their journey, or he was going to die trying.